CAST OF CHARACTERS
(For Easy Reference)

Cody Musket — Former US Marine aviator, call sign "Babe." Hall-of-Fame retired baseball player, now active as the founder and force behind a private, covert anti-trafficking operation involved in the rescue of children.

Brandi Musket — Wife of Cody. Activist and spokesperson for Planned Childhood, a privately-supported foundation which provides shelter for trafficking victims and orphans worldwide.

Knoxi Musket — Daughter of Cody and Brandi.

Baker and Elena Rafferty — Husband and wife team, head of Muskets' security.

Ryan Maxwell — Son of Sabre Maxwell (deceased). Ryan is a quantum sciences researcher and developer for the US Dept. of Defense.

Jeremy McNair — Nineteen-year-old Los Angeles Dodgers draftee, son of Tanner (Sly) McNair, who was a childhood friend of Cody.

Alexis (Alex) Blanca, alias Glorietta Zomata, alias Annabelle (Annie) McNair — Teenage victim of traffickers who heroically escaped from Mexico.

Robbie and Peaches — Teenage couple (pregnant) on the run from underworld figures.

Keyshawn (Hawker) Harris — Former US Marine pilot, friend of Cody, now Acting Director of the Texas Rangers.

Kenny (Sleeping Wolf) and Adrian (Silent Arrow) — Native Cherokee brothers, friends of Cody. Former Army Rangers.

Star and Hutch — Entertainers. Former military specialists. Covert fighters under Cody's employ.

Virginia Cutter — Undercover DEA.

Rolfe Sagan — Shifty, unscrupulous news reporter.

When your pain from seeing the suffering in your world is greater than your fear of doing something about it.

Knoxi's World

The Cody Musket Story, Book three

James N. Miller

Lions Tail
BOOKS™

Cover by Delaney_Design.com
Proofreading by Wordsmith Proofreading Services
Special thanks to Johanna Morisey, Betty Snyder, Martha Black, and Lisa Worthey Smith

Printed and bound in the United States of America

INTRODUCTION

Knoxi's World extends the Cody Musket Story into the next generation. Of the three books, this one might be your favorite if you love even more adventure with romance, and especially if you like to be surprised with a little futuristic science in the mix.

An international coalition of power brokers is attempting the largest corporate merger in history, a shadow movement which will enable them to enslave millions without impunity. Knoxi Musket, a freshman basketball player at the University of Texas, discovers this plan, but the elites are too well protected. Can anyone stop them?

You will be familiar with most of the characters if you have read the previous two books in the series, and you'll meet some intriguing new figures — some good, some evil. Sometimes deliverance arrives through the most unlikely sources.

—James N. Miller

THE CHOPPER

South Miami Beach, Florida

Something was wrong. A helicopter missing for sixteen years suddenly appears on the beach like a sleeping ghost of the past. And while thousands are lining up to get a glimpse, a sudden infestation of sharks invades the shoreline.

In the predawn hours along Florida's east coast, everything seemed normal at first. Silent waters were awakened by the usual morning calls of seagulls combing the shallows. Timeless beaches were refreshed by cool morning waves that lapped upon the shores. Golden rays began to break through thin morning fog, bringing another day of sun-n-fun for humans determined to leave their footprints, if only for the moment, in such pristine sands.

Dawn's early light had forever come to these waters like clockwork, making the miracle of daily stability seem routine. But the welcome light of day this particular morning would expose a chilling spectacle — a stunning mystery no one was prepared for. This day would be anything but routine.

A Beltway News Network crew scurried frantically, setting up for a live video report to be broadcast from sandy South Miami Beach. The view here had oft made the perfect vacation postcard, but today officials in hazmat suits dominated the picture. Federal agents had cordoned off the area where the helicopter had mysteriously appeared on the beach the night before. Deputies in riot helmets and body shields stationed themselves along the perimeter to prevent gathering crowds from overrunning the area.

Finally, the broadcast began . . .

"Good morning, ladies and gentlemen. Ron Worthy, BNN, reporting live from South Miami Beach, Florida.

"A huge crowd of onlookers grows by the hour, thousands now trying to get a glimpse at what some are calling the smoking gun in the untimely disappearance of legendary Tejana music star Glorietta Zomata who has been missing for a decade and a half.

"Authorities have closed off the area around an old-style Bell 206 Twin Ranger helicopter which seemingly materialized out of thin air last night around six o'clock Eastern. This craft disappeared sixteen years ago from Austin Texas, and with it, supposedly, the seventeen-year-old Glorietta.

"Witnesses reported nothing out of the ordinary until after 6 p.m. last night, when, suddenly, the helicopter appeared on the beach sitting just as you see it now behind me. No one saw it wash up, no one saw it fly in, and no one can explain why the bird appears to have not aged a single day.

"The singer's mysterious vanishing has immortalized Glorietta's music. It is said that her live performances made her audiences fall in love with her, and that her sudden departure made her a legend.

"Early responders from the Miami-Dade Sheriff's Office report the chopper is riddled with bullet holes. There is visible smoke damage to the interior. It could not have flown far in this condition.

"The registration number, N5106T, still clearly visible on the tail boom, matches FAA records. Is someone pulling off a well-orchestrated hoax in order to reignite Glorietta's music?"

The reporter turned and looked toward the chopper. "I'm standing here a hundred yards away from the helicopter, and I would remind viewers that if you look beyond the Twin Ranger and out to sea, you're looking into an area known as The Bermuda Triangle."

He turned again to face the camera. "The region, sometimes called 'The Devil's Triangle,' is famous for mysterious disappearances of ships and planes, tales of space and time warps, magnetic disturbances, and other unexplained phenomena. But this bird was not flying in the Triangle when it went missing. So, how did it disappear in Texas sixteen years ago, then end up here last night?

"Will forensic experts be able to determine what happened? Was the beloved singer on board indeed as the legend would have it? Will they find any remains? Does this Bell 206 Twin Ranger hold the keys to the mystery? Glorietta's fans certainly hope so.

"Ron Worthy reporting live from South Miami Beach."

Hook 'em Horns!

Sixteen years earlier

Cody Musket was in hiding, and his family wasn't talking. After being pronounced dead twice at Methodist Hospital in Houston, Cody had been restored to life through a top-secret medical technique invented by Ryan Maxwell, an unknown US Department of Defense researcher whose laboratories do not officially exist.

Subsequently, Cody's inner circle had arranged for him to have a "timeout" from public life because he wanted to escape the controversy surrounding his sudden resurrection, and he needed time to recover physically and emotionally at his own pace.

His friends and family had managed to sneak him out of the hospital and onto a native Cherokee reservation in Oklahoma where he was welcomed with open arms. He had been sequestered there for the past seven months. Life with the Cherokee was good, and he had benefited from their quietness, discretion, and friendship. Meanwhile, the world never stops.

~   ~   ~

University of Texas Campus, Austin, Texas. "Good evening, ladies and gentlemen. Welcome to the brand-new Roger Simmons Center. In case you don't know me, I'm University of Texas Athletic Director, Colt Durham."

The audience laughed, then applauded as the well-known and popular UT athletic director gave himself an unnecessary intro.

"What a great way to kick off this brand-new fall semester, and what a privilege for me to introduce someone else who needs no introduction. So let's give it up for Texas University Women's Basketball Coach Kristy Willis!"

The audience extended a rousing reception to their coach who had led the Texas Lady Longhorns to the Final Four NCAA Tournament three seasons running. Coach Willis acknowledged her warm reception, then raised her hands to quiet the enthusiastic crowd.

"Students, faculty, alumni, Athletic Director Durham, and members of the press, welcome! You already know why we're here. Now, I'm going to make it official. Eight days ago, I received a text from Knoxi Musket which simply said, *"I'm all in!"*

A deafening applause erupted as the coach now confirmed the rumor that had been circulating all week — Knoxi Musket would soon become a Lady Longhorn. Texas University burnt orange T-shirts with Knoxi's facial image imprinted had already appeared around campus.

Behind the backdrop curtain, Knoxi wrestled with the butterflies. A crowd of about four thousand had packed the new Roger Simmons Convocation Center to welcome her. She was accompanied backstage by her friend and protector, Elena Rafferty, and by special friend Jeremy McNair, a 19-year-old baseball phenom who had recently been drafted by the Los Angeles Dodgers.

Jeremy, like his father Tanner, always fancied himself as the coolest among the sly. "Don't be scared, Knox. These people gonna love you, jus' like I do. This ain't nothin' afta' that speech you made in Rome last January."

"Do I look nervous?" She rolled her eyes. "What gave it away?"

"Well, for one thing, you gotchur shoes on 'na wrong feet! Here, lemme change 'em for you." Jeremy knelt down.

"Jeremy McNair, don't you dare touch my shoes! You're worse than your daddy!"

"*Ha-ha!* See there? You gon' be fine!"

As the applause continued, Knoxi looked through a small opening between the curtains and peered out at the crowd. She focused on an individual sitting directly in front of the stage wearing a press badge. "The only thing that bothers me," she said, "is Rolfe Sagan from BNN sitting right on the front row. He hates my dad and thinks our whole family is delusional."

"Don't worry. He ain't gon' bully you. Elena and your mom are here, and besides, if anybody mess wi'chu, they gon' deal wid me."

The audience settled down as Coach Willis made her brief remarks and formal introduction.

"As you know," the tall coach reminded, "it's been a traumatic year for Knoxi, with the accidental shooting seven months ago of her father Cody and the subsequent events. She couldn't decide whether to stay with her sequestered father to help him recover faster, or to accept a basketball scholarship and follow in the footsteps of her mother, Brandi, a former All-American at Stanford. We gave her a third option, and she wisely took it!"

The crowd stood and acknowledged their coach once more with brisk applause. She held up her hands for quiet again.

"The Muskets have been active for two decades fighting human trafficking, saving distressed children. Knoxi herself has a storied past, having engineered her own escape from traffickers at age six. She has appeared on the covers of *Sporting News* and *African Sunrise,* and has spoken on every continent. She speaks three languages, is an outstanding student, and has received seventeen basketball scholarship offers from other universities. What an honor to introduce now. Knoxi Musket, welcome to the University of Texas!"

Knoxi was jolted by the fresh applause — thousands of hands moving so quickly she could feel the breeze. She pranced gracefully toward the podium, her bouyant ponytail bouncing and swaying 'neath her Texas team cap. The UT band played the Texas fight song while cheerleaders performed acrobatic maneuvers exhorting everyone to reach maximum volume. The stage boards underfoot rumbled from the vibes.

Knoxi was no stranger to the noise, having grown up listening to huge crowds cheer her father when he played baseball. Now, they cheered for her, applauding as if she might single-handedly deliver a national championship to the university, though she had not yet played a single game.

Being a Musket, she had learned one lesson very well — never let momentary mass delirium trap you in its crosshairs. She thought of her father's self-admonition by which he had excelled at his sport: *"Stay within yourself, don't lose your head, do your best, and have fun doing it."*

Knoxi raised both hands, displaying the familiar *hook 'em Horns* gesture, a staple of Texas Longhorn culture.

"Hook 'em Horns!" she screamed into the mic.

The building came unhinged. Students waved UT towels in the air, making a sea of burnt orange. The noise level increased again.

"Thank you for such a rousing rush!" she yelled, giving rise to more whistles and cheers. After a few moments, anxious to hear Knoxi's remarks, the crowd quieted again. Knoxi looked toward the balcony and saw her nervous mother Brandi, waving and beaming.

"Some have asked why I chose Texas. Why not Baylor like my dad? Why not Stanford like my mom? Texas is where I belong. I wanna study law under Matt Wellington, and I can intern with the Texas Legislature during the summers. I have plans to enter politics someday, and Texas is the best fit for me." She waited while the audience clapped again.

"When Coach Willis first approached me, she made me feel comfortable even though I'll be the smallest player on the team at five-nine. Thank you, Coach Willis, for this amazing opportunity!"

Her new coach came to Knoxi's side. "As agreed, we have time for several questions from members of the press. What would you like to ask Knoxi?"

The first individual to stand was Rolfe Sagan of Beltway News Network (BNN). Knoxi braced herself. Sagan was a household name, with a reputation for being a bully during interviews.

"Knoxi," he asked, "how's your father?"

"He—he's recovering nicely, Mr. Sagan. He should be able to attend his Hall of Fame induction ceremony next summer."

"So, Knoxi, in the past months you've been making broad statements about human trafficking. You talk about your faith and how good always wins out, when clearly that is not the case. Do you plan to continue those outdated remarks as a representative of this fine university? If so, how can you justify it?"

The room fell silent. Knoxi cleared her throat. "Uh, Mr. Sagan, I believe —"

"And about your father," he interrupted. "Is he still suffering from that delusion about going to heaven and all that hocus-pocus?"

Kristy Willis stepped in. "Let's limit the questions to basketball-related subjects, shall we?"

"Pardon me, Coach," Sagan argued. "I was not aware you were planning to muzzle the press tonight. I'm doing this university a favor."

"It's okay, Coach," Knoxi said. "I don't mind." She gripped the lectern with both hands. "Now, Mr. Sagan, anything I say publicly will be strictly my own opinion, not someone else's. I'm grateful this university accepts me as I am. I leave all the drama to journalists who've fallen in love with their own spin each time they profile someone to make them fit the prejudices of their readers."

"What did you say? Profile? I am the leading journalist in America. I'm also an Atheist. You religious people are the biggest profilers of all. You're so naïve that you would call me a profiler? Do you know who I am? Go ahead. Be frank, be specific. Don't talk in generalities."

"Okay. As long as we're being frank, I know who you are, Mr. Sagan. You are one of the most influential UT alums in the world. You are the man who has everything, and a man who has nothing."

"That sounded rehearsed. Let's cut to the chase, Knoxi. In all your speeches, you claim to see miracles, but you speak in generalities. Miracles? Can't you see that what you call a miracle is just a natural-occurring event? When's the last time you saw a blind person made to see? A crippled person walk? An instantaneous healing like you read about in your Bible?

"If I didn't know better, Rolfe, I'd say you are baiting me. So, let me ask you a question first, then I'll answer yours. Do you know the purpose of the prostate gland?"

A sudden silence caught everyone by surprise, and the not-so-mild-mannered reporter seemed off his game. "What? The prostate? Are we getting personal now? Should I ask you about the purpose of your uterus? How personal do you wanna get with me, child?"

"You asked for frank, Rolfe. I'm being frank. Do you know the purpose of the prostate gland? It's found only in males, of course."

A thin applause with a few laughs waved through the crowd. The uncomfortable administrators and faculty had never seen a public discussion of this nature between a powerful alumnus and a freshman student. Was this even the right forum for this conversation?

Knoxi answered her own question. "The prostate secretes an alkaline-balanced fluid to protect the sperm and equip it to survive when it reaches the more acidic environment of the female body. It also provides just the right chemical to enable the sperm to bore into the female egg and fertilize it. Without the prostate, normal conception would not be possible."

"My god, young lady, you sound like a rambling medical journal. So, you memorized all that, but what's your point?"

Athletic Director Colt Durham decided to declare the meeting over. He was not about letting a veteran reporter bully an eighteen-year-old UT freshman on his watch. He stood to his feet and started toward the microphone, but one look at Knoxi's poised face and steady-as-she-goes body language made him find his seat again.

"My point, you ask?" Knoxi folded her hands confidently on the podium. "The prostate is a male gland created with the female in mind. If you believe that all of creation was caused by a mindless entity with no ability to reason, to think or plan, congratulations; you have more faith than I do, sir."

Brandi stood up from her seat in the balcony to show solidarity with her daughter, as did others.

"Rolfe, I spent a week last May in Mozambique with a missionary couple who feeds over ten thousand orphans every month. We spent the second night in a mud hut next to a garbage dump. I mean, it wasn't exactly a five-star in Malibu. A woman brought us her two children who were lifeless and cold. Their eyes were open, and . . . and they were both covered with flies."

"Knoxi, Knoxi, you're getting way off the subject."

A large man in a Texas Longhorn cap stood and pointed at Sagan. "Hey! Shut up! Show some respect!" Sagan sat back down.

Quietness descended upon the gathering once again.

Knoxi's huge blue eyes now glistened with visible tears, softening the audience in the afterglow of her passion. "This—this woman . . . she wanted me to hold her babies and pray for them. I mean, the way they smelled . . . I didn't want them at first. Then, I was so ashamed of myself that I took them and held them next to my heart. I don't know how long I prayed — maybe three, four minutes, maybe just thirty seconds.

"All of a sudden, I felt these two little lifeless bodies warm up. They began to cry. I mean, I was so happy. But I looked around and everyone who had gathered acted like it was commonplace. They've seen it before. The babies and mother were ushered away from there and taken to a feeding center."

"Knoxi, I can think of at least ten other explanations for what you saw."

"Mr. Sagan, do you have any inner peace at all? I've been frank and I have answered your questions. Please give me the same consideration."

"Peace? Hell no!" He paused, then glanced to his left and to his right. He composed himself. "I mean . . . nobody has peace in this world. Nobody. Don't further delude yourself, child."

"Rolfe, I made a choice to trust God long before I saw my first miracle. I believe because I want to believe. I trust God not because I see miracles, but rather, I see miracles because I trust God."

Knoxi stepped from behind the lectern and stood in front. "The truth is, Mr. Sagan, I've made my choice and you have made yours. My choice has brought me peace. Yours has not. But we don't have to hate each other just because we disagree."

The students and faculty responded with a standing ovation, but clearly, there were dissenters.

Knoxi raised her *hook 'em Horns* gesture one more time. "Listen everyone! Don't forget that Glorietta Zomata will be performing tomorrow night at the Erwin Center following our Texas barbeque feast. All my teammates and coaches will be there, so come join the party!"

As Knoxi was escorted toward the exit, things heated up. Elena Rafferty, her personal bodyguard, and Jeremy, her boyfriend, had gotten separated from her, squeezed out by a host of suddenly-aggressive reporters, fans, and apparent outsiders. Knoxi sensed danger. They were no longer moving, the crowd pressing closer and closer. Some began shouting racial slurs, anti-Christian hate, bullying their way through the crowd and reaching toward her with snarling faces. She wasn't prepared for this.

She felt someone tugging at her arm. She turned to look. A small female police officer was pulling her sleeve.

"Come with me," the Latina officer said, her voice trembling, tears on her face. "We need to get out of here. *¡Prisa!*" ("Hurry!")

The young woman gave Knoxi an orange hoodie to wear as a disguise and began pulling her away. Her face was familiar, but Knoxi couldn't place her. She was frail, but ravishing, with soft, brown curls falling around her shoulders, a smooth, round face and dark charismatic eyes. She was in a hurry, distressed, panicky.

With the hoodie over her head, Knoxi bent low and followed. "What's wrong? Where are we going?"

The trembling woman begged Knoxi to trust her. *"Por favor, señorita, confía en mí, ¿de acuerdo?* ("Please, miss, trust me, okay?")

"Okay," Knoxi replied. "But let me call my mom and boyfriend first. My bodyguard is here too."

This obviously concerned the officer. *"Confío en ti, pero ¿puedo confiar en ellos?"* ("Can I trust them?")

"*Sí!* Of course!" Knoxi was becoming edgy. "Of course you can trust them! *¡Por supuesto usted puede confiar en ellos! Okay? ¡Ellos son como mi familia!"* ("You should trust them completely. They're like family!")

"*Está bien, 'tá bien!"* ("Okay, okay!"), the young woman said, glancing around nervously. "Call them. Tell them to meet us in that room over there underneath the stairs." She pointed toward a gray metal door. "I have a key."

As she approached the door, Knoxi texted Elena, Brandi, and Jeremy. Her nervous guide looked around again, covering her face.

Knoxi's curiosity suddenly paid off as she looked deeply into the sad brown eyes of the young woman. *"Se quien eres,"* ("I know who you are,") Knoxi whispered softly. "You're Glorietta Zomata. You're supposed to perform tomorrow. Who are you hiding from? *¿Por qué te disfrazas de policía?"* ("Why are you masquerading as a police officer?")

"It's okay." Glorietta tried to calm herself. "I speak English good. I'll explain to everyone when we get inside."

Just then, Brandi and Jeremy arrived.

"Wassup, Knox? Did we miss something?" Jeremy's eyes grew to the size of golf balls. "Whoa! You're Glorietta!"

"*Shhhh!*" Knoxi shook her head. "C'mon, let's get inside."

Elena showed up out of breath. "What gives?"

Glorietta glanced around again as if to make certain no one was watching, then hurriedly opened the door. After they entered, Glorietta frantically closed and locked it. The room was pitch-black.

"It's dark in here," Elena said. "Where's the switch? *¿Dónde encender la luz, huh?*" ("Where is the light, huh?")

They stood in the darkened room for what seemed an eternity while Elena felt along the wall for a light switch. Suddenly, Elena stopped and listened. They had entered the room as five. Now, she heard a sixth breath sound.

Knoxi sensed as much. Even in the musty darkness, she knew someone was behind her. Just then, two huge arms surrounded her and began pulling her backward. "*Ughh!*"

Death Trap

The five women held their collective breath in the dark utility room, stricken by the bitter reality that they were not alone. Elena found the light switch and flipped it on. They turned to behold a well-dressed man the size of Guadalupe Mountain holding Knoxi in his grasp.

"I want every cell phone tossed into that bucket," his grisly voice demanded. "And if anyone tries to leave through that door, I will snap this lady's neck. We have men stationed on the other side of that door waiting 'till I come out, so don't think you're gonna go anywhere until I say so. Now, cell phones in the bucket! Do it!"

They dropped their phones as instructed into a bucket filled with soapy water.

The deep voice was that of a tall, heavy-set male, clean-shaven, with a square jaw, pug nose, and shaved head. He wore an in-your-face tat on his right forearm which displayed four letters: USMC.

He looked professional enough with his white long-sleeved shirt, tie, pressed trousers, and a pair of Claiborne Extraordinaire loafers which did not come cheap. With sleeves rolled up to his elbows, ripped forearms, and hands as large as bowling balls, he was The Hulk dressed to kill.

He reached down with one hand, pulled a gun from his front pocket, and looked at Elena. "You're just like me, I can see it on your face. If you have a weapon, remove the mag and drop the gun in the bucket. Now!"

Elena noticed that his pistol, an Italian Staccato .45 automatic, was not equipped with a silencer. Was the room soundproof? Would he risk firing the weapon knowing that others might hear and send help? What about his associates supposedly stationed on the other side of the door? Was it a bluff? He was wearing an earpiece; he was definitely equipped for communication with someone.

Knoxi was keen to see the complete transformation of Jeremy's face. His forest-green eyes, usually cute-n-sly, were now fierce like a junkyard animal wanting to rip apart an intruder. Brandi reflected terror on her face. Glorietta cowered in the corner sobbing.

Elena stared calmly into the killer-eyes of their adversary. She slowly pulled her Beretta M9 handgun from beneath her evening jacket, removed the magazine, and dropped it into the bucket with the phones. "What is it you want?" she inquired. "Why were you hiding in here?"

"All we want is Alex. I walk out with her, everybody else lives. That's the deal."

"Alex? Who's that?"

Glorietta whimpered, "Uh . . . that's me. They want me. My real name is Alexis Blanca. I'm from Nogales." She covered her face. "Nogales, Mexico."

Knoxi's head was exploding with each heartbeat. The cold gun barrel against her right temple and the huge left hand choking her windpipe darkened her vision. She could hear the triggerman's teeth grinding. Was he as nervous as she?

Her father had drilled her repeatedly with the words, "If you want to handle others, learn to handle yourself first."

Cody had told her of being held as a human shield by two Taliban warriors in Afghanistan. It was life or death for himself, for his comrades. Cody had instructed Knoxi in martial arts, had even taught her the moves he had used that day to free himself. She had practiced over and over, but this was different. This wasn't just practice.

Mother and daughter looked into each other's eyes. Brandi's were tearful. Knoxi's were perfectly clear. This man was letting no one go. They had seen his face. Brandi understood, got the message.

Knoxi had always been Cody; she had lived that way, would die that way.

Knoxi's hands and feet began to fly so fast it startled everyone including their ungracious host. She was able to snatch away the pistol while twisting herself into position to administer a groin kick. She planned to follow up with a crushing blow to the larynx, then use the pistol if necessary.

But the big man quickly came to his senses. He forced her fingers to release the gun, dropping it to the floor. He caught her fist before it could reach his throat and seized her by the neck with his other paw.

Knoxi coughed, a sudden struggle to breathe. Frantically, Elena thrust her hand into the bucket with a splash, searching for her pistol and magazine. That's when another unexpected event occurred.

It began with a shout, followed by the blunt thud of Jeremy's head crashing into the ribcage of the malefactor. Jeremy's assault had come like a blur, catching the would-be killer before he could move a single muscle. Like a runaway locomotive did Jeremy's legs drive the Hulkish aggressor into the back wall, forcing the iron-chested behemoth to fight for breath while trying not to collapse in a heap.

Jeremy staggered backward a few steps and fell to his knees, obviously bell-rung by using his own head as a demolition ball. The big man stood up and administered a powerful blow to Jeremy's nose rendering him motionless and face down on the floor, then he reached for his Staccato .45, seized it before Knoxi could retrieve it, and aimed it at Knoxi's head.

Brandi screamed, *"Nooo!"* She closed her eyes and placed her hands over her ears.

A gunshot resounded like a cannon discharge in that tiny room. The ringing boom was followed by the sounds of a collapsing table and the soapy mop bucket overturning. The smell of spent gunpowder visited every nostril. Glorietta held her ears and sat in the corner screaming hysterically.

Brandi's knees collapsed. With eyes tightly closed, she saw flashes like lightning passing from right to left. Then she heard a distant voice.

"Somebody help me. Jeremy's hurt!"

The voice seemed faint, other-worldly. Brandi lost all the air in her lungs as she finally opened her eyes. Knoxi was kneeling over Jeremy, saying, "Mama, help me. Jeremy's hurt bad."

The fallen figure of the Hulk-man lay in a pool of blood, his eyes open, a hole in his temple.

Elena was all business. She holstered her smoking Beretta which still dripped with soapy water. "Is anyone else hurt?"

Knoxi coughed. "My neck. I couldn't breathe for a few seconds, and his fingernails dug in." She put her hand to her throat and realized she was bleeding.

Suddenly, came a pounding at the door.

"Orlando! Orlando, ¿qué está pasando? ¿Por qué no está utilizando su dispositivo de comunicación?" ("Orlando, Orlando, what's happened? Why won't you answer?")

"Who's that?" Brandi whispered, trying to calm herself.

"His associates," Elena whispered back. "And they wanna know why Orlando's gone dark. We don't know how many of them are out there, and they don't know how many of us are in here."

"What're we gonna do?" Knoxi asked. "Jeremy may need a hospital. How do we get outta here?"

Elena stood next to the door and addressed the voice on the other side. "Uh, no speaky, yawl. Listen, dawlin', does anybody out there speak English? If so, I can tell yawl what happened just as quick as a midnight ace in Laredo."

A different voice answered. "You'd better talk fast then, darlin'. Where's Orlando?"

Elena turned around and whispered to Brandi. "So, now we know there are at least two." She faced the door again. "Uh, my bosses sent me down here from Fort Worth jes this mawnin' on a mission. I'm 'fraid I got bad news for you, sweetie pie. We are claiming Glorietta as our property. It pained me to put poor ol' Orlando down, but he jes wouldn't cooperate."

All was quiet at first, then someone on the other side began barking out commands, sending several subordinates scrambling. "*¡Prisa! Ve a investigar! ¡Descubre quién es esta mujer!*" ("Hurry up! Check out her story!")

Elena whispered to the others, "They didn't buy it but it bought us some time. He told some guys to check out my story. That'll keep 'em busy for a few minutes."

"So sweetheart," the English-speaking voice said, "best give it up now. Nobody here believes your story. Who are you?"

"I am your worst nightmare, Loverboy. We don't like you Mexicans comin' into our territory. Keep yo little fanny on the otha' side of the river or us Texans are gonna fertilize the territory with you. Now I'm sure you don't want the police here any more than we do, so let's break it up afore it's too late."

She walked back toward Knoxi. "Can Jeremy walk? I notice he's sitting up. We don't have much time."

"Yeah, yeah. I ain't totally useless," Jeremy slurred. "I guess I sort of made a fool outta m'self, huh? *Ha!* Stupid, stupid. I nearly got us all killed."

"Oh, honey." Knoxi used a clean wet towel to wash the blood from his mouth and chin. "You were so brave. You saved my life."

"She's right, Jeremy," Elena said. "Straight up. You had no choice, and don't ever let yourself believe otherwise. You understand, young man?"

"Well I trained in martial arts my whole life. Cody and my dad taught me. Cody wudda thrown that piece of garb in the trash. Straight up, as you say. I'm bigger than Cody. I shudda taken that guy."

Elena helped Jeremy to his feet. "The difference is, the dead man on the floor was more than an expert. He was a killer. To be good at that, you have to train for it until you think of yourself as a killer. You don't ever want to carry that raw edge on you, son. Believe me, I've been there, and so has Cody. Now, can you walk?"

"Yes, ma'am."

"Brandi, check the dead guy for some sort of ID and see if he has a phone. We need a way to communicate with the outside world. Gather up our wet cell phones; best not to leave anything behind that'll identify us."

Elena turned to Knoxi. "Your boyfriend's eyes look dark and puffy. See if you can find some ice in that freezer over there. He may have a broken nose. Maybe a concussion."

Everyone waited a moment for Elena to collect her thoughts. "Nobody make a sound," she said. "I need to hear them. They don't know I speak their language."

"Orlando's clean." Brandi knelt beside the body. "No ID, no phone."

"What's keeping them from just rushing in here?" Knoxi asked.

"Same thing that keeps us from going out there," Elena said. "They don't know our numbers or our weapons. As soon as they figure out the Fort Worth story is bogus, they'll come right through that door. Count on it!"

Brandi stood up again. "So, where are all the people who work in this building? Didn't someone hear the shot? This room isn't soundproof."

"It's nearly ten o'clock, Mama. "Most of 'em have gone home."

Elena agreed. "This building emptied fast. I wanna know who gave Alex the key to this room and why Orlando was waiting here."

"Good questions," Brandi said. "They knew Alex was coming. Orlando was waiting. They were gonna do the job in this room, then put the parts in those disposal bags over there and. . ."

"Right," Elena said. "They hadn't counted on Alex bringing friends with her." She looked at Alex sitting in the corner. "Somebody set you up, honey. We're gonna find the answers, but first we gotta get outta here."

"Get outta here?" Jeremy fumed. "How you plannin' to do that?"

"I did my homework, Jeremy. The schematics show a crawl-thru door inside that mop closet. It leads to Section C."

"What about the body?" Knoxi wanted to know.

"Leave it. We'll call the police as soon as we find a phone."

"*No, señora!*" Alex whimpered frantically. "*Please, no policía!*"

"No police? Why not?"

"I'm illegal here. Pólicia will send me back to Nogales. I will end up back at factory where they throw the bodies."

"What? What bodies?"

"I cannot be Glorietta anymore because cartel know my identity now. I can't be Alexis anymore because police will send me back. Ohhh, I get you all in trouble. *Es muy peligroso.* (It is very dangerous) You should just leave me. I will get you killed."

"No, no," Elena said, intending to calm her. "*Discutiremos esto más adelante, okay?*" ("We will discuss this later, okay?") I wanna hear your story as soon as we're in a secure place. We're not leaving you." Elena bent low and looked into her eyes. "*¿Entiendes, señorita?*" ("Do you understand, young lady?")

A spark lightened the young woman's face. "Why? Why you help me? This is America. I'm nobody. Americans, they want only profit."

Elena quickly back to business. "Brandi, pick up Orlando's weapon. We might need it. Careful, that Staccato has a hair trigger. Make sure the safety's on. Somebody hand me that small toolbox and hold this flashlight steady for me while I hunt for that trap door."

Alex wiped her face and stood to her feet. "I hold the light for you."

DODGER BLUES, PINK HEARTS

With a shaky hand, Alex held the light while Elena located the trap door inside the closet. Elena removed eight bolts and pulled the four-foot-square panel off the wall.

"Come on, we're runnin' outta time," she said as she let them pass through first. The opening led to a stand-up utility tunnel where they stopped and gathered.

"Follow me," Elena whispered. "Are you okay, Jeremy? You look a little wobbly."

"We have him," Knoxi said as she and Brandi supported him. Alex continued to hold the light for the group as Elena led them through the short tunnel. Jeremy had to stoop since the passage was not tall enough for him to stand up.

They came to a louvered utility door which opened into Section C of the Simmons Center. Elena listened intently before opening. She could still hear the distant conversation of the hostile men they had left behind in Section B, but she heard nothing else.

She inspected her weapon, took a breath, then spoke. "Alright. I'm going first. There is an office directly across the floor about thirty yards away. The building is dark except for the service lights. It should be safe. Wait for my signal."

Elena made it safely, picked the lock, opened the door, and entered. The spacious conference room was superbly arrayed with burnt orange and gray leather and a large oak table surrounded by matching chairs and cabinetry. A ginormous, intimidating picture of Bevo, the Texas Longhorn mascot, covered an entire wall. One landline phone occupied the table, but the connection was dead.

Elena motioned for the others to come one by one. After they had all arrived, she laid out her plan. "We should keep our voices down and the lights off. You can check that fridge for food. There might be something edible. Everybody get comfortable and stay here. I should be back in a few minutes."

"Where are you going?" Brandi's face was distraught. "Elena, what are you doing?"

"Going hunting."

"What?" Knoxi mirrored her mother's confusion. "Hunting for what?"

"Trust me." She departed through the door and closed it behind her.

"Mama, what if she doesn't come back? It's too dangerous."

"Look, baby, we don't have any choice. This is what Elena and Baker do. I'm sure she'll obtain a phone and several other things we can use."

Brandi and Knoxi found breakfast croissants and bottles of cold spring water inside the fridge. They passed them out to the group.

Knoxi sat down next to Alex. "Tell us what you meant about the bodies in Nogales. And why did you seek me out earlier in disguise? Did you think I could help you?"

"Is—is not what you think," she began. "I living in Juarez. My mama, papa murdered 'bout four year ago. I was an only children."

"An only child? You have no brothers or sisters?"

"Si. No brother, no sister. No parents. I was thirteen. I have no work, no skills. I was good singer." She smiled. "I love to sing, but nobody listen."

Knoxi walked to the fridge to get another bottle of cold water. "Go ahead, Alex. I can hear you."

"So this man, tall handsome, come to me and invite me to Nogales to work in clothing factory. They make designer jeans — Azteca Calientes designer jeans." She put her hand over her lips and trembled.

Suddenly, Jeremy startled everyone. "Did you say Azteca Calientes? Like these I'm wearing? You mean those owners are responsible for what happened to you?"

"Uh . . . Si, Mr. Jeremy. They very bad men. They make us do things. They treat us like —"

Jeremy jumped up, unbuckled his belt, pulled off his jeans one leg at a time, and dunked them into the trash with considerable prejudice. "I ain't wear dese no more!"

Suddenly the air went out of the room. It wasn't so much Jeremy's bizarre, out-of-character behavior, but his big blue and pink boxers that stole the show. Brandi reminded everyone to hold down the noise.

The three women, mouths wide open, sat in total disbelief for a few seconds. Brandi seemed the most concerned. "Jeremy, honey, you've been injured — your head. Maybe you should sit down, sweetie."

But Knoxi found Jeremy's behavior more entertaining than worrisome. "Jeremy McNair!" Whispering, her face fiery red. "I didn't know you wore sports boxers with blue polka dots and pink hearts!" She snickered and clapped her hands together silently.

Alex unexpectedly dropped her head to the table, shaking with uncontrollable laughter. She held her hand over her mouth to muffle her laughing voice. "Oh, Mr. Jeremy, sexy pink hearts! *Muy caliente!*" ("Very hot!")

"I ain't wear dem jeans no more. And for evabody's information, these dots are Dodger Blue."

Knoxi decided to stir the pot. "For everyone's information, Jeremy knows how to use proper English. He knows ain't ain't a word."

Jeremy lunged forward and tried to grab Knoxi's arm, but she scooted away into the adjoining office squealing like a mouse with Jeremy in hot pursuit.

After they had disappeared into the other room, Elena came through the front door carrying an armful of men's clothing. Brandi and Alex were too distracted to notice.

"Wow, Ms. Brandi. I think Mr. Jeremy, he recovered quickly."

"I'm not sure *that's* what you call recovery," Brandi answered.

Elena stood quietly, now listening as well. "He may not remember this tomorrow. He may have a concussion."

Brandi's edginess grew. "Is he dangerous? Might he hurt Knoxi or himself?"

"I doubt that," Elena said. "He cares deeply for her. Still, concussions are serious. Jeremy should be evaluated."

The women could hear Jeremy talking quietly while Knoxi giggled. In a few moments came complete silence from the other room. Brandi was compelled to move nonchalantly toward the open door. Eavesdropping was not her favorite thing, but . . .

She stopped and stood just shy of the opening. Jeremy was trying to choke out an apology. "I'm sorry, Knox. I . . . I might as well come out and say it. I—I'm scared. I've never been afraid of nothin' in my life. I mean, I've been sheltered. My parents, they such kind people. They raised me to be the same. We give money to help people just like Alex, but I—I ain't . . . I mean . . . I never met anybody like her before. I ain't never seen evil like I saw today. Right now, I'm just plain scared."

"Well, Jeremy, that means you've grown a little today. We're all scared. I am so proud that you are a kind, considerate man with such high expectations for yourself. Now, listen to me; I love your Dodger Blue, and we've known each other since we were three, but you need to put some pants on. You hear me? Tomorrow you'll be embarrassed if you even remember this."

When the couple joined the other three in the main room, Elena tossed Jeremy a pair of large trousers. "Here. See if these fit."

Brandi wanted to know where the trousers had come from.

"I took 'em off those banditos. I have three pairs here. Shirts and cell phones too."

"How did you get these?" Knoxi asked.

"I told you I was going hunting. They never knew what hit 'em. I left all three of 'em tied up in the ladies' room in their skivvies."

"What happens when the authorities find Orlando's body?" Brandi asked. "Your bullet will be found in his head."

"The syndicate has a second crew working that room right now. They'll have that place squeaky-clean in no time. I want to hear Alex's story before we think about calling the authorities. We've suspected the existence of an underground movement involved in trafficking for over a year. Possible South Texas law enforcement officers involved in some sort of sick alliance with Mexican businesses and even Mexican police. If Alex is a link, we may have stumbled onto something tonight."

THE PUREST MUSIC

"Those trousers look good on you Jeremy. Perfect fit." Brandi was in a more jovial mood.

"Yes, ma'am, 'cept I don't like wearin' pants some monster left his own sweat in."

"How's your head?" Elena used a small flashlight to check his eyes. "You should rest. Try to sleep. We'll have to sneak outta here later tonight."

"So, what's the plan?" Knoxi asked. "When can we leave?"

"I spoke to Baker. I briefed him. He's gonna call some people and buzz me back ASAP. Might still be bogies in this building. Not safe yet."

"Uh, señora, you husband? He good man?"

"Yes he is, Alex. Good husband. Good father."

"What did Orlando mean when he say you just like him?"

"He was wrong, Alex. Don't ever let an enemy tell you who you are. It'll usually be a lie."

Knoxi spoke up. "Alex, do you feel like telling us about the bodies at the factory in Nogales? What were you talking about?"

Alex took a burdensome breath and lost the brightness in her eyes again. "I was born in Juarez. When I lose my parents, I'm thirteen. This tall man, Pablo Cisneros — handsome, friendly — he offer me job in Nogales at jeans factory. I have no choice."

"*¿Te mudaste a Nogales?*" (Did you move to Nogales?") Elena asked.

"Si, he recruit me. After I move there, I discover all workers are women. No men. They give us tiny room for sleep. Let nobody leave.

No vacation. No days off. We are like prisoners. Policía guard us, how you say in English, twenny-four-seven. Then I notice some women disappear. I see men take them away. They never come back. Four women."

Knoxi and Elena traded a brief glance. Brandi came and sat down with them. Jeremy rested on a sofa in the other office with an icepack on his face.

"One night, Pablo come into my room. He drunk. He . . . smell worse than horse, like dead body. Bloody fingers. He make me —" She hid her face. "Por favor. I cannot tell you what he do to me."

Brandi and Knoxi reached across the table, but Alex got up and went into the corner. "*Por favor*. No touch me." She held up her arms. "Please, no touch me." She sat down on the floor and hid her face.

"Okay, Alex. You don't have to say any more. We won't —"

"Later, I find out I am pregnant." Her lip tremored. "Pablo come and say he want a son . . . want to train him to take over business someday. He want my child to grow up and be killer like him. Every night I beg God to save me from that place before my son born, but nothing happen."

No one spoke. No one breathed. Even Elena showed tearful eyes and swallowed hard.

"After Zorro was born, I —"

"Excuse me, Alex," Brandi said. "You named your son Zorro?"

"Si. Yes, I did. El Zorro means the fox. One day he escape like a fox and bring justice. I name him Zorro!"

"Where is the boy now," Elena wanted to know.

"I dunno if he alive or dead. I thought they would let me be his mother, but after he five months old, they come take me away from him. Three men, they work for Pablo. They take me to the junkyard behind the factory. They . . . they do things to me I cannot say. Beat me, whip, bite. Finally, I play like I am dead. The last thing I remember, I am falling, falling. But when the sun come up . . ." Alex didn't finish. She sat alone in the dark corner wringing her hands.

Knoxi spoke delicately, "Alex, do you want some water?"

"The worst thing was their eyes," Alex sobbed, trying to catch her breath, oblivious to all else. "When the sun come up, I wake up in deep pit, garbage dump. That's where I see them, their eyes open — the four missing women." Her hands tremored covering her face.

"I try not to scream, so I think about the last time I was happy; my son sitting on my lap. I made faces for him and he laugh and laugh and laugh. Musica, musica, his laughter was like music. And I think; if God make something so pure, so sweet, God must be good. It is the only thing give me hope to keep going. The purest music God ever make is the laughter of a child. I can still hear him."

A silence louder than words overshadowed them — sweet, bitter, unthinkable. Elena finally broke the spell, asking quietly, "Alex, how did you get away?"

"They thought I was dead. I climb up to top of hole and just walk away. When I come to the gate, I see one of the men. He was not one who hurt me, he only watched the others. He open gate and let me out. He say he will tell nobody. I have no clothes. He give me his big T-shirt. He pull it over me for cover. I have to sneak away, but they keep my son." She dropped her hands and rocked back and forth, moaning and crying.

Her story was paralyzing. For a frozen moment, no one moved. Elena, Knoxi, and Brandi wanted to embrace her, but the three could only watch the grieving seventeen-year-old who had asked for no touching, no hugging. Then, seemingly out of nowhere, Jeremy approached, tears running across his smashed nose and down his swollen cheeks. He had heard it all from the other room.

He reached down with his massive arms, gently lifted the young woman off the floor, and cradled her like a child. "Shhh, li'l mama. It's okay. We gone get ol' Zorro back. Straight up. We ain't lettin' this stand."

Alex let him carry her to the other room and place her on the couch. He sat on the floor next to her until she stopped crying.

A Flying Leap

Baker called Elena back at 2:30 in the morning. Everyone perked up. It was the call they had been waiting for. Baker was on his way in a Bell Twin Ranger helicopter and would be hovering above the Simmons Center in quiet mode within an hour.

The group of five had been napping, still hunkered down in the first-floor conference room. Jeremy's nose was still swollen and his joints now ached. Everyone was still curious to know how Alex had progressed from being a sweatshop slave to becoming Glorietta the singing sensation in such a short time. But that story could wait.

Now, they focused on how to get from the UT campus to a safe location, and how to construct a story which would explain their visible injuries. No one could know they had been in that utility room earlier.

Another question was what to do with Alex. She could not continue as Glorietta, at least for the present, because it would be too dangerous. If she used her old identity, Alexis Blanca, normal immigration channels would deport her back to Mexico where she would be in even greater danger.

"Okay, listen up, everybody." Elena had called them all together. "Baker has chartered a helicopter and pilot and will be here in about one hour. He'll give us a ten-minute heads-up and let us know exactly where they'll pick us up. We need to be diligent because this area may still be a hot zone."

"How do we explain to the university that Glorietta won't be performing at the Erwin Center?" Knoxi brought up.

"That's one thing we need to work out. Baker has already been in contact with allies in the press, medical profession, and immigration. We're working on a plan to get Alex a new identity for at least the short term so she can stay in this country until the rats are cleared from the nest."

Knoxi wrinkled her nose. "Rats? Nest?"

"Use your imagination, Knox. I hear this lady jus' fine." Jeremy set aside his ice pack. "We gon' set a rat trap, right?"

"*You* won't be setting any traps, Jeremy, but we have some specialists who will," Elena said. Once the rats start to scatter, we'll divide and conquer."

"Divide and conquer? *Qué significa eso?* " Alex asked. "Uh, what does 'divide and conquer' mean?"

"It means we gonna find Zorro, li'l mama. I told you we gonna get little Zorro back. So, 'bout how old you think he is now?"

"My son exactly *dos años y tres meses, cinco días y dos horas,*" she answered with a soft smile, placing her hand over her heart.

Jeremy waited. "And?"

"It means two years, three months, five days and two hours," Knoxi said.

"Well," Jeremy gulped. "Seems to me like he old enough to ride! What can I do?"

"You're doing just fine, young man," Brandi said. "Your father will be so proud that you've become such an encourager."

Knoxi grinned at her able and athletic boyfriend. "That goes for me as well."

At that moment, Elena froze. "Did anyone else hear that?"

Alex began to shake all over. "*Sí! Algunos hombres fuera de la puerta. ¿qué hacemos? ¡Siento tanto que te metí en este lío!*"

"I hear them too," Knoxi confirmed in a strong whisper. "Several men speaking Spanish . . . checking the building . . . looking for us."

"Everyone get in the other room," Elena said. "Stay quiet. I got this."

The door to the conference room was locked. Elena had made certain of it. She was hoping the snoop-dogs didn't have a key. She crouched underneath the oak conference table. From there, she had a clear line of sight to the door, but she would be hidden in the shadows. She drew her Beretta and waited, her speeding pulse pounding inside her head.

The men on the outside tried to open the door. One looked through the glass and shone a flashlight into the room. A moment later, they were gone.

Just then, Loverboy's phone buzzed in her pocket. It was Baker. "Our position is one-five miles east of campus," he told her. "Sitrep?"

"Physically our status is the same," she reported quietly. "All hands safe in Section Charlie. We have unknown hostiles at large."

"Okay," Baker acknowledged. "Can you get to Door 12 if we create a diversion in Section Alfa?"

"Affirmative. Door 12 estimated sixty meters from here. Let us know when to move. And honey, we must not get the police involved."

"Oh, they're involved, all right," Baker hollered. "They're gonna help us escape. LZ in sight at twelve o'clock, two miles. We have permission to land on the helipad near the door. Be ready to move on my command."

Elena briefed everyone. "Make sure we leave behind no evidence that we were here. We must be ready at a moment's notice."

Five minutes passed. Suddenly, they were alerted when they heard sirens, horns, and a series of small explosions. Knoxi peeked between the blinds which covered the window. Two large fire rescue vehicles and one police cruiser drove past the Simmons Center.

Baker called again, sounding desperate. "Change of plan! Change of plan! Can you get to the roof?"

"The roof? Stand by. Looks like the stairway to the catwalk is about thirty meters away. What's up?"

"Go!" he shouted. "Go now. The helipad has been compromised, but the diversion is in progress, so you should have a clear path. Go!"

"Change of plan!" she told the others. "Follow me. Expedite but stay quiet." She gave the two handguns she had taken off Loverboy to Brandi and Knoxi, and kept the Staccato and her Beretta.

They made their way through the dark building to a dimly-lighted utility stairwell, then took the catwalk to the door which opened onto the roof. They stepped outside. A low-level overcast had moved in and a mist was falling. The unlighted Twin Ranger was hovering over the westernmost portion of the roof, unable to come closer due to the presence of guy-wires and communication antennas. Elena led the party across the roof toward the chopper, but their path was dark and slow with vents and other surface obstructions impeding their progress. Suddenly, they heard small arms fire. Bullets began ricocheting near them, bouncing off the flat-roof tiles and striking the nearby vents.

Alex screamed and fell into a fetal position fully exposed on the roof surface. The other three women found cover next to a utility turret. Baker, still aboard the helicopter, had come prepared with an assault rifle and began shooting at the attackers. His muzzle fire, clearly visible in the open door of the aircraft, created just enough light to illuminate a pathway to the helicopter. He continued firing to provide cover for everyone to get aboard.

Elena also returned fire toward the hard-charging hostiles. Knoxi and Brandi joined in, firing from behind cover. Two of the enemy fell, and the rest finally took refuge behind an air conditioner unit. Elena told Knoxi and Brandi to make a run for it. She would stay and cover them.

But Elena had lost track of Jeremy and Alex. When she gazed behind, she was horrified to see Alex lying on the roof in the line of fire. At that instant, Jeremy seemed to appear again out of nowhere. He seized Alex on a dead run and bolted toward the door of the hovering aircraft.

Elena decided to run for it as well, using both pistols as her own cover fire. Jeremy made it to the helicopter with Alex, but Elena fell about twenty feet behind him. Now, the four remaining gunmen charged, automatic weapons firing at will. Bullets began punching through the cabin of the chopper putting the ship in serious peril, and Elena was hit, unable to get back on her feet.

Baker released his safety belt, hoping to go rescue his wife, but Jeremy unexpectedly flew right past him, leaped from the open door of the helicopter, hit the surface running and sprinted toward Elena. The nervous pilot, distracted by the gunfire and the sudden departure of Jeremy's 220-pound frame, was unable to keep the chopper steady. He drifted too far above the surface, panicked, then turned the craft around and headed east to escape the gunfire.

"Go back! You're leaving two behind!" Baker yelled. "Go back!"

"If I turn back now, we're all dead! I can't take that chance!"

Then, the chopper fishtailed as if something had collided with a skid.

The pilot screamed, "What was that!?" He fought to regain control.

Baker looked out through the rear sliding door. Filling his vision was a large African American male with a swollen nose and two black eyes hanging on to the skid with one arm and holding his precious Elena with the other.

FIVE MINUTES

The Twin Ranger had just cleared the rooftop at the Roger Simmons Center. The streets directly below were nearly deserted at 3:30 a.m. A half mile away, however, the student housing complex was coming to life. The gunfire and low-flying helicopter had awakened a sleeping University of Texas campus. Vehicles were moving full-speed-ahead approaching the site of the battle.

But most aboard the chopper failed to notice. Knoxi resembled a scarecrow, the life having drained from her dimpled cheeks. She tried to speak but struggled against hyperventilation. She was still recovering from scrambling across the rooftop trying to outrun real bullets fired from real guns.

She finally caught her breath. *"Baker!* What are we gonna do? Jeremy's gonna fall! What if he drops Elena? We have to land! *We have to land now!"*

Jeremy was swinging in the wind underneath the skid while holding Elena. He had managed to get a solid grip on Elena's collar, but the neck of the lace zip jacket wasn't built for the stress. Her 125-pound body was limp, lifeless. The collar began to tear. The zipper in front began to rip open. Baker realized that within minutes Elena would slip completely out of the garment, leaving Jeremy holding only an empty white jacket with orange lace.

Pilot Marty Luna focused on getting them out of bullet range while Jeremy struggled to hang on. Baker feared that the young hero, already suffering from the blow to his head, might lose consciousness.

Then Brandi coughed. "I smell smoke! Baker, I smell smoke!"

Something was burning. Toxic smoke now swirled about the cabin before being sucked out through the open door. Marty looked back. "I can keep it airborne another five minutes, maybe a little longer if we shed some weight. Maybe I can set 'er down long enough for the healthy ones to get off, then fly Ms. Rafferty to a hospital."

"The kid's losing Elena!" Baker shouted. "He can't hold on another five minutes. What's your airspeed?"

"I've slowed to eighty knots!"

"Reduce airspeed another forty knots! We might be able to get the two of them on board if we slow down. Getting 'em aboard will reduce drag and give this helo a longer range."

"Roger that."

Baker fastened a safety harness to his belt. As the aircraft slowed, Jeremy got the message. He was able to loop one leg over the strut, then lift the limp body of Elena high enough for Baker to slip a harness around her waist and pull her inside. Jeremy's strength finally gave way, but the three healthy women pulled him on aboard and buckled him into a seat.

Jeremy reached up and caught Baker's arm, breathing rapidly, panting, gasping. "How's . . . how's —"

"She's alive, son, barely." Baker cut away the jacket and blouse around Elena's waist. "Looks like a bullet went clean through." He brushed Elena's face while Brandi worked to stop the bleeding. "I didn't know if . . ."

Then he snapped his head around and shouted to Marty. "Get to the clinic where we left our van earlier. It's only 'bout two minutes from here. After you drop us off, it's another three minutes to Moon River. I'll drive over and pick you up. Can you keep this smoker in the air long enough?"

"Affirmative. One turbine's overheating. It musta' been nicked by a bullet. I'll make it work. It's the least I can do."

"Can you stay below radar? I don't want ATC to track us."

"Negative, not in this area. Too many obstructions and low visibility, but I have another idea."

Marty called Austin Area Approach Control. "Austin Approach, Twin Ranger Zero-Six-Tango departing UT campus squawkin' VFR."

"What are you doing?" Baker shouted.

"I'm gonna try to throw 'em off," Marty answered as the return call from ATC crackled in his headset —

"Twin Ranger Zero-Six-Tango, read you loud and clear. Proceed VFR. What is your final destination tonight, sir?"

Marty calmly replied, "Sir, we're headed toward Moon River Ranch, will be dropping below radar coverage shortly. Uh, by the way, we've spotted what looks like a commotion at one of the UT buildings. You might wanna check it out. There is another helicopter involved, might be a practice military op, maybe National Guard. The other chopper is headed south. Do you copy?"

"Affirmative. We have no military aircraft scheduled this morning. Do you still have the other helicopter in sight?"

"Negative, we are now IMC, can't see a thing at our six."

Baker was still hyper. "Do you actually think that'll work?"

"Not really, but worth a try. They'll be searching south for an unidentified helicopter while we're headed north. I'll switch off the transponder when we get close to the clinic so they won't know we landed there. We'll be below their radar by then anyway."

"You ever see action before, Marty?"

"No, sir. I was in the reserve, but —"

"You did fine. Just get us to the clinic, then fly this thing to Moon River Ranch and hide it."

While they approached the clinic, Baker filled Brandi in. "I had this prearranged just in case we needed medical help," he said. "The clinic is managed by Susan Winters. She's a trusted friend and one of the best ER docs in Austin. Her clinic isn't scheduled to open until next week, so there will be no other patients. She'll be discreet. We can't afford for any of this to go public since we may be dealing with some powerful people."

"What happened with plan?" Alex wanted to know. "How come they knew we were coming and shoot at us on roof?"

"Ma'am, we're not sure. But apparently, our transmission-blocking technology succeeded only in blocking the police. The bad guys intercepted our transmissions and deployed to stop us."

"Fortunately, they have no idea who we are," Knoxi said.

"We gotta keep it that way," Baker warned. "I already have someone working on a cover story."

They were met by Dr. Susan Winters and her husband John, a former Green Beret medic. The landing pad at the new clinic was unfinished, forcing the helo to set down on raw dirt. Everyone exited quickly so the pilot could make his departure immediately. Smoke and dust filled the air, whirling and spinning up through the turning rotor blades until the ship was airborne again.

Alex and Knoxi supported Jeremy and guided him to an examination room where John was to evaluate his injuries. It was discovered that, in addition to a concussion and possible broken nose, Jeremy had been grazed by three bullets and had strained his left shoulder while hanging on to the skid with Elena.

Susan and Brandi prepped Elena for surgery. The bullet had gone straight through her body, but internal surgical repairs were necessary.

Knoxi walked to the end of a short hallway, sat down on a small sofa, and began to cry. The emotional drama now took its toll. She dropped her head into her hands, powerless to stop the tears. Painful fatigue began to set in — aching shoulders, knees, feet.

For a moment, she was six years old again, standing among the captive children at the compound in Central Librador, wondering where she was, missing her family. She remembered how impossible things seemed. Why would mean men steal children from their mommies and daddies? Did the children do something bad? No!

Someone needed to do something about it, but she was too little and she was afraid.

She remembered gazing up at the stars, wondering if they were the same stars she had seen from her home on the other side of the world. The despair that night was more than she could bear. But then, from her subconscious mind, she heard her father's voice — familiar words he had delivered to a graduating class at the US Naval Academy when she had accompanied him to Annapolis:

> *"When your pain is greater than your fear of doing something about it, you must act."*

She had then bowed her head to say a prayer. Her new friend Ruben, a homeless child from Venezuela, a fellow captive, had come over to hold her hand when he saw her standing alone crying. He didn't understand much English, but he knew she was saying a prayer, so he gripped her hand and bowed his head with her.

Now, twelve years later, seated at the end of the hallway in the unfinished clinic, she felt a trembling hand slip into her palm again.

"Ms. Knoxi, you no need to cry. Jeremy gonna be okay. Ms. Elena too."

Knoxi opened her eyes. The tender hand belonged to Alex. Knoxi brightened her face and wiped her tears, then glanced toward the other end of the hallway and saw Baker walking toward them.

"Doctor says Elena can be moved in a couple of days. She'll need a month to recover." He came and sat on the floor next to them, leaning his spinning head against the wall.

"I need to go get the pilot," Baker said. "He's hiding the helo in a barn at a small ranch that he inherited. We can't afford to let the authorities find it. Forensics will point to us."

Brandi joined them. "That's gonna be hard to do, since the farm is only a short distance from town."

"We'll figure some way. We just need a little time," Baker said. "Somebody wants this little girl dead." He reached up and placed his hand on Alex's shoulder. "My wife nearly died for you tonight, young lady. I'm gonna find out who these people are."

"Why . . . why these bad men try to own people, hurt children, hurt women? Why they steal my son from me?"

Baker stood to his feet, drew his Navy Colt from his belt, and installed a fully-loaded magazine. "Because they can," he said bitterly. "They do it because they can."

Alex's brown puppy-dog eyes looked up at him. "Why you go to all this trouble for me? Why you all help me?"

Baker ground his teeth and holstered his weapon. "Because we can." He turned his hardened face away and forced his steps toward the exit.

Alex called out to him. "When I look at you, *Señor* Rafferty, I know God is good."

Baker froze, fumbled with his cap, slowly placed it on his head, then left the building.

Lock Down

After Baker left to pick up pilot Marty Luna, Susan emerged from the tiny operating room and sat in her office chair. John, her husband, had put his Army medic experience to good use treating Jeremy. He left Jeremy resting comfortably and headed to the pharmaceutical dispensary to fill two prescriptions that his big patient would need in the coming week.

Susan invited Brandi, Knoxi, and Alex into her office. "Please be seated, ladies. I should examine all three of you," she said. "In the immediate aftermath of traumatic events, injuries are not always apparent."

Brandi was the first to respond. "Thank you, Doctor. I'm concerned more about my daughter and Alex first. Those fingernail gouges on Knoxi's neck could get infected, and I don't know how long it's been since Alex has had any medical attention."

"Yes, I understand. And please, call me Susan. I don't need to know exactly what happened tonight, but I can tell you that authorities have locked down the UT campus. No one goes in or out. My husband is monitoring emergency transmissions."

"Uh . . . so, did they find any—any bodies?" Knoxi asked.

"They aren't saying. John's on the phone now with a friend in the department. We might know more in a few minutes. Let me have a look at your neck, Knoxi."

Knoxi began unfastening the top buttons, then became aware of dried bloodstains on her blouse. She looked at the doctor.

"Whew, I don't know what I was thinking," Susan said. "These stains blend with the orange trim on your blouse. I missed it. Perhaps you ladies should all change. I have a shower with several robes and a closet full of clothes down the hall."

~   ~   ~

Meanwhile, Baker approached the farm where pilot Marty Luna had taken the helicopter. Something was wrong. The beacon atop the barn was not rotating. He refrained from calling Marty by phone for fear of being monitored.

Baker turned off his headlights, installed his night-vision goggles, and approached slowly. When he saw no movement, he rolled down the window and listened. Bird sounds echoed across the field in the humid morning air. The sun hadn't risen yet, but the eastern sky was beginning to lighten.

He moved the vehicle ahead slowly and caught sight of a figure walking toward him waving his arms. He hit the brakes and took a close look. It was Marty. He sped up and pulled alongside him. "Why are you walking?"

"I—I hit the ground strong. The helo barely made it in. Had to put the fire out after I crash landed. I pulled the bird into the barn with the tractor, but didn't want your vehicle to attract any more attention to the barn."

"Okay, son, good thinking. Nice job. Get in." Baker turned the car around and headed back toward Austin.

Marty glanced at Baker as if afraid to ask. "Sir, how's your wife?"

With no expression, Baker answered. "She'll make it. Thank God, she'll live."

"By the way," Marty said, "I found this on the floor of the helicopter." He handed Baker a handgun.

"What? You found this? This is Elena's. That's impossible. I was certain she dropped it on the roof where she was shot."

Marty's closed eyelids gave away his exhaustion. "Well, we don't need to leave that kind of forensic evidence behind, right?"

A long, awkward silence followed. Finally, Marty asked, "Mr. Baker, why did you call me in the middle of the night for this job?"

Baker never answered, never flinched, so Marty spoke again.

"I—I mean you must know at least a hundred helicopter jocks you could have called. Why me?"

Baker forced a sigh as if getting something off his chest. "I just learned of your whereabouts recently. I been keepin' up with you."

"What are you talking about? Who am I to you?"

Baker deliberated and dropped his eyes. "I knew your father."

"You? You knew my father? Congratulations. I never did."

Baker was uncertain. Had he gone too far? Said too much?

Marty pulled off his cap, looked across the field, and crossed his arms. "My dad was killed on some crazy half-cocked mission in Chechnya. Some say it was unauthorized. Of course, the records are sealed, so nobody knows what really happened. My mom still believes my dad was a hero." His heavy breath fogged up the inside of the passenger window. "But he's dead now, so what difference does it make?"

"Makes a difference to me," Baker said. "Makes a big difference to the ambassador and his wife and two children. Made a big difference to eight embassy personnel who got caught in a crossfire worse than what we saw tonight."

"You were there? You saw what happened?"

"I was his commanding officer. The mission *was* authorized, but we went beyond . . . I mean, it was *my* call to move the perimeter. A miscalculation. Technically illegal. But your dad climbed aboard an abandoned armored vehicle and held off at least fifteen hostiles so the rest of us could get the hostages out."

Baker slowed the car to a full stop, but kept his hands on the wheel and looked straight ahead. "When your father finally fell, it inspired three locals to pick up and use the weapons our fallen fighting men had dropped in the street. All hostages saved, but your father and the rest of the team . . ." He turned his gunmetal-gray eyes toward Marty. "I alone survived. I got the medal. I've never forgiven myself."

Marty cleared his throat. "So my mom was right?"

"Son, I'm thankful that I've lived long enough to tell you what happened. And tonight, people I love were in trouble. I needed someone on the double, somebody I could count on if all hell broke loose. Like I said, I knew your old man."

"But I lost my nerve. I left your wife and the tall kid on the roof."

"No. You were the captain of the ship. It was *your* call, and you made the right one. Another two seconds and we'd have all died. I have no idea how Jeremy — I mean, how do you figure that kid? Yeah, it is what it is."

Morning crickets sounded off in the nearby field. The sun was rising.

"Well, Mr, Rafferty, about Chechnya; maybe yours was the right call too. Like you said, it is what it is."

~   ~   ~

Brandi stepped out of the shower at Susan's clinic. She donned a fluffy powder-pink robe and made her way down the hallway to the examining room where Knoxi and Alex had already been seen by the doctor. Just then, John came in with some news.

"The police are investigating. Get this: they found no bodies, but they're gathering lots of DNA evidence — blood, hair, prints — stuff like that."

"No bodies? How's that possible?" Brandi asked.

"Cleaners. The bad guys removed their dead before the cops got there. They even cleaned up bullets and shell casings."

Knoxi tightened the waist belt of the blue robe she had borrowed. "I don't understand why the police didn't get there earlier."

"Maybe they did. Reportedly, two police officers died in the line of duty tonight at the campus. No details."

"Oh, I no like police," Alex said. "I do not trust cops."

"What if some of those bad guys were cops?" Brandi said. "Maybe the others covered for them saying they died in the line of duty. I still don't understand why someone didn't call 911. That place shudda been crawling with police after the shooting started. Didn't anyone see the helicopter taking gunfire?"

"It happened between three and four in the morning — too early," John reminded. "Not enough reliable witnesses around. The few 911 calls they received came off like pranks. One eyewitness reported aliens landing at the Roger Simmons building and a UFO with orange lights over DKR Stadium. One even reported a helicopter and a Russian Mig in a dogfight over the capitol building."

Knoxi and Alex began laughing. "Oh, I'm so sorry," Knoxi said, trying to straighten her face, "but I needed to laugh."

"One other thing," John said. "Reports are circulating that Gloria Zomata has been either killed or abducted."

"Abducted? Killed?" Susan snickered. "By whom? Aliens?"

"Her agent has declared her missing. That's all I heard. It's a developing story."

Alex gasped. "Oh, how do we ever get it straighten out?"

Baker walked through the door. He had dropped Marty off downtown and then had stopped by an all-night diner and purchased sausage and egg tacos for the group. He laid out a feast on the entry table. "Dig in. I've got some things to tell everyone." He stuffed half a taco into his mouth and continued talking.

"I've never seen so many emergency vehicles downtown. The campus is locked down. The helicopter incident has everyone stirred up. The low visibility last night worked to our advantage because no one got a good description of the helo. The word is that Glorietta is either dead or missing."

Brandi jumped on it immediately. "That's the perfect ruse. If the Mexican cartel believes Glorietta is dead or abducted by a rival group, she's safe for now. Thanks to Elena's gangster-girl act, the bad guys are lookin' in the wrong direction."

"Exactly." Baker crammed down the remainder of his taco.

"Wait," Alex interrupted. "So I have to disappear? Maybe witless projection?"

Knoxi was amused. "No. It's called *witness protection*. But that's different."

Baker added clarity. "We're trying to protect you by taking you out of play." He guzzled half a bottle of Edwards Plateau spring water.

Knoxi apologized and explained further. "Alex, sweetie, if the bad guys believe you're trying to get back your son, they may kill him. But, if they believe you've been kidnapped or killed by someone else, they have no reason to harm him when we start pressuring them."

"But I have no name. I cannot be Alex or I will be sent back to Mexico."

"I'm working on that too," Baker informed her. We can get you a new identity and you can start all over and stay in America. Give us a couple of weeks. Meanwhile, enjoy being out of circulation. Wear a disguise."

"Maybe I become . . . uh, how you say, *dumb blonde?*"

The Tejana Heartthrob

With the early-morning breakfast meeting concluded, Susan left for her shift at the hospital. John was now in charge of the clinic. He led Baker and the three women to makeshift sleeping quarters for some shuteye.

Late in the afternoon, Elena finally opened her eyes. She scanned her surroundings in the small operating/recovery room. John was the first to greet her.

"Howdy, Ms. Rafferty."

"Ugh, who are you? Where's my husband?" She was scarcely audible.

"Your husband is down the hall. I'm EMT John Winters. My wife, Dr. Susan Winters, surgically repaired your bullet wound this morning."

"S . . . surgically repaired?"

"How much do you remember, ma'am?"

"My—my side hurts. Um, the last thing I remember was looking down and I . . . I was . . . flying through the air." She squinted. "Flying through the air, I think."

Jeremy's large frame suddenly appeared in the doorway. He had been horizontal all day in the next room dealing with a strained left shoulder, concussion, and minor bullet creases on his arms and hip. Elena's weak voice had drawn him from his bed rest. His nose was still swollen, his knees wobbly, his left arm in a sling. Staring at Elena, Jeremy's lips curved into a shallow smile.

John pointed to Jeremy. "Do you remember this big guy, Elena?"

Elena stared for a moment, squinted again, then held up a shaky right arm. "Come in here, you crazy-ass kid. Don't ever let me catch you doing something that stupid again."

"Yes, ma'am." He stepped toward her. "You got my word on that."

Baker entered behind him. "Welcome back," he said to his wife. "The women are waking up in another room. They're coming to see you."

Then he rolled an armchair toward Jeremy. "Here, son, have a seat. You shouldn't be walking around."

Baker pulled another chair and sat next to Elena's bed. "I know it's sudden," he spoke quietly, "but we need to talk business when the others get here. So, how do you feel?"

"Like I got kicked by Bevo," she winced.

Alex, Knoxi, and Brandi came into the tiny room. "Kinda crowded in here," Knoxi observed. She bent over and put her cheek next to Elena's face. "Elena, you're so heroic." Then Knoxi looked up at Jeremy. "So how 'bout your memory? What do you remember?"

With his Hostess-Twinkie grin on, he answered proudly, "Blue polka dots and pink hearts!"

"Oh, me too!" She squeezed him, her eyes shining, cheeks flushed. "And I'm *sooo* proud."

Alex stood in the doorway quietly watching Knoxi embrace Jeremy. Brandi noticed.

"So, Alex," Brandi inquired, "can you tell us how you became Glorietta? How did you go from being a slave to a Tejana heartthrob?"

Jeremy gave up his armchair to Alex, entreating her to sit down. He sat on the floor next to Knoxi in the corner.

"I 'ventually made it across border," Alex began. "I wandered into big orchard. Big oranges." She held up both hands to show how big. "I live in orchard for five days. Sleep. Eat. I have only old T-shirt I bring from Mexico. Want no one to see me."

"You don't need to tell us everything," Brandi said.

Baker agreed. "We only need information which will help us understand who your contacts are, how you were discovered and promoted, that sort of thing. Understand? My wife can translate if necessary."

"No, no, sir. I speak good English, right Knoxi?"

"Well," Knoxi began with a hesitant smile, "it . . . it's not too bad. I mean —"

Brandi was quick. "We can work on the English later, Alex. Just tell us what we need to know to help you."

"One night, I was asleep in orchard under a tree. I hear rattlesnake. I look in time to see snake bite me on left ankle. I ran — bad thing to do. Never run after snake bite. Four days later, I wake up in clean bed. Pretty gown. No more rotting T-shirt."

"Was it a hospital? A clinic like this?"

"No, it was the people who owned the orchard — Cole and Linda Reyes. They realize I am serious crime victim. It take me three months to recover. They say they know about Nogales pants factory. Say they will protect me. I trust them. They want me to work for them. I was happy until I realize what work they want me to do."

Baker couldn't hide his disgust. "Don't even say it."

"They take me to Laredo, to Open Season Bar — big Tejano music festival. Tony Coleti is playing. I know all his songs. They give me pretty dress, spend money on my hair. I think my prayers are answered, and then . . . they take me to room upstairs with two men waiting." She stopped talking — reluctant eyes, hard memories.

Knoxi offered a tender smile. "It's okay, Alex. You don't need to tell us every detail."

"The two men tell me to take off my dress. I tell them I have bite marks all over, other scars. I tell them they will not like what they see, then I run, run, run. They chase me down stairs.

"I hear loud music playing. I run, jump on stage and tell Tony Coleti I come to audition for his band. I have no shoes, torn dress. I see him call for the officers to take me away. He think I am crazy person." She stopped again to catch her breath.

"Alex! Tell us what happened!"

"I get the job! All the drunk men in crowd say, 'Let her sing! She pretty! Let her sing!' So he ask me to sing and I get a job!"

Jeremy exploded, "*Woo-hoo!* Li'l mama! You cooool as cupcakes!"

"Soon I get my own band. Everything good for one year. I thought if I could make enough money, I could pay someone to get my son back. But last week I find out my manager, Traci Calhoun, she steal all my royalties. I threaten to turn her in so she betray me to the cartel. They send bad men after me so I wear police disguise at university. I try to find Knoxi."

"Why did you look specifically for me?" Knoxi asked, surprised.

Alex froze, then tried to explain. "I wear police uniform so I can get close to you. I knew your face already because I . . ." She went silent again.

"Where did you get the police uniform?" Brandi wanted to know. "It looked authentic."

"I sing at police benefit last month. They give me uniform to wear for program, tell me to keep it."

"Quite a story." Baker pondered. "No doubt there's more, but that's enough for now."

Then he turned to Knoxi. "You need to enroll in your classes. Your student ID will get you through the security check. We need your eyes and ears on campus. Play it as if everything is normal."

Knoxi protested. "But what if someone saw me go into that utility room? What if someone recognized me on the roof?"

"No one did. That would have made a huge news story. No one's reporting that. No one knows where the helo is either, but that'll change if we don't get it moved."

Brandi spoke. "It's hard to believe no one recognized us."

"One other thing," Baker breathed hard. "We gotta leave this clinic as soon as Elena can be moved. Hospitals and clinics are the first places they'll check. I have two agents coming over from Houston to help us put our plan together — Starsky and Hutch."

"Starsky and Hutch? Those two?" Brandi looked at the others. "Oh, I can't wait. Everyone get ready to be outraged."

"I thought those guys were jus' movie characters," Jeremy said.

"In your dreams," Brandi snickered. "Just wait'll you meet 'em."

After the meeting, Jeremy arose and started gingerly toward the door. Brandi and Knoxi held his arms and steadied his steps as he returned to his bed in the next room. Alex watched with wistful eyes.

"Ma'am, how's your pain?" John asked Elena. "I can start another IV."

Before answering, Elena noticed that Alex had remained behind after the others had left. Did she want to stay and talk?

"Uh, give me a few minutes, John. I can manage the pain for now." Elena bit down hard as the burning hole in her middle section brought tears to her weary eyes.

"Understood, ma'am. I'll be back in a few." He nodded to both women as he left.

Elena motioned weakly to Alex. "Come closer, child. It's just the two of us now. Tell me about it."

AM I A KILLER?

Alex stood beside Elena's bed in the small recovery room. She had wanted to talk, but standing this close, she could now see the pain on Elena's face. She had never been a gunshot victim and could not imagine what Elena must be feeling. "Oh, Ms. Elena, I think I go and then come later if you hurt too much."

"Está bien. ¿Quieres conversar en español?" ("It's okay. Do you want to talk in Spanish?)

"Uh, no, not Spanish," Alex answered. "I want to practice speak in English, learn how to speak English like American."

"You'll learn if you're around Americans who speak English as a first language. But something else is on your mind, isn't it?"

"Ms. Elena, I want to ask . . . ask you something, but I not know if it is right for me to say." She clammed up and tried to hide the sheepish grin on her lips.

Elena managed a warm smile. "I see how you look at him, niña. If I were your age, I'd look at him the same way."

Alex's cheeks blushed redder than the Rose of Monterrey. "You already know my secret?"

"It's no secret, child. You've fallen hard for him."

Alex frowned and placed her fingers over her mouth. "How many people know?"

"You are easy to read, honey."

"Si," she admitted. "From the moment I first see him. But, Jeremy and Knoxi; I think they lovers, no?"

Elena chuckled. "Ouch, laughing hurts. Uh, sweetie, they've been friends all their lives because their fathers were high school friends and both played professional baseball. Jeremy has just become a professional like his father."

"So, Knoxi want to marry a baseball player?"

"I've never heard them speak of marriage. I know they're good friends. Everyone assumes they'll marry someday, but that doesn't mean they will."

"I don't think he even notice me. Knoxi rich, pretty, smart. I dunno why he would love someone like me — so plain, poor, helpless."

"Alex, the way you see yourself is the way others will think of you. We all believe you are one of the most amazing young women we have ever met. You're a survivor. Strong. Talented. Loving. That's the way you should think of yourself."

"Jeremy so brave, but I fall down when bullets start. I am so afraid. Can't move. He pick me up and put me in the helicopter."

"Is that why you fell in love with him? Because he saved you?"

"No," Alex insisted. "I love him when I see him first time. And I—I love even more when I see blue dots and pink hearts on boxers!"

"*Ha-ha-ha!*" Elena interrupted, unable to stop herself. "Oh, honey, you're gonna make me lose my stitches!"

"Jeremy jump off building and catch helicopter and never let go of you. I see movie once —"

"Honey, he could practice that move a hundred times and probably never do it successfully. But when everything depended on it, he made it work. That's exactly what you did when you climbed from that pit and drove yourself forward when most women would've laid down and died."

"Jeremy get injured because he help other people. I only want to help myself and my son. I no want to help anyone else. I no trust anyone — no police, no Border Patrol, no Mexicanos, no Americans." She blinked back a tear. "Why Jeremy risk his life for me?"

"Because he couldn't pass you by, Alex. He couldn't leave you there. And, he couldn't just sit in that helicopter and watch me slaughtered on that rooftop either. I won't underestimate him again."

"I only want to kill people. I want to tear the eyes out of the men who left me with bites on my breasts. Men who beat me with belts, take my son from me. When I kill them in my dreams, I not sorry. Last night you shoot Orlando and you not sorry."

"Ohhh, sweetie." Elena reached her hand toward Alex. "Come closer. I want to be touching you when I tell you something you must always remember."

Alex scooted the chair closer and sat down. She closed her eyes as Elena brushed her dark hair with her fingers.

"Alex, if you plan to kill someone and you keep thinking that way, you will soon think of yourself as a killer. And if you carry out your plan, you'll never be the same again. Becoming a murderer doesn't bring you peace."

"I sorry," Alex said. "I want to be different, but I have only one goal."

"Hun, I hadn't planned to shoot Orlando. I wanted to avoid it, but I had to fire my weapon to protect people I love, including you. That's not murder."

Alex looked up. "I tell you why I dress like cop and come to Knoxi for help. When I am bit by snake, I am asleep for several days. I have dream about a shining man — big, scary, beautiful. He say to me, 'Trust this woman.' And then I—I see Knoxi's face in dream. I never forget face. I look for her everywhere I go, but I never find her until I see her on stage at university."

"Why didn't you tell Knoxi that?"

"I was 'fraid she think I'm crazy."

"Alex, those prayers you prayed every night; they were answered. That man you saw was a messenger from the Lord. Knoxi would not think you're crazy."

"Ms. Elena, why did you tell me you were just like Orlando before?"

Elena swallowed a sip of water and drew a deep breath. "When I was your age," she began slowly, "I was a blood-money street fighter in Chicago. All underground. My boss, my boyfriend, was Ricardo Muniz. He kept most of the money like your manager, and he was a cruel sadist. I finally got the nerve to say 'get lost.' By then, I had learned to hate, and I wanted to kill him."

"Did you ever fight to the death?"

"Once . . ." Elena shut her eyes.

"I'm sorry, Ms. Elena. I should not ask that. Please, forgive me."

"Ricardo wanted me to throw my next fight. I refused. He kidnapped my kid sister, Mona. She was thirteen. She was all I had. I was one angry Puerto Rican chick with lethal hands and a big chip on me. I broke into the warehouse where they were holding her. I shot three of Ricardo's men and beat Ricardo until my hands were bloody with two broken fingers."

Alex was riveted. With very word she was drawn deeper into the story. She stared silently through big misty eyes.

"Mona had been beaten. I helped her walk, but I was weak and exhausted. I had cut myself breaking in, and I was bleeding. We made it out to the street, but we walked right into a big cop. I didn't trust anyone, especially cops, especially *black* cops. Mona and I could hardly stand up. I lost the grip on my weapon and dropped it. At that moment I wanted the cop to pull the trigger and end it for us. Living made no sense anymore."

Elena's voice faded. Alex wanted to hear the end of her story but pain and fatigue were overcoming her new friend. "Maybe I leave you alone now, eh? You tell me the rest later?"

"Uh . . . wait." Elena took another sip of water then labored to continue. "This cop, he asked us if we had ever prayed. He put down his gun. His kindness . . . so unexpected. He drove us home. He—he became like a parent to us. He's the reason I became a police officer. I still get texts from him."

"So, Ricardo; you beat him up and he died, no?"

Elena's eyes were slowly losing focus, but she was determined. "Ricardo? He lived. Years later, I was a cop. I convinced him to enter rehab and hook up with Teen Challenge. He was so desperate." She cleared her throat. "He got clean and became a fanatical Jesus follower. Now, he pastors a street church in Chicago. He runs his own halfway house for convicted felons. True story."

JUST ONE HAPPY FAMILY

Next morning at 7:00 John woke Baker who had spent the night camped out in the reclining armchair next to his wife's bed.

"Security cams are picking up a vehicle nearing the gate," John said. "It's approaching slowly. Might wanna check it out."

Baker was awake immediately. "Is it a cherry-red Gran Torino with a bonus white stripe?"

"Affirmative. Nice ride for an antique. You know 'em? Looks like two occupants."

"Starsky and Hutch. Right on time."

"Starsky and Hutch?"

"Let 'em in."

Elena awoke sounding stronger. "Oh, don't let those two fools near me," she said. "If they see me like this I'll never hear the end."

"My wife's still upset 'cuz when she had a kidney stone two years ago Hutch impersonated a doctor and told her they had found a matching knife, fork, and spoon inside her bladder."

"Good thing I didn't have my Beretta on me," she said.

John left the room and returned with a breakfast tray. "I gave the green light to your guys outside, so they're on the way in." He placed the tray in front of Elena. "So why did they name themselves after fiction crime-fighting characters?"

Susan walked into the room. "Yeah, I was about to ask the same question."

"Their real names are Hunter Star and Cat Hutchinson," Baker told them. "Their last names gave 'em the idea for the Starsky and

Hutch routine — part of their cover. They team up for automobile stunt shows and kids' benefits, and they sell ice cream at athletic events. Nobody suspects what they do when no one's looking."

"They're still epic twits if you ask me," Elena said.

"What she's not tellin' you is these guys are former military spooks. They've adopted this comedy act to help 'em cope. Things they've seen. Things they've had to do . . ."

"Both possess IQs over 160," Elena admitted. "But they can be so outrageous. I love these guys and hate every minute of it."

"Hutch is a motion-picture stunt driver," Baker commented. "Star has invented everything from a remote-controlled fish-scaler to his own biodegradable bird poop that doubles as a surveillance listening device."

Someone tapped on the door and opened it slightly. "Excuse us, ma'am, are you the chick who got butt-shot playin' on the roof?" It was Hunter Star.

Elena appealed directly to Baker. "C'mon, honey. Please tell me we brought along our bug spray."

The two new faces invited themselves in. "So, how soon can we move out?" Hutch asked. "We need to expedite."

The duo had alarming news. The Mexican cartel had moved at least fifteen operatives into the Austin area to look for the helicopter and to search the region for Alex.

"We've picked up voice transmissions that indicate they plan to search this clinic at 1700 today," Star reported. "We've been listening for the past twenty-four hours."

"Also," Hutch informed, "Azteca Calientes is planning to shut down their jeans factory in Nogales and move it somewhere else. They're scared. That girl Alex has 'em scramblin' for cover. They don't know who snatched her, or whether she's alive or dead, but they're takin' no chances."

"Is it true she's Glorietta?" Star asked. "I wanna meet this little *chiquita bonita* who escaped from Pablo Cisneros. He's wanted by every legit law-enforcement body in the hemisphere and protected by every underworld figure on the planet."

Brandi entered the room with Alex and introduced her.

"Pablo does not believe I am dead?" Alex asked, her voice trembling. "What if he hurt Zorro?"

"Excuse me, ma'am. Did you say Zorro?" Star made no attempt to hide his fascination. "I love this chick already."

"*Ha!* You love *every* chick already," Hutch said.

"Yep, Star's the hot bachelor of the two," Elena told Alex.

"But what about my son? He only two years old."

Star swallowed hard. "Well, I—I don't think Pablo can afford to hurt the little guy, cuz if he does, he loses his bargaining chip with you. That little fox is Pablo's best hope to stay a free man right now."

Both agents were dressed for the part. With bell-ringer jeans, racing-striped tees and wing tips, they looked ready for a '70s series of their own. Hunter Star was over six feet with shoulder-length black hair, while Cat Hutchinson was a stocky five-eight with a pug nose. Neither resembled the actors who had played the original Starsky and Hutch characters, but everyone liked to call them Starsky and Hutch, and the two comedians used it as cover for their clandestine activities.

"We gotta get Elena ready to travel," Star said. "We've found a secure place on Lake Travis a few miles from here." He walked a couple of steps toward Elena. "After we get you set up at the lake, Hutch and I are off to Nogales. From there, we launch Dracula and let him poop all over the jeans factory across the border."

Alex looked confused. "Dracula? Poop all over factory?"

Baker snicked. "I wasn't kidding about the bird-poop surveillance. Dracula is a stealth drone. Star designed it. Hutch operates it. The poop is water-soluble tech-craft that'll listen to the bad guys 'til it washes away on its own."

Hutch stepped in. "If they decide to move, we'll know where. Our eavesdropping should tell us who the deep pockets are behind this operation. We wanna put this entire cartel out of business."

"We suspect this factory is just the proverbial tip of the iceberg," Star said. "The Mexican border runs right through Nogales. We'll launch the drone on the American side and direct it across the border to spy on the company."

Hutch tightened his demeanor. "The difficult part is doing all this without anyone noticing. We'll launch Dracula in the wee hours."

"Mexicano police protect Pablo," Alex insisted. "They guard women like prisoners. What you do about police? What you do about federales?"

Hutch handled the question. "Our intel will be transferred by satellite back to our office in suburban Houston. Our associate there will log all intelligence and analyze. We can devise ways to get around the police and federales."

Star pulled up a chair and sat next to Elena. "So, do you figure on travelin' this morning? We have 'til five this afternoon to get you moved before Pablo's guys show up."

"I'll go if you give me a ride in your GTO."

"Uh . . . Dracula's in the back seat and the poop's in the trunk, but I'll squeeze you in if you show me where you got shot."

Hutch rebuked his partner. "That was plain rude! Why should she show *you* first? I'm the one who drives the car! I fly the drone! You're just the —"

"Hutch!" Elena interrupted. "How's Farah?"

"Uh, she's a sophomore this year at A&M. She—she's flipped over this guy who's a real piece of work. I mean . . ."

"Oh, Lord, have mercy on us," Elena moaned. "I don't even wanna know what *you* consider a piece of work. Get me outta here."

Alex frowned. "Huh?"

Baker shrugged. "Just one happy family."

BLOOD ON THE SADDLE

The drive to the Lake Travis hideout lasted nearly two hours. Morning fog and winding roads made the driving slow. The curves were difficult for Elena. The pain meds John and Susan had given her did not completely compensate for road stress.

At last, they turned off the main road and drove through a security gate which featured a cattle guard and a stone marker which read, "Full Count Ranch."

The long brick driveway weaved its path between gigantic white rock formations and zig-zagged around hickory, Texas Sage, and Bald Cypress trees. With a trained eye, one could see security cameras nestled among the rocks and branches. The land was rustic natural, no fences, no landscaping, only scant signs of civilization. Soon, a magnificent hacienda made of stucco and red oak came into view.

A covered veranda with hand-carved lantern posts was adjoined to the arched entryway to the home, and the colorful front gardens were punctuated with adobe pottery of old-world vintage.

"Who owns this?" Brandi wanted to know.

"Terry Lowe," Baker answered. "A friend of Cody's. Pitched for the St. Louis Cardinals. The Lowe family is traveling in Europe so they won't be here. We're here with their permission."

As they slowly approached the large Spanish-style home, Baker issued a warning. "We should stop here while the dynamic duo checks it out." He pulled his van to the side of the road and allowed the GTO to pass them by.

Suddenly, the large double doors swung open and a familiar figure stepped out onto the veranda.

"Mama! It's Daddy!" Knoxi threw open the door and hit the ground running. "When did you get here?" she asked her father. "Did you decide to leave the reservation early?"

"My family is in trouble. Where did you think I'd be?" He wrapped his arms around his daughter, then hugged Brandi who had joined them.

"Uh, Daddy, this is Alex. She's a new friend."

"I know all about your new friend."

Cody extended his warm hand, but Alex threw her arms around Cody's neck. "I see your face many time, sir. My cousin in Juarez have your baseball card."

"Hello, sir," Star greeted Cody. "I see you've already cleared the premises."

"That's affirm. The building's secure," Cody said. "I brought two friends with me. I'll introduce you."

He motioned toward two men who had suddenly appeared. It took only a moment to realize these two were identical twins — middle thirties, sculptured cheekbones, rock hard faces, dark gray eyes, their heads shaved Mohawk style.

"On the left," Cody said, "is my brother Sleeping Wolf, and on the right, my brother Silent Arrow. They've offered to help keep us safe while we sort things out."

Brandi tried to hide her snickering. She knew these two from her trips to visit Cody at his hiding place among the Cherokee in Oklahoma. They were lock and barrel matches for the Muskets' friends Star and Hutch — always scheming, always looking for ways to be outrageous. The stone-faced, stoic countenance was all part of their act, especially when meeting people for the first time.

Between the two, Sleeping Wolf was the best gamer, speaking few words and sandwiching them between authentic-looking "Indian" hand signs.

"I am one called Sleeping Wolf," he said, keeping his hands moving. Great honor to . . . guard family of one called *Looong*

Musket." He extended his hand to Star and Hutch, but neither could decide how to respond.

Brandi and Knoxi giggled. They couldn't help themselves. Knoxi hugged the two Cherokee brothers. "Thank you, gentlemen. We needed a laugh." Then she smirked at Star and Hutch. "In the years I've known you, I've never seen you guys look so white."

"Sleeping Wolf extended his hand again. "Just call me Kenny. My brother Silent Arrow goes by Adrian. We've seen some of your cool videos. Your car stunts, kiddie shows — ummm, bad medicine."

"Hey, I can already see we're gonna like you guys," Hutch said. "We should hang sometime."

Adrian finally spread a smile across his tight lips. "I hear you got some serious horses under that hood. I've never seen your car in person."

The four comedians gathered around the red GTO and exchanged pleasantries while Baker and Cody carried Elena from the van to her bed in the ground floor master bedroom.

Jeremy complained of dizziness as he labored up the steps and onto the veranda. Knoxi and Brandi walked beside him for support. Alex followed behind them carrying a small bag of Jeremy's things as they walked through the front door.

The spacious entry opened into a huge family/activity room which covered nearly half the bottom level. The rustic stone floors, frontier oak ceiling beams, and polished wooden inlays filled the senses with the brightness and elegance of simplicity. Two French doors led into a private parlor containing decorative baseball trophy cases, a small couch, a coffee table, and three kick-back chairs.

In the front yard, still hanging around the GTO, Star and Hutch talked shop with Kenny and Adrian. They bonded, sharing stories about fast cars, defense techniques, families, and missions they had conducted.

Suddenly, from behind the house, a blood-chilling plea for help pierced the humid morning air.

"Help! Somebody pleeeese help me!"

The four men scrambled and were forced to dive for cover when a strawberry roan quarter horse came galloping around the corner at breakneck speed. An empty chestnut saddle rode on its back. The horse ran across the driveway toward tall grass and began to slow, finally coming to rest about fifty yards in front of the house.

Kenny and Adrian walked slowly toward the panting, snorting animal. Kenny whistled softly and the horse looked up. Adrian then walked alone toward the beast with small steps. He took the reins and spoke in a whisper as he stroked the horse's face.

When Kenny followed he made a shocking discovery. The saddle was dripping with fresh blood. The horse's missing rider was seriously injured.

Having earned the horse's trust, Adrian mounted up and began backtracking to find the rider. Kenny, Star, and Hutch climbed aboard a four-wheeler which the two Cherokee braves had brought with them on a trailer.

When they reached the rear of the house, they were surprised to see five riders coming toward them.

"Who do you suppose those people are?" Star watched the horsemen intensely.

"They aren't friendly," Kenny said. "I'd bet on it."

Meanwhile, Adrian had located the rider who was lying face down. He checked for a pulse, then turned the rider over. It was a young girl, a teenager. She was pregnant, maybe six months, bleeding from the waist down. She was dressed in a sports top and jeans which were at least twice her size with no belt. She had no shoes, her bare feet hidden by the long legs of the jeans. She had been trying to get away from somebody and had left in a hurry.

The four-wheeler arrived. "We got trouble, gentlemen."

The men dismounted from the vehicle. "She looks bad," Hutch said. "We need to get her inside." He looked up and saw the five horsemen approaching. "Weapons, guys."

The riders were armed. They pulled within ten yards and stopped. "We're takin' the girl, ladies. After that, you can have a nice day."

The spokesman was a long, wiry individual with a smug expression, bushy beard, and a red Stetson. He carried his shotgun in a careless position, draping it over his forearm while sitting on the horse. The two individuals on either side of him carried themselves professionally. They appeared to know how to handle horses as well as weapons. They both carried handguns, and their eyes never ceased scanning in every direction. These two were dangerous.

Star spoke up. "Any of you guys a doctor?"

"I am," said a man sitting on the left flank.

"Well then," Hutch grinned large, "do you know what appendicitis looks like? Get down here, a couple of you guys, pick her up. She's all yours."

"Good thing you come along," Kenny said, with a strong countenance. "She not well. Need *strooong* medicine. You fix girl."

Two of the men got down and approached on foot. Adrian reached into the floor of the four-wheeler, whipped around with a spear in his right hand and hurled it at the lead horse's feet. All five horses reared, forcing the three remaining riders to grapple with the reins. The careless lead horseman dropped his shotgun.

In the same blink of an eye, Star and Hutch brutally took down the two men who had wanted to play doctor. Kenny picked up the fallen shotgun and fired two shots into the air. The spooked horses bolted into a dead run, leaving the three remaining riders lying on the muddy turf.

Adrian tossed Star a handgun from their four-wheeler, then helped Kenny load the young woman on board the vehicle.

"I'm gonna round up those horses," Adrian said. "I'll see you guys in a few." He mounted the lead horse and rounded up the runaways.

Kenny transported the injured girl to the house on the four-wheeler.

Star and Hutch dealt with the bad guys. "Well, gentlemen. This has certainly been a nice day for us, but not so much for the girl you guys mutilated. Everybody get on the ground. Prepare to be searched for weapons. Then, you're coming with us 'til we get to the bottom of this."

"You can't do this!" the tall spokesman ranted. "I'll torpedo you with a lawsuit that'll bury you. All of you. You're holding us against our will. Do you know who I am?"

"Let me guess," Star said. "You're a guy who wears a red Stetson and leads a posse to apprehend a scared pregnant girl who's bleeding to death. Your doctor wouldn't know the difference between appendicitis and a botched abortion, and you aren't very good at playing cowboys and Indians. How's that so far?"

Hutch followed up, "What about attempted murder? Do you know what that means? Either way, you better hope that little girl doesn't die."

"That girl is none of your business! You're interfering with a private family matter. What do you care anyway? Who are you guys?"

"Us?" Hutch looked around. "We're the four guys who don't like five-to-one odds against kids."

Star observed, "No wonder the girl wanted outta the family."

~ ~ ~

Cody, Baker, and Kenny carried the injured girl inside while Star and Hutch herded the captured riders into a basement room and locked the door.

Brandi called Susan at the clinic while Knoxi listened in.

"You absolutely must stop the bleeding," Susan said. "Some uterine bleeding will stop on its own, but the fact she fled across the countryside and fell off a horse doesn't help. It might have damaged the placenta or even killed the baby. Is she conscious? Can you find out what happened to her before she got on the horse?"

"She's bleeding. I can't stop it," Brandi said. "I can't wake her. She's really pale."

"Keep her perfectly still. She needs to be airlifted," Susan said. "She needs an ultrasound to determine the extent of injuries. John's on the phone now arranging a medevac. I'll tell you how to evaluate the baby's heartbeat if you have a stethoscope."

"No. We—we don't have one here."

"Robbie . . . Robbie, did you . . . get away?" The young woman was now semi-conscious, as quiet and weak as a falling feather.

"Who's Robbie?" Knoxi asked.

"Where am I?" the victim wanted to know. "Did Robbie . . . did he get away?"

"Who is Robbie?" Knoxi asked again. "You are among friends."

"My boyfriend. He—he fought them off. Tried to . . ." Her voice failed.

"Uh, what's your name? Can you hear me?" Knoxi listened but heard only soft breath sounds.

Brandi completed her call. "They're arranging a medevac. What did the girl say? Looks like she's drifted off again."

"She said her boyfriend's name is Robbie and he tried to fight for her. So, I mean maybe we should check on her boyfriend."

"*Cody!*" Brandi yelled toward the other room. "We have to send Kenny and Adrian."

Cody appeared at the door. "What're you talkin' about?"

"There is another victim! His name's Robbie. There's no telling what those guys did to him."

"He could be injured or dead," Cody said. "The Cherokee brothers are world-class trackers. They could mount up and backtrack, but I'm gonna give 'em the option of either taking the risk or not."

"Susan's arranging an airlift for the girl," she told him. "We've gotta get the sheriff involved, Cody. We can't hold those guys captive in the basement forever, and we can't let this girl or her baby die."

"Do we even know her name?"

"No, but I think it's time for Cody Musket to come out of hiding."

"It's time," he said. "But I didn't know I would run into such a mess this soon. Seems like I attract violence."

"Maybe God puts you where you can help," she said. "Remember Braddock, the old medic? Something about being in the wrong place at the wrong time because someone needs you there?"

THE NATIVES ARE COMING

Kenny and Adrian gathered up an array of weapons. They were going hunting for a heroic young man who might be dying or held against his will. There was no choice to be made. Their faces reflected disgust — the bloody teenage girl against five ruthless men. They prepared themselves in case they met more of the same in the woods.

They removed the saddles from the captured horses. They would ride bareback, bringing along a pack horse to carry weapons, first-aid supplies, and even some jerky.

Kenny had already determined which among the captive animals was the lead pony. She was the smallest of the group, a spirited blond mare with a high step. He would ride her and hold the reins lightly. She would lead them right to the spot.

As they mounted up, the mare began to fidget. She bucked on all fours for a few steps, then settled down. Perhaps she didn't like strangers, or maybe she was nervous carrying a rider bareback for the first time.

The success of a two-man raiding party counted on speed and surprise. They had no idea who might be waiting, but Kenny and Adrian would paint their faces and take the fight to the enemy if necessary.

"Hey," Adrian rumbled, "The natives are coming."

His tight-lipped partner responded with a slight grin.

The horses maintained a brisk pace until the winding trail led to a secluded ranch-style dwelling about three miles from where they had started. Kenny brought the feisty mare to a halt and tied the reins to the trunk of a small tree. The other horses slowed down and stopped. They hid them in the trees.

The men planted two spears and a handgun in a nearby crevice — a location they designated as "point alpha." Staying hidden, they continued on foot toward the large ranch house, carrying the remaining weapons past Purple Sage trees and Rosemary shrubs which made good cover. They stopped about forty feet from the house and crouched behind a fallen live oak. After they pulled out the remaining weapons, and armed themselves bodily, they stashed their bags, designating this location "point bravo."

The brothers split up, with Kenny moving left along the tree line and Adrian the other direction. Each man took a position with a good view. The building was a triple-decker — three floors with large glass windows. Curtains were drawn, rooms dark, no lights. A quiet country mansion.

They listened for human sounds, but heard none. A barn behind the house showed no proof of life either. The barn door was wide open and several horses grazed on the green lawn as if someone had left in a hurry.

Kenny pulled up his cell phone to alert Cody with a situation report but then things began to happen. A commotion stirred in the upper rooms. They glued their eyes to the top-floor windows but saw nothing. Kenny put away his phone.

After a moment, a curtain opened and a wiry young man with dark wavy hair appeared through the glass. He frantically rolled open the window and threw down a long rope, leaving it dangling. The tall youngster climbed out onto the rope and began sliding down.

Could this be their package? They had no physical description of Robbie, but this guy fit the scant profile. He did not appear to be injured but was clearly desperate to escape.

Then another individual appeared at the window above. "You're makin' this too hard, Stanton!" It was a balding, heavy-set man with a bushy-blond mustache, glaring down and yelling at the youngster on the rope. "You'll be lucky if you can walk after your old man gets through with you this time!"

Next, a cowboy wearing buckskins, a hat, sidearm, and red leather chaps emerged from the side door of the house. He positioned himself on the ground directly beneath the youngster who was still suspended on the rope. The decked-out cowboy looked up at him. "A lot easier to come on down, Houdini, 'less you wanna stay up there all day. This time, I got these waitin' for ya'."

The cowboy produced a pair of handcuffs, then pointed toward the porch where a set of leg-irons awaited. "And them thangs right there'll keep you 'til yer daddy comes back."

Kenny touch-dialed Adrian. "Don'tcha just hate cowboys?"

"Roger that with passion," Adrian snapped. "But since the boy isn't harmed, we should contact the sheriff and let him handle it."

At that moment, things got a lot more complicated.

The boy yelled, "What did yawl do with Peaches? She got away, right? *Ha!* Otherwise, my dad wudda come back by now. I told you she could outride any of 'em!"

"Rob, yer daddy always gets what he wants," the cowboy said. "You should oughta know that by now. You gotta jes' accept it. He's gonna —"

"*Noooo! Never!*" The boy let go the rope, fell straight down upon the startled cowboy, horse-collared him, and wrestled him backward to the ground. Robbie broke free and took off toward the trees, hobbled, limping."

Four more cowboys came around the corner running and yelling. They subdued the conflagrant youngster, shoved him onto his belly and attempted to cuff him. Robbie still would not surrender. The cuffs were gouging his knuckles, wrists, and forearms, but he managed to kick one cow puncher squarely on the nose, sending him rolling on the concrete. Finally, one of the men produced a police Taser.

Kenny bristled up, "Time for a rodeo."

"Copy that!"

Kenny watched Adrian's silent arrow strike *Taserman* in the knee. The individual dropped the stun gun, yelled, limped toward the house and tripped, holding his pierced knee. As Adrian prepared for another shot, the other four ducked behind a thinning hedge next to the house.

Three more arrows arrived in quick succession, each silent, each finding the toe of a cowboy boot. Amidst screams of pain and terror, no one knew where the arrows were coming from. That didn't seem to make any difference to Robbie who managed to apply his good leg to the backside of the fifth cowboy as he ran for his life. Robbie limped to the line of trees and disappeared.

Now, the only remaining entity to deal with was the chubby man in the upstairs window. But when he looked out and saw two whooping, screaming warriors from another era headed full speed toward the house wearing red war paint and waving spears and arrows in the air, it was game over. He bolted upward like the tomcat who'd just chewed through the power cord, banged his head on the upper window frame, tried to crawl back inside, but passed out and left his legs hanging outside the window.

"Nice boots!" Adrian yelled.

"Go to bravo and gather up everything then meet me at alpha," Kenny said. "I'm gonna try to head the kid off before he steals our horses."

"*Whoop! Whoop!* I love this kid! He's trouble!"

~ ~ ~

Robbie limped badly but kept moving. He ducked behind a rocky ledge for cover and spotted the horses. He untied the lead mare and managed to mount her.

"You . . . horse thief." Kenny had just arrived. With all appropriate hand language mixed in, he continued. "Me . . . Sleeping Wolf. You . . . no steal horse. My horse."

Robbie turned back to look. "Who—who in tarnation are you guys?"

"Dismount, Ahusaka."

Robbie stayed put, staring at Kenny. "*Ahusaka?* What's that? Something like *Kemosabe?*"

"It very great honor when Cherokee brave give you Indian name," Kenny said. "Ahusaka good name."

Adrian arrived out of breath just in time to answer Robbie's question. "Robbie Ahusaka. It means 'Robbie who sprouts wings.'"

Robbie was not impressed. "Nice war paint. Very authentic. Where do you get that stuff?"

"Walmart. *California Shaded Rose* with matching nail polish," Kenny said.

"*Lipstick?*"

"Yeah, we brought it just in case," Adrian volunteered. "Never know when you might need some good war paint! I'm Silent Arrow. You can just call me Adrian. And my brother Sleeping Wolf, he goes by Kenny."

"We'd like to chat more, Robbie, but we gotta move," Kenny said. "Don't worry about giving up the horse now, your ankle's swelling. You hit the ground hard when you flew off that rope."

Adrian spoke again as they began riding back toward the hacienda. "We found Peaches, Robbie. I have to warn you, she's seriously injured."

"Did they shoot her? They were gonna force us to abort our baby. My dad's the one who's behind all this. He brought in some quack doctor. I saddled two horses and broke Peaches out of the upstairs bedroom. I didn't want them touching her. We were gonna just ride as far as we could and take the rest of the horses with us, but they caught us before we could —"

"You fought off ten men so you could save your girlfriend and child?"

"She . . . she's my wife. Don't ever tell anyone she's my girlfriend! You hear me? Not if you know what's good for you."

"Save it, son. We'll be there in a few minutes. They've airlifted Peaches to —"

"Airlifted!? What's wrong with her?"

"Is your dad a tall white dude? Dark hair? Likes to wear a red Stetson and carry a twelve-gauge popgun?"

"Damnation and pass the hand grenades! You've seen my dad? I hope you guys still like to take scalps!"

"We captured him. We plan to turn him over to the sheriff."

"The sheriff? No! He's the one who turned Peaches over to my dad's looney-creeps. It's underworld stuff and it's huge. Goes all way south of the border."

"What do you mean?" Kenny asked.

"And he ain't my real dad, neither. I just found out last year. He's not my real dad, but Peaches is my real wife despite what anyone says."

"So, you said something about south of the border? Mexico? You got any proof?" Adrian asked.

"Tell you later *after* I see Peaches. Just don't call no sheriff. You hear me?"

PEACHES

Kenny called Cody during the horse ride to fill him in. Cody informed him the medevac for the Jane Doe had been postponed due to mechanical issues.

"That might be a good thing," Kenny said. "We dunno if this kid is tellin' the truth. But what if we put that girl on the helo and a hit squad is waiting for her? Should we trust this sheriff?"

Soon the raiding party returned. Robbie's concerns about the sheriff presented an unexpected problem. What law enforcement agency should they call? They couldn't just let the suspects go.

And what about the cowboys at the ranch house? They didn't seem to be killers or skilled fighters. After all, one tenacious teenage boy had given them all they could handle. They were just cowboys. But they were complicit in unlawfully detaining two minors. Cody and Baker decided to hear Robbie's story before making a next move.

Peaches continued to stabilize, in and out of consciousness. Susan and John were on their way from the clinic to evaluate her.

"I just came back to the world," Cody mused with Brandi. "Already I'm up to my ears in alligators. Before I was shot, I was complaining cuz my life was too quiet."

"Chew on this for a moment," Brandi suggested. "We've encountered three young kids in the last two days who need serious help. Could this all be just coincidence?"

Meanwhile, Star and Hutch left for Nogales as scheduled. They would launch Dracula the drone over Azteca Calientes Clothing Works to drop a substance on the roof which resembled bird feces, but which was charged with electronic snooping nano receptors. They sought to gain intel for a plan to bring the company down. They hoped to free the slaves and recover Alex's son Zorro alive and well.

Robbie was accompanied by the Cherokee brothers into the room where Peaches lay. They would sit nearby, hoping to learn what she had been through.

"Hey, Peach," Robbie whispered. "You awake?" He waited, brushing strands of hair from her face. Her eyes remained shut.

"I—I'm not hurt, Peach. See? I'm here in one piece. You gotta fight! Don't give up."

Her swelling eyes opened partway. "Oh, Robbie. You shouldn't have . . . I mean, your father isn't gonna give up. Save yourself."

"He's *not* my father I told you!" He stopped himself, refocused, and lowered his volume. "He stole me when I was born. And you're my wife. I gotta show him he can't bully me or you."

"No, I'm not your wife. It was annulled, remember? I'm just . . . I'm just . . ." Her breathy words weak, sluggish, forlorn. "Robbie, you're such a sweet boy. You . . . tried . . . tried to help me, but —"

Robbie slipped to his knees beside the bed. "Peach, listen to me. If there's a God anywhere in the universe, I swear you *are* my wife. No man can change that."

"I'm nowhere as brave as you Robbie. Forget me. I don't know how to fight these men."

"That's not true. You're the bravest woman I've ever seen. I don't care if you are just fourteen. You hear me?"

Adrian put his hand on Robbie's shoulder. "Come with us, little brother. Your wife needs rest. They need to come in and make sure she isn't bleeding again, and we need to have a talk, okay?"

The three men walked quietly down the staircase, through the spacious living room, and into the adjacent parlor. They were joined by the others. Jeremy was no longer wobbly in the knees. Brandi was the last to arrive, reporting that Peaches was now holding her own — asleep again, but no bleeding.

After everyone was introduced, Cody questioned Robbie. The first question he asked the youngster was his age. He also asked about Robbie's father, or the man who claimed to be.

Robbie said that Abdulla Stanton owned the ranch where the Cherokee warriors had rescued him. He added that he could've made it okay alone and didn't need their help. He was a full seventeen years old but did not know who his *real* father was. He had learned a year earlier that Stanton had abducted him when he was an infant. In the process, he had murdered Robbie's parents. Now, Robbie had sworn to break free and take his precious Peaches and their child with him.

"Peaches is the best thing to ever happen to me," he said. "When I first saw her in that shop in Mexico, I totally fell on my face. Have you ever loved something so much that nothing else in life mattered?"

Brandi offered a pleasing smile and held onto Cody's arm.

"I couldn't bear the thought of what was going to happen to her," Robbie continued. "I promised I'd get her outta there. At first, she didn't believe me, but—"

"Hang on a second," Cody interrupted. "Get her out of where?"

"That slave shop in Nogales," Robbie snapped. "That's where!"

Jeremy perked up. "Nogales? Your Peaches is from Nogales?"

"No. She's from Brownsville. She's American. Her parents died in Hurricane Francis two years ago. She was picked up by these guys who said they were from a modeling agency. Her real name is Sophia Gonzales. I named her Peaches. She likes her new name."

Everyone seemed stunned, so Robbie saw it as a challenge. "Okay, I get it! I'm just some stupid kid who likes to make up stories. Nobody ever believes me!"

Knoxi spoke up. "I believe you, Robbie. We all do."

Alexis fired off a burning question. "How . . . how you get her away? You steal her?"

Robbie looked around the room. "My father, uh, I mean Abdulla, told me he would one day turn over his empire to me. I only had to learn how to run the business. But I wanted to be a cowboy, livin' in the rough, wranglin' livestock." He made a motion like roping a steer.

"Abdulla would take me to his factories and tell me how much money he made. He said he was helping all these workers because they had no homes to go back to. It never seemed right to me; the stench, the conditions. When I started hearing what some of the men did to the women, I didn't believe it."

"So, what about Nogales?" Jeremy wanted to know. "How did you get Sophia, er, Peaches outta there?"

"When I found out Abdulla wasn't my father, I confronted him. I shudda known better. I demanded to know who my parents were. He said it didn't matter cuz I was better off this way. To prove it, he would show me a side benefit of being in the family. He took me to the Nogales factory and said to take my pick of any girl under twenty. I would take her to a local hotel and make sure she could barely walk the next morning — my chance to prove my manhood." Robbie lowered his head and gnarled his teeth. "Like, anybody can be a man. All they gotta do is—"

Alex reacted, "*Ohhhh!* Mr. Robbie, tell me you didn't."

"Nogales — that's where I saw Peaches. She was . . ." He cleared his throat. "Two men drove us to the Modern Inn and Suites on the American side. These guys went with us to make sure I lived up to my . . . my manhood. When we got there . . ."

He paused and took a breath. The room was so quiet that each could hear the others breathing. But even more captivating was the story that followed.

Modern Inn and Suites, Nogales
One year earlier

Robbie had opened the door to Room 1141. A tearful, trembling Sophia Gonzales followed him in. He closed the door behind him, telling the two watchdogs to wait outside. He gave them each fifty dollars and told them to bring him back a bottle of tequila, and to purchase a bottle each for themselves. He gave them another hundred to wait outside while he took his turn first with the girl. One of the men went for the booze and the other stayed outside the door.

Sophia pleaded, "*Por favor, señor* —"

"It's okay," he interrupted her. "We both speak English. I'm not here to hurt you."

She sat down on the bed, her voice shaking. "Please. I know you are the son of Abdulla Stanton. I—I should be honored, but please don't —"

"I'm not gonna hurt you. Don't you understand English?"

She began unbuttoning her blouse. "I try to please the other men. I don't want them to hurt me. I can make you very happy. Please don't let those other two men —"

"Don't you understand? I'm not here to hurt you. And don't ever call me the son of Abdulla Stanton again! You got that? I'm not his son. I got no last name."

"But don't you think I'm pretty? I will be very nice to you."

"*Stop!*" He held her hands to prevent her from removing her blouse. "I—I couldn't possibly . . . I mean, of course you're pretty. You're the most beautiful thing I've ever seen. I want you, but . . . I mean, not like this. Not in this place."

She crossed her arms. "So—so why exactly did you bring me here?"

He walked to the large window and pulled back the curtain. "We need to get rid of those guys. I want to get you outta here."

"This is a joke, right?"

"What've the other men done to you? How many men—?" He withdrew when he saw the pain in her swollen brown eyes.

She began buttoning up her blouse. "You don't want to know about the other men . . . what they do to me."

His eyes hardened, his skin red-hot. "Nobody's gonna hurt you again. I want you to marry me. Like, tonight. I know how to bribe a judge into marrying us. At least I learned something from Abdulla. So, how old are you?"

She lost her breath, her unbelieving face contorted. "You are one crazy person. Who are you really? I mean, marry you? I'll be fourteen in two months."

"That just means I get to see you become a woman. But you gotta start thinking like one! We're gettin' outta here. You're gonna become my wife and we're gonna change our names. Trust me."

"Those men out there are dangerous," she choked. "How are you gonna get past them?"

"You mean *we*. How are *we* gonna get past them? We gotta work together. First, we wait 'til they get really hammered. After that, we have options."

"What? You don't have any other plan? Do you know how *violent* some men get when they drink?"

"Look on the bright side," he chuckled. "Do you know how *stupid* they can be when they're drunk?"

"I don't even know your name."

"Robbie. My first name is Robbie."

"Well, Mr. Robbie. If you're for real, why are you doing this?"

"Because . . . because I want a better life than Abdulla has. When I saw your face, I knew I had found it."

"You'll change your mind tomorrow. You'll go back to Abdulla and I'll —"

"No! I won't! And you're not going back to them guys, neither!"

"Oh, you're a such a *toolkit!*" She stood with hands on hips. "So what's the plan? Wait 'til dark and send up the *Bat Signal?*"

"Will you listen to me and be serious? First, we gotta take their cell phones and steal all their clothes."

"Freakin' brilliant!" She threw up her hands. "I'm so glad you finally got serious!"

"Slap me," he said. "Real hard!"

"Oh, now I see." She glared. "You're playing a game! You made a wager with the two pricks outside the door. How much? You bet them I wouldn't hit you, right?" She slapped him so hard he nearly lost his balance. "You're worse than any of 'em!" she screamed. "Here's for all your gaming and fun! I hope you really enjoy this!" She slapped him again under his right eye then drew back her fist, targeting his nose this time.

He caught her hand. "That's enough!" He walked to the mirror and grinned. "That looks perfect."

Then, while she stood in stark disbelief, he pulled off his trousers and shirt. "Here," he said, "go into the bathroom and change into these, then hand me all your clothes."

"You're gonna wear *my* clothes? Are you going to beat me first?"

"Look, haven't I proven anything to you?"

"Proven what? That all the pervs like you aren't locked up yet?"

He grabbed her shoulders. "Now, listen to me! We're either gonna die tonight or we're gettin' outta here. Are you on board?"

"So . . . you actually meant those things you said to me? You think I'm beautiful?"

"Look at me. Don't I look like a boy who means what he says?"

She studied him a moment, her youthful eyes now acquiescent and tearful. "No, sir. You look like a *man.*" Her voice mellowed. "You're the first man I have ever met. Tell me what to do."

"Get ready to fight," he growled. "You gotta trust somebody or this nightmare will never end. You hear me?"

No longer trembling, Sophia placed a warm hand on the side of his face. "Who are you, Mr. Robbie with no last name?" She stared into his strong eyes, then carried his clothes to the bathroom and shut the door.

Robbie's lips fell silent, his staring eyes seemingly lost in the nebula between his present reality and that room back in Nogales. Everyone in the parlor remained motionless. It was as though no one had taken a single breath for the past ten minutes. Was he making this up? Alex, on the couch, had drawn herself into a tiny ball, hugging her own knees. Brandi covered her lips with one hand to contain her emotion.

Knoxi finally spoke with an anxious whisper. "What happened next, Robbie? Don't stop there! What did you do with her clothes?"

"Sophia, er . . . Peach came out wearin' my shirt and pants. She looked funny with my clothes. They were way too big. She handed me her stuff. I knocked over furniture and scattered her clothes around the room. I even sprinkled tequila around and took a swig to make my breath smell. I poured the rest down the sink and threw the bottle on the floor."

Robbie began to pace, his voice getting louder and louder. "Peach hid in the closet. I invited our two wasted attack dogs inside. I told 'em Sophia was drunk in the next room and that she liked to play rough. They bought it. I told 'em to leave their expensive clothes with me since this chick was a fighter and the stuff they were wearin' was too pricey to mess up."

Robbie chuckled. "*Ha!* They took off everything, threw it down, and raced each other to the room expectin' to find a ripe peach. When they got inside, I locked 'em in. We left with their car keys, their cell phones, all their clothes, and me wearin' Calientes low-risers and a pair of brand-new boots."

"Man, you one bad dude!" Jeremy was perculating. "So where'd you go after all that?"

"Peach and I ditched the car and drove a rental straight to Galveston. I got a judge to marry us. I listed my last name as Earp."

"*Earp?*" Knoxi clapped her hands with delight. "*Ha-ha! Earp?*"

"We lived in a beach cabin at Galveston for six months and laid low. We had plans to head to Wyoming, but Abdulla found us and sent state troopers to hold us. The local sheriff's office here went and picked us up."

"Is there anybody you trust? Any law enforcement agency? Any person?" Cody wanted to know.

"No, sir. We trust nobody. Everyone wants a slice. It was easy for Abdulla to annul the marriage, but that was just paperwork. I know what my responsibilities are, marriage license or not. Peach doesn't understand that yet."

"Peaches is scared," Brandi weighed in. "She's pregnant, and that's hard enough on the nerves, but she went through so much even before you met her."

"Yes, ma'am. Even after we settled at Galveston, she was shy about letting me touch her. I, uh, didn't force her or nothin'. But after a few weeks, she changed." He took a deep breath to clear his mind. "I mean, I know she's scared, but I can't let her give up." His eyes teared up for the first time. He compensated by growling and tightening his jaw.

Knoxi placed her hand on his shoulder. "Robbie, it's okay to let your emotions —" She stopped and thought better of it. "What I mean is, the two of you have been fighting all alone, and you are both so brave, but —"

"Abdulla is a very powerful man," Robbie interrupted. "He has major corporations and newspapers behind him. He openly believes he's more powerful than God, and a lotta people believe him. I mean, like, no matter where we turn, somebody's waiting for us."

Jeremy asked an obvious question. "So, look, if Stanton's so powerful, why does he care about messin' wit you? And why kill your baby?"

Knoxi offered an explanation. "He's a sociopath who believes Robbie has stolen his property. In Abdulla's sick mind the only way to set things straight is to recover his property and kill the baby. Sociopaths can be without conscience when someone stands up to them."

"Guess where Abdulla is now, son."

"Where's that, sir?"

"He's in the basement below, tied up."

"Here? Abdulla is here?"

"That's right. He's not a very big man right now."

"Well," Robbie countered. "You better hope the sheriff doesn't find out."

As the meeting broke up, Susan and John arrived to check on Peaches. They brought alarming news.

"Our scanner just picked up three county sheriff's vehicles. They're headed this way. And we got word just minutes ago from a contact in the Austin Police Department. Seems they're widening the search for the mystery helicopter. Moon River Ranch is on the list to be searched immediately."

DON'T SHOOT THE SHERIFF
(And Please Don't Shoot the Deputy)

Cody went to the front window and looked down the long, curvy driveway. No sheriff's vehicles yet. The Cherokee warriors had left immediately. Cody knew exactly where they were headed. They would hide their prisoners, making certain they would not be found. Everyone but Cody and Brandi would stay hidden when the county sheriff vehicles showed up.

It would be tricky dealing with the sheriff and his men. Were some of the deputies just following orders, unaware of the crimes they were covering up? Would they possess a search warrant?

If the sheriff found Abdulla and his henchmen, it would be a disaster. He would file multiple charges against Cody and the entire group, Peaches and Robbie would be turned back over to Abdulla, and the underworld would know that Cody was now a player.

In a few minutes, three sheriff's department vehicles pulled up. Cody watched through the blinds. The deputies stood by their cars while their boss walked toward the front door. The sheriff wore a gray wide-brim hat on his head and a low-hanging sidearm on his right hip. His tight britches were stuffed into his tall, shiny black boots. The man himself was a small, more odious Barney Fife, a dried-up boomer who had missed his stagecoach and who squinted in one eye. He was not carrying any paper, but might have a warrant in his breast pocket.

Cody decided to preempt the knock. He opened the door and walked onto the porch with a smile and an extended his hand. "Good morning, Sheriff. How did you find me? I thought this was a safe location." He waited for the sheriff's reaction.

The sheriff stared for a moment. It was obvious he didn't recognize Cody. "I, uh, yessir, my name's Bill Colton. I'm sheriff in these parts."

"Good to meet you, Sheriff Colton. I've heard about you."

Colton still struggled to recognize Cody. "Are—are you alone here, sir?" He scratched his chin, his squinting eye now blinking rapidly.

"No, sir, I'm not. I have my wife with me. I had hoped no one would find us here."

"May I ask, sir, why you don't want to be found?" His deputies now began to spread out, casting glances in every direction.

"Expecting trouble, Sheriff Colton? Are you looking for suspects? Escaped prisoners? Bank robbers? Dangerous people in these hills I should be worried about?"

"Sir, do you recognize this?" Colton held up a blue, fiber-shaft hunting arrow with sleek green feathers and a screw-on tip. "We pulled four of these outta some guys up the road here. You know anything about this incident?"

Cody handled the arrow, studied it carefully. "This arrow should be easy to trace, right? I mean, aren't these custom-made?"

"This arrow? You can find this at any Lowes. No prints, no traceable serial numbers. Impossible."

"So, that's why you came? To ask me if I use a bow and arrow?"

"Uh, well, sir, we're searching for a teenage girl. 'Bout five-five, dark hair, Mexican. She may be injured."

"Have you issued an Amber Alert? How old is she?"

The sheriff tilted his head. "One thing bothers me, sir."

Cody handed the arrow back. "You mean besides a missing teenage girl who may be hurt, with no Amber Alert issued?"

The sheriff's eye stopped blinking. "Quit playin' games with me, cowboy. Tell me who you are."

"Sorry, Bill. My name's Cody Musket. I been sequestered here off and on for the past six months. I was shot and died, but then —"

"Yeah, yeah, I knew you looked familiar. So you been here the whole time? How come no one's ever seen you?"

"Well, like I said, I've been here off and on. I didn't want anyone but my inner circle to know my whereabouts for the past seven months."

"Yeah, I remember you all right, Musket. You were a good man 'til you became a religious fanatic. For all I know, you're a sociopath. I don't buy your story 'bout bein' here before. You and I both know you got the girl inside. Step away from the door."

"Now hold on, Mr. Sheriff. I wanna see a warrant."

"You don't want to do this, Cody. We don't need a warrant in my county. We're comin' in and there's nothin' you can do about it."

"So, Sheriff Bill Colton, are you threatening to perform an illegal search in this private residence? You have no reason to believe I've abducted anyone, no probable cause for entry, and no warrant." He increased his volume to make sure everyone heard. "Do your deputies know the penalties for being complicit in such an illegal action? Come back with a legal warrant signed by a judge and I'll gladly comply."

The sheriff stepped closer, his right hand resting on his holstered revolver and his left hand on Cody's chest. He lowered his voice. "Now, let's keep this between us. You don't want to start this fight. You have no idea who you're dealin' with. I'm comin' in either way."

"Tell me who I'm dealin' with, Bill." Cody glanced about. "Right now all I see is your deputies who may or may not support you in an illegal act, and a man with a badge and gun who just moved so close to me that if you draw that pistol, I'll have you on the porch before you can clear the holster. After that, I'll file charges against you with the Texas Rangers."

"Now, Mister Marine Corps, sir, how long has it been since you practiced any of that martial arts crap? I bet you've forgotten too much of it to go up against the likes of me."

"Some men never learn, Sheriff. And some men never forget."

Colton's right hand shook as though the gun handle were red-hot. He backed away, growling under his breath. "Have you ever heard of Abdulla Stanton? He's good at gettin' rid of cockroaches like you. He's the one who owns this territory."

"So, does Stanton own you?"

"You started this fight and you'll regret it. I'm comin' back with a warrant ASAP. I'm leavin' my men here to make sure nobody leaves this place. If that little girl dies, I'm comin' after you, mister-religious-fanatic-turned-predator. After that, all bets are off!"

The sheriff departed at a hard pace, burning rubber, swerving around the tight curves as his vehicle disappeared from view. Cody caught sight of a reflection coming from the wooded area adjacent to the house. He turned, looked closely, and discovered that Robbie had somehow obtained one of the scoped rifles Baker had brought along, and had observed the entire exchange from the cover of the trees. Robbie was now making his way back toward the house, doing his best to remain hidden.

Cody received a text from Kenny. *"No worries, I had him whole time. U gotta talk 2 Robbie b4 we rename him 'Wrecking Ball.'"*

"Copy that," Cody texted back.

"HAWKER"

After the sheriff drove out of sight, Cody stood stoically on the veranda. He must remain unflappable. He contemplated his next move in light of the sheriff's strident departure and his animated pledge to return with a search warrant.

He nodded at the three deputies staring in his direction. How far would they go in defense of Sheriff Colton? Could one or more of the deputies become an ally? He must find out. That would be a good next move.

Fortunately, none of them had seen Robbie sneak off with a rifle into the wooded area near the right flank of the house. That could have gotten ugly in a heartbeat. What should he do about this undisciplined son of thunder who seemed so anxious to fight a war, and who might jeopardize everyone's safety? Robbie had never known a father. Cody had seen it before.

He opened the front door and reentered the house. Brandi met him head-on with twinkling eyes and a cell phone. "We got it," she said proudly. "Listen to this." Everybody gathered.

Brandi pushed the *play* button. The audio and video quality of Cody's recorded confrontation with Sheriff Bill Colton was exceptional, a possible game-changer. Nothing on the recording would suffice as evidence in a court of law, but on social media it could be a knockout punch to the sheriff's reelection run.

"I placed the phone in the window to record it, and left it there during the whole meeting," Brandi said. "Tomorrow, Bill Colton will be the guiding light of social media."

Everyone applauded. Then Cody had a request. "Could yawl give me a moment with my wife?" Everyone obliged.

Cody put his arms around Brandi and kissed her, then with an extended embrace he would not let go. Brandi relished feeling his beating heart next to hers. She knew his secrets, his thoughts. He had just lived through a treacherous encounter with a man who did not mind torturing and killing the helpless. Cody needed to unwind.

Finally, he stepped back. "Where's Knoxi?"

"I dunno. She disappeared upstairs earlier. She's been talking to someone on the phone. Sounded like . . . sounded like she was making a dinner date with some person at the campus. Is that possible?"

"Hmmm, she has a head on her shoulders, but I'd like to know who she was talking to." Cody rubbed his chin.

"That's because you're still the daddy and you wanna control her life forever. Get over it. You still have two sons at home and . . ." She did not complete her thought.

"And what?"

"I have an uncomfortable feeling about Robbie," she said. "I know he's a brave young man, but don't you think he might need a little fatherly advice?"

Cody shook his head. "He won't respond to advice. With him, it's gonna take something stronger."

"I hear you. And in the FYI department, I too would like to know who Knoxi was speaking with." Brandi looked about to make sure no one was listening, then she whispered. "So—so which one of us gets to snoop around and find out?"

Cody wore a bland grin as he walked toward the stairwell and looked upward. He turned to Brandi again. "How are the two patients? What does Susan say?"

"Elena's recovering quickly. Susan says Peaches needs bed rest, but the baby is healthy. She sees no evidence that Peaches was assaulted. Robbie must've gotten her away before that so-called doctor could use any instruments on her. Susan thinks the bleeding was from the horse ride and the fall."

"Boy or girl?"

"Girl," she said. "Robbie thought it would be a son, but he's happy about the girl. By the way, what should I do with the video?"

Cody was non-committal. "Lemme think about it. It might be more effective if we just threaten to release it." He turned and walked toward the parlor. "I'm going in here to make a call. I'll tell you about it later." He entered the parlor and shut the door behind him.

Cody's heart began to pound as he dialed an unfamiliar number. When a friendly female voice answered, his nerves calmed.

> "Good afternoon. Texas Rangers Division. How may the Rangers be of service?"

"Good afternoon ma'am. I'm calling Captain Keyshawn Harris."

> "May I ask what this is regarding? And whom shall I say is calling?"

"Tell Captain Harris . . . tell him it's Babe calling. I have information about an investigation."

> A few seconds later, "This is Harris. Who's this?"

"Hello, Hawker. Long time since Afghanistan. How did a butt-ugly Marine flyboy from Nebraska end up in Austin?" ·

> "Cody? Musket? Babe! Is this for real?"

"It's me, Hawk. I need help — somebody I trust. Congrats on your promotion — interim director of the Rangers." Cody explained his predicament in "thirty words or less," mostly centered upon Stanton.

> "You have Stanton? The mega industrialist? The guy with shady ops in Mexico and lotsa holdings in Texas banks? Tied up in your basement? You bought yourself a lotta trouble. The Rangers have tried to build a case against him, but — Look, you can't hold

him. It's unlawful. You gotta be deputized, have a warrant. You know all that, right? You might pull that off in a third-world country, but not here."

"Well, then how 'bout a sheriff named Bill Colton?"

"Don't tell me you got him in your basement too."

"No, but I had a run-in with him, and things are . . . uh complicated."

"Colton's dangerous, one of the most corrupt elected officials in the state. He's linked to a crime syndicate, but we can't connect the dots, and nobody will testify against him. A family of five on Highland Boulevard was going to testify, but . . . never mind, I'll text you the file. It's not pretty."

"Okay. Meanwhile, I'm sending you a video we just now obtained. It might force Colton to cooperate if I threaten to wreck his reelection bid by releasing it on social media. It can't be used in court, but it ties him to Stanton. Maybe you can investigate that angle to build a legal case."

"Careful. This guy would slit your throat and not even say 'excuse me.'"

"It wouldn't be the first time somebody killed me."

"Well said, Marine. But, I can't overlook you holdin' Stanton against his will. If he files charges . . ."

"Understood, Captain. Watch for that video."

After Cody ended his call, he opened the door and invited Robbie in for a powwow.

WRECKING BALL

After Robbie walked into the parlor, he closed the door and sat across from Cody on the small couch. Cody was good at not giving away his feelings. Even Brandi had oft complained that his eyes were unreadable.

"Good to hear your wife's doin' better, Robbie. Looks like the baby's healthy too. Susan says she needs bed rest."

"We'll repay you for all this somehow," he pledged. "You don't know this, sir, but I had your back while you met with that sheriff."

"Did you notice Kenny watching your back while you were watchin' my back? And are you aware how carelessly you carried that weapon when you were sneaking around out there?"

"You saw me? How? And why did somebody need to watch my back? I never asked for your help."

"Cardinal rule when in hostile territory — make sure your own people know where you are at all times." Cody handed Robbie his phone. "Check out this text I got from Kenny."

Robbie read the message about the wrecking ball.

"Wrecking Ball? That's the perfect name for me. That's exactly what I wanna be — a wreckin' ball!"

"Do you realize you endangered the lives of everyone here? If you had been spotted it would have told the enemy everything they wanted to know."

"But I was careful! And I wanna get rid of all those guys! I'd rather kill 'em all!"

"Is that who you want to be? A killer? Is that who you think you are? You must not like yourself very much."

"*Ha!* You're absolutely right! I hate myself!"

Knoxi tapped on the doors and pushed them open a few inches. "I brought you guys some coffee." Both men nodded. She entered and set the tray on the coffee table, then slipped out.

"Why do you hate yourself, Robbie?"

"For bein' born mostly. For bein' raised by a psycho. For goin' along with his evilness all those years. For waitin' so long to figure things out."

Cody lifted his cup to take a sip. "So, you think you have things figured out? You think your roots are your fault? Like . . . like you've lived your whole life in the wrong place at the wrong time?"

"That's about it. I owe the world for who I am, for what I've done. How do I ever fix that? I'm tryin' to face it like a—a man."

"Becoming a man is about a lot more than just bein' a wreckin' ball and apologizing for who you are, son. And, you have bigger issues than just taking another man's firearm without asking."

Cody stood and walked to the window. He parted the blinds with his thumb, gazing out at the three deputies who were hanging together in one of the three vehicles.

He turned around. "The first thing you gotta know is who you are, Robbie. After that, the rest will fall into place." He leaned against the wall and folded his arms. "Let me ask you a question: What motivates you the most? What inspires you?"

"Honestly, sir, I'd say hate. Hate inspires me most. I hate myself, I hate the traffickers, and I hate Abdulla for makin' me what I am."

"What motivated you to fight off ten men to save Peaches and your child? Was it hate, or was it something else?"

"I guess . . . I guess it was something else, maybe."

"Maybe?"

"For years, I followed Abdulla around and wanted to be just like him. I helped him steal. I even delivered several women to hotel rooms. I never went inside, but I knew something was wrong. They would cry. They would — I mean, it seemed so easy. I just turned and walked away, until . . ."

"Until you found out Stanton was lying all those years? Until you saw Peaches in that place?"

"It won't leave me alone, night and day." He placed his hands over his ears. "The things I let them do to people. I still hear them. So, what does that make me?"

"Robbie Earp is the man who set aside his hate long enough to fool two dangerous older men into letting down their guard at the hotel. Robbie Earp's the man who inspired an abandoned teenage girl to fight for her freedom. Was that hate?"

Cody walked back to his seat and poured another cup for himself and one for Robbie. "Son, I like the Robbie motivated by love a heckuva lot more than the one inspired by hate. You can always determine someone's character by asking one question: Who do you honor? What does honor mean to you?"

"I—I don't know if I follow what you mean, sir."

"My point, Robbie, is that you turned down a life of wealth and power because you did not consider the life of a predator to be honorable."

"So, how do I pay everyone back for what I did? How do I get rid of all the images in my head?"

"Some things cannot be paid back, Robbie, but you *can* be forgiven."

"I don't wanna to be forgiven. There's no getting off scot-free."

Cody leaned forward and folded his hands on the coffee table. "Robbie, I know a fellow Marine Corp pilot named Shawn who had a checkered past. He was a wild kid in high school. He was black and summa the white kids picked on him . . . insulted his family, his black heritage. It made him bitter."

Robbie nodded and squeezed both hands around his cup.

"So, ironically, he had one friend and one friend only, and he was white, the son of a state representative. One Saturday morning, the friend invited him to borrow his pickup and go hunting on his family's large ranch in Nebraska. The whole family was gonna be outta town. Shawn accepted the offer.

"But he put the rifle in the seat without securing it in the gun rack. He hit a bump and the gun discharged. The bullet went right through his boot but missed his big toe and managed to shoot through the floorboard and destroy the front tire." He chuckled.

"Shawn was afraid this powerful state representative would come down on him like a blitzkrieg. He apologized over and over and offered to pay all the repairs. He even went to the repair center and the tire store and offered to put everything on a payment plan, but State Representative Buddy McDonald had already paid the bill."

Robbie looked up. "So what happened to Shawn?"

"What happened? Buddy McDonald told Shawn he was so impressed by the way he stepped up and took responsibility that he saw greatness in him. Then, he chewed him out for using a friend's truck without having proper gun safety knowledge. When I flew with him in Afghanistan, I knew him as First Lieutenant Keyshawn Harris, Weapons Systems Officer in command of an FA-18D, with enough firepower at his fingertips to level the entire downtown area of Austin, Texas. Today, the former truck-shooter is in command of the Texas Rangers."

"So, he never paid it back?"

"Depends on how you look at it. Shawn used it as a valuable lesson on humility. He pays it back every time he frees someone, every time he takes a predator off the streets. Accepting someone's forgiveness humbled him and changed his mind about who he is."

Robbie was quiet. Cody wondered what his thoughts were.

"You see, son, you fly into a rage and become like a loose bowling ball. You live your life by primitive animal instinct instead of virtue. You seem hell-bent on getting yourself beat up or shot because you think you deserve it. All the while you're playing into the hands of your enemy. You say you don't need our help, but if

Kenny and Adrian hadn't shown up earlier you would be in worse shape than Peaches right now."

Cody finished his cup, then set it down. "If you and your Peach hadn't worked together, you wudda never gotten out of that hotel room at Nogales. Teamwork. You gotta learn teamwork. We want you to be part of our team, but you have to do what we say. Is that perfectly clear?"

"Yes, sir."

"And until you've had proper firearms training, you will not even touch a firearm around here."

"Mr. Musket, I have one question."

"Call me Cody. And what's the question?"

"I heard your wife and Knoxi prayin' to Jesus when you went to wait for the sheriff. So, does someone up there really listen? And, how does someone like me square things with God?"

"It's already squared. Jesus paid in blood for all the stuff we've done. You can't pay God back for that kind of love, but you can be forgiven if you just ask. He punched your ticket. Just hold onto it and keep it where your heart beats. And yes, I'm living proof. Someone listens."

HEROES AND COCKROACHES

C ody stayed seated, watching Robbie leave the parlor. Had he reached him? Peaches was his soft spot, a good place to begin.

He pulled up the video of his conversation with the sheriff and played it again. Brandi had sent it to his phone. Sheriff Colton could return with more deputies and a warrant any moment. What could he do with this recording? After consulting with Baker again, he decided to play the video card sooner rather than later.

Cody opened the front door and approached the deputies, carrying a full pot of coffee and a stack of throw-away cups. "Howdy, gentlemen, would anyone like a cup of brew?" Each of the three men accepted his offer.

"Thanks, Mr. Musket," one of them said, extending a warm hand. "I'm Ulysses Fox."

The other two men offered no hand and no greeting, but accepted the coffee.

Deputy Fox opened the door and stepped out. "What an honor, sir, meetin' you my first day on na' job. I served twenty-one years. Injured in a chopper accident, got a discharge, and here I am." He nonchalantly strayed a few feet away from the vehicle. Cody followed casually, sensing something was up.

Fox's appearance would have made the perfect law-enforcement recruiting poster. He was tall, lean, and barrel-chested like Tanner McNair, Jeremy's father, his best friend from high school. The deputy had a friendly, well-traveled face and eyes that had seen trouble.

"Well, Deputy, you look like an Army guy. Delta maybe?"

"Special forces weapons sergeant. How'd you know?"

"Army guys always say 'chopper.' Navy and Marines say 'helo.' I also noticed your blood type taped to the heel of your boots. That's a *dead* giveaway for Delta, in a manner of speaking."

"Yessir," Fox said with a deep chuckle. "Old habits never *die,* in a manner of speaking."

"I notice you constantly scan to the perimeter with your eyes, Deputy Fox. You're all business. I bet you never miss a thing, right?"

"Yes, sir." He looked toward the tree line where Robbie had stood earlier, and nodded his eyes. "Yessir, that's correct, sir."

"Cool," Cody said. "Heard anything from the sheriff yet?"

"Not yet, Mr. Musket, but we're always here for you. Call me anytime. Here's my card." The business card carried contact information. All deputies carried them.

Cody walked calmly back to the veranda and entered the house again. Immediately, Brandi wanted a report. "So, how did that go?"

Cody examined Fox's card thoroughly. On the reverse side, he found three words scribbled: *"Watch ur back."*

"Cody, what happened?"

"That big deputy is an ally." Cody's game face was on.

"How do you know?"

"He saw Robbie in the woods and never said a word. He gave me his card. Check out the back."

She turned it over. "Watch ur back? Who is he?"

"Ulysses Fox, former Delta. He knows something isn't right. He must've hand-written this earlier hoping to pass the message to me. I wouldn't be surprised if he's undercover FBI or Texas Rangers."

Cody sent a text to the number printed on the deputy's card. It read, "Watch yours. Protect your cover. Take a look at this video. Delete this message."

Brandi exhaled a weary breath. "So now what?"

"I'm going back out there." Cody left the house again.

"Howdy again, gentlemen. Can you get a message to your boss? Tell him I have some vital information. He'll want to see it. Tell him to come now."

In fifteen minutes the sheriff screeched to a halt in front of the house. This time he marched up double time and banged on the door. Immediately, five more vehicles showed up.

"Hello, Bill," Cody said with a grin. "Let's have another chat."

"Don't be so smug, Musket. I got an army here this time."

Cody looked up to see six deputies approaching the porch with hands on weapons. Fox came alongside the others.

"I know a game when I see it, Colton said. "You're hiding people. Do my deputies have to draw their weapons before you let us in?" The sheriff's eye twitched randomly as he wiped his sweaty forehead.

Cody lost his thin smile. "I'm unarmed and you outnumber me, but this should even the odds." He pulled out his phone.

Colton's face narrowed. His lip curled into a silent snarl as Cody played the video at the lowest volume setting.

"Between you and me, Sheriff, you'll be a social media star by morning. When I release this video, you're gonna be wanted by people on both sides of the law. How's that gonna affect your reelection bid?"

"I'll have you in jail before tomorrow morning," Colton growled under his breath. "Extortion! Blackmail!"

"Don't stroke your own ego, Musket." Colton spat on the porch in front of Cody's feet. "The people support me because I keep undesirables like you away. They pay me to make the hard decisions."

"Was it a hard decision to get rid of that family of five before they could appear in court? Did you suffocate them one-by-one yourself or did somebody do it for you?"

"*Ha!* That's old news. We caught the suspect. He hung himself in jail."

"You mean the Rabbi? The one they proved later was in Huntsville at the time of the murders?"

"How come you know so friggin' much about my county?"

"I have sources. You were once a capable lawman, Colton, but you decided to stop living the day you started accepting blood money instead of fighting for the victims. Now, you're just a bitter old man who is tired of livin' and afraid to die, and nobody'll even watch your back unless you pay 'em. It doesn't have to be like this."

The sheriff moved nose-to-nose with Cody and responded through clenched teeth. "Every day I look for more ways to hate you religious crusaders. You're weakening the foundation of my America. I fight my *own* battles, and I despise everything you stand for."

Suddenly, the windows rattled. A moment later, a thundering sound like that of a thousand horses' hooves echoing through the hills surrounded the hacienda. The noise seemed to come from every direction as two helicopters burst onto the site, skimming above the swirling treetops, slowing down, and finally hovering. A terse, electronic voice crackled through the air.

*"Everyone place your hands on your head and get
on your knees; by order of the Texas Rangers!"*

As the Rangers continued to hover, three unmarked black SUVs raced up the final stretch of driveway and stopped. A six-man SWAT team spilled out of the vehicles and took up aggressive positions.

"Federal agents! Remain with your hands over your heads. You will be disarmed and read your rights! You are all under arrest!"

Cody, on his knees like the rest, was approached by one of the men. "Mr. Musket, you are not under arrest. I'm Agent Timothy D. Comer, FBI. This is a joint operation with the Texas Rangers, sir. Rangers' Acting Director Harris sends his regards." He shook hands with Cody. "And, thank you for your service, Mr. Musket."

As the sheriff and his deputies, including Fox, were led away in cuffs, Brandi came out to join Cody. "What about —"

"*Shhh,*" Cody whispered. "No one must know he helped us."

"What do you think will happen to the sheriff's department? How much disruption will this cause for this county?"

"I think God just smiled on this county," Cody said. "Now, the people can elect a real sheriff." He watched as Deputy Fox was the last to be placed in a vehicle. "I think I know just the man for the job, if he isn't already employed elsewhere."

Incident at Moon River

The FBI and the Texas Rangers headed back to Austin with their prisoners. The joint task force saw it as a unique opportunity to apprehend Stanton and Colton in one operation and possibly compel the two material witnesses to turn on each other. It would be a tricky legal procedure, but it was worth a shot.

After the authorities had departed the scene, everyone decided it was chill time. Sunset turned the evening sky to orange, while the entire company enjoyed a Texas barbeque feast catered by Danny's, a popular stop along Good Night Trail. Time to unwind, knowing that no one would invade tonight, and the satisfaction that some dangerous people were in custody.

Brandi questioned Cody. "Have you heard anything from Star and Hutch about their Nogales mission?"

"I got a text," Cody said. "They spent the day loading up. They plan to leave at first light tomorrow and be in Nogales by sundown. They'll launch the drone after midnight and fly a circular pattern over the factory."

Cody's cell rang. It was Captain Harris. He told Cody that the video, which names Stanton as an associate, was an eye-opener. Until then, they had no information linking Stanton with Colton. The recording provided enough information to get the necessary warrants.

"We're pushin' it, Babe. Gonna be a slippery slope trying to get these guys to incriminate each other and turn over evidence linking them to bigger fish in exchange for leniency."

"Leniency?" Cody gripped his phone tighter.

"Sometimes it's the only way to get things done," Captain Harris told him. "These guys could be just the tip of the proverbial iceberg. Incidentally, you don't know anything about a missing helo, do you?"

"Missing helo? I heard some rumblings, but . . ."

"Yeah, that's what I figured," Harris said. "I didn't expect you to know anything."

"So, you're investigating that too?"

"Yep, but it doesn't concern you." Harris exhaled heavily. "Uh, by the way, do you remember when we were in Pensacola and stole that T-28 so we could fly to Atlanta and see those two chicks? We ran outta fuel and landed at a private airport and hid the bird in a barn. We got it out of that barn just before NCIS arrived."

"Uh, yeah. We . . . were in such a hurry we didn't check the fuel before we took off, right?"

"You always did like to live on the edge, Musket. I hope I don't see a warrant for your arrest someday." The call ended.

"Baker! We gotta get that helo outta the barn at Moon River. The Rangers are on to us. It's due to be searched tomorrow."

"Your Texas Ranger friend told you that?"

"Loud and clear. Made up some story about — Never mind, we gotta do something about it. Like now!"

Baker yanked his cell phone from his pocket and called Marty. No answer, so he left an urgent voicemail.

"I can't reach Marty," Baker said. "If I don't hear back in thirty minutes, I'm going over there. He's scheduled a truck to move the helicopter at 2300 tomorrow."

"That'll be too late," Cody said. "We should go now."

"I have another idea," Baker said. "Let me take one of your guys from the Cherokee rez. Either one of 'em can handle himself. You and everyone else stay here. We may not be as safe here as you think, so watch your back and guard your family."

Cody agreed. Baker took Kenny and departed for Moon River. Cody gathered everyone else and informed them. John had just arrived from Austin to check again on the two patients. He reported that both women might be able to travel by the next morning.

"Where's Knoxi?" Cody asked Brandi. "I don't want to lose track of anyone tonight."

Brandi shrugged her shoulders. "She went upstairs again with her phone in hand. It isn't like her to be so secretive. I have no idea who she's calling."

~   ~   ~

While Cody and Brandi talked downstairs, Robbie silently entered the upstairs room where Peaches lay. He tiptoed over to her bed and sat down on a chair beside her. He wanted to tell her so much, but he was afraid. He kept his voice barely above a whisper.

"Hey, Peach girl. How you feelin?" He waited. "Peach, you awake?" She did not respond, but Robbie decided to keep talking.

He reached for her limp hand. "We're gonna have a baby girl, Peach, *not* a son. She's a fighter just like you. I wanted to name her Strawberry, but that didn't sound good with Earp. I mean, Strawberry Earp? Are you kidding me? I think *you* should name her."

He moved his chair inches closer, and spoke softer than a breath. "A lot happened today. I—I mean Abdulla was taken into custody." He squeezed her hand but got no response.

"So, see, Mr. Musket . . ." Robbie cleared his throat. "I mean Cody came down on me 'cause I almost got us killed today. You know me. *Ha!* I just rush into everything before I think, right?"

"Listen, Peach. Seriously. Cody . . . he believes in teamwork — like, we should look out for each other. He even promised to teach me to shoot; I mean really shoot good, the right way. Nobody ever took time for me before. It was almost like havin' a real dad for fifteen minutes. He showed me what honor means. Abdulla never did that. And, there's somethin' else I gotta say . . ."

He stroked her dark hair away from her eyes, hoping she would open them, but they remained shut.

"This is important, Peaches." He pulled in a deep breath. "All this time, I thought the reason I saved you was to spite Abdulla, to wreck his plans because I hated him so much. But, Cody said — Uh, don't laugh, okay? He said love is when you care about someone else more than you care about yourself. Right then, I learned something. See, I didn't help you just to get revenge on Abdulla, and I didn't marry you just cuz you please me." He took a moment to see if she would respond, then glanced back at the door to make certain no one else was listening.

"I'm afraid to tell you this next part. I'll practice while you're asleep, okay? So . . . so, here goes. I love you, Peach. I know that now. I shouldn't get my hope up, but maybe someday you'll feel the same."

She breathed comfortably, but her eyes remained closed.

"One more thing," he whispered. "Listen to this: Cody said Jesus paid for all the bad stuff I've done. I just gotta ask Him to forgive me. He even said Jesus can change me into a better person, maybe even a good person. So, like, I know it sounds crazy — Me? A good person? Me? Forgiven?"

He kept his voice down to a quiet whisper. "I mean, hell's bells! You'd be freaked outta your mind if you could hear me talkin' like this."

He brushed her hair again. "Yeah," he sighed. "That's all I got to say. I'll be back when you wake up."

As he turned to leave, Peaches lifted her weak right hand and reached for his forearm.

"Please . . . don't go."

～　　～　　～

Baker and Kenny finally arrived at Moon River and approached cautiously. Both men sensed trouble. Baker had still not been able to reach Marty by cell. He had left Marty several messages.

They drove at 15 mph over the cattle guard onto the property, but stopped when they noticed a dim light ahead. Faintly it shone through a shallow ground fog. Baker turned off the car lights and rolled down the two windows. Both men sat silently, listening.

"It's a trap," Kenny said. "Back outta here!"

Baker slammed the SUV into reverse and gunned the motor. He turned back to face the road behind him and backed up about a hundred yards. When he stopped, Kenny was no longer in the vehicle.

His cell phone beeped a frantic text from Kenny: *"RPG! Get outta the car! Now!!!"*

Baker grabbed his weapon pouch off the front floorboard, then burst from the vehicle and hit the ground running. He dove into a drainage ditch just as his vehicle exploded. He felt the concussion and the hot windy blast, but most of the energy passed above him as he lay in the bottom of the ditch. His eyes suddenly burned from the blowing dirt and smoke. He coughed.

His ears rang, his entire body was numb, but instinct and experience told him that if he stayed near the vehicle he would remain in great danger. Whoever had launched the rocket-propelled grenade would be there within minutes to make sure no one had survived.

He struggled to climb from the shallow ditch, then realized he needed a situation report from his partner. Was Kenny still in one piece? He scrounged around the bottom of the dry ditch and found his phone that he had dropped. He was surprised to see another text: *"Stay hidden. I got this."*

Baker hunkered down again. After what seemed an eternity, he sensed someone standing over him. He raised his weapon. It was Kenny. "Come on. I took care of it. You okay, Baker?"

"I think I'm in one piece," Baker said, trying to clear the smoke and cobwebs from his head. "So, what's the situation?"

"Two hostiles dead on the road." Kenny helped him out of the ditch. "I have their weapons. I also confiscated their hand-held launcher and two RPGs. Let's check on your friend and then find a vehicle and leave the site. It won't be long before this place'll be crawlin' with state troopers and local cops."

"Uh, yeah, of course. Lead the way." Baker tried to shake it off. His body felt like it weighed four hundred pounds, the fatigue excruciating. "We . . . we need to get someone to remove the helicopter from the barn and get it outta here by morning."

Kenny responded. "Remove the chopper? That's not gonna be possible. Somebody already beat us to it. Take a look."

Baker wiped the grit from his eyes and tried to ream out his ears with his fingers. Then, he stopped cold. A chill swirled up and down his spine as he blinked twice. The light they had seen while approaching the ranch had come from the barn. The doors were wide open, the dim lights were burning, and the helo had vanished.

They hid in the hedges while Baker attempted to call Marty again. Finally, an answer. "They came right through the . . . the door, sir. I—I couldn't . . ."

"Marty? Where are you? Are you injured?"

"I'm dead, sir. They wanted to know where it was, but I dunno where it went. It's . . . gone. The chopper. I didn't give 'em any names. Told 'em my partner was Sp . . . Spiderman." His throat rattled, "Please tell my mom about . . ."

"Marty? Where are you?" Silence.

Moments later, they found Marty's body. It wasn't pretty. His cell phone was still planted inside his clenched palm. The helicopter was indeed missing. There were no tracks, no signs of a trailer or tractor. It was simply gone.

Baker's vision began to narrow as peripheral blackness encroached upon his sight. "I need to go see his mother. Somehow I have to tell her his death made sense. That part would be a lie."

Lightheaded and fatigued, he finally sat down on a bale of hay next to Marty's body.

Kenny noticed a book lying a few feet away on the floor of the barn. He stepped over and picked it up. It was an open Bible with a bloody fingerprint on the page that read:

> *"Blessed is the one whose transgressions are forgiven,*
> *whose sins are covered . . ."*

Kenny returned with the open Bible and handed it to Baker. "Tell his mother that his last hour was his finest, and that a brave warrior has gone home. That part would be the truth."

TERRORS BY NIGHT

Cody had slipped into bed with Brandi, but his mind wouldn't settle down. Would Star and Hutch be successful launching Dracula in Nogales tomorrow night? What about the helicopter at Moon River? Should he trust Captain Shawn Harris, his friend and acting director of the Texas Rangers? Why had he been unable to reach Baker by phone in the past hour? Was Marty okay?

He didn't have to wait long to get some answers. When his phone sounded off it jarred his senses, scrambling his thoughts into tiny pieces. *That must be Baker!* He grabbed it off the nightstand, but it wasn't Baker. It was his buddy, Captain Harris.

"Cody! You gotta get outta there, man! Get your family out now! We have reason to believe they've sent a hit team. They could be there already. Were sending a couple of vehicles to pick you up!"

"A hit squad? Why?"

"A sniper was waiting when the FBI delivered the sheriff's men to the Austin branch," Harris informed. "The shooter killed three including the sheriff. Agents shot and apprehended the hitman, and before he died he said there's a contract on Stanton's life. Stanton is just a smaller fish after all. Someone wants to make sure he doesn't talk, and your people are a loose end. They're comin' after you."

"That's scary," Cody said. "I mean, how far does this thing go?"

"You've stumbled onto something that's getting bigger and bigger, man."

"What about Fox? Deputy Fox. Is he okay?"

"Don't worry 'bout Fox. I see you've already made him."

"I gotta call you back Shawn. We're mobilizing right now. I'll ring you back when we —"

"Wait, Cody!" he interrupted. "There's been a disturbance at Moon River. An explosion. You know anything about that?"

"Moon River?"

"C'mon, Babe, stop the ruse. What are you hiding? You gotta level with me or I can't help you."

"Okay, okay. First of all, it's more than just my family over here. We have wounded who can't be moved in the middle of the night, and—"

"So what about some girl Stanton's gunning for? She may be our star witness now that the sheriff is out of the way."

Cody had nothing more than a slow, deep sigh into the phone.

"Cody?"

"Yeah," Cody conceded "We have her."

"Don't you know that girl is a target?"

"Well," Cody said, "with Stanton in custody I figured we were all out of danger. But —"

"We're coming to get you all. I don't trust any law-enforcement agencies in your area right now. We'll get some of our people there as quick as we can. I dunno about landing a helo there at night with the hills and everything."

Cody responded. "There's room to land in the front. I can direct 'em in. How soon can you be here?"

"Could be as much as an hour to deploy everyone, but will expedite!"

Cody jammed the phone deep into the front pocket of his jeans. Too much to digest. One thing at a time. The hit squad must be the immediate priority. He could check on Moon River later — *Oh, God, I pray Baker and Kenny made it out.*

Cody placed Adrian in charge. He was a highly-trained former Army Ranger. He mobilized rapidly. They needed more people, but it was what it was. He designated the word "ox" as the password and ordered all lights off.

Knoxi and Brandi were both trained in the use of handguns. They would wait at the top of the stairs and drop anyone who attempted to climb up. Jeremy, who also knew how to use a weapon, would be stationed behind the counter in the kitchen and would shoot anyone who attempted to come through the back door.

Cody took Robbie aside and gave him a three-minute tutorial on firing a handgun — install mag, pull slide, remove safety, point, shoot. He told Robbie to stay with Peaches, and to not allow anyone to come through the door without the password.

Elena, barely able to walk, volunteered to watch the front of the house and alert Adrian if she spotted movement. She would stay inside and use night-vision equipment to observe through the windows. She was armed. They did not expect the hostiles to attack from the front, but someone needed to keep watch just in case.

Adrian scanned in every direction with his bogie-tracker, but the invaders had employed a jamming device. Adrian would be forced to do this the old-fashion way. He quietly opened a window on each side of the hacienda and listened. He whispered the password and moved up the stairs, passed onto the north-side balcony and listened again. His senses had been correct. Two subjects were moving in opposite directions through the woods about forty yards away. He alerted Cody by text.

Just then, gunfire erupted on the other side of the hacienda — a long volley of shots from an automatic assault weapon ricocheting and cutting through the walls of the bottom floor. An emotional shockwave rocketed through the house when they heard a loud scream coming from Jeremy's station. Cody was closest so he ran through the living area toward the kitchen. Before he could arrive, three individual shots fired off in rapid succession. Cody hit the floor.

All was quiet. Cody regained his focus quickly enough to realize those last three shots had come from Jeremy's gun. As he digested the sudden odor of spent powder, he felt a vibration in his right front pocket. He reached in and pulled out his phone. It was a text from Jeremy — "*Got him!*"

He slithered carefully around the bullet-battered furniture on his way to the kitchen. Jeremy was crouched on the floor, breathing heavily with his large hands pressed against his temples and the handgun lying on the floor beside him.

"Are you hurt, son? Did you get hit?"

Jeremy stared blankly at a lifeless, bloody body wearing black ninja clothing which lay in the back doorway. The intruder had just invaded someone's home for the last time.

"Jeremy?" Cody knelt and tried to get him to return to reality. His eyes were unfocused and distant. Cody had seen it before. "Jeremy, I need you to focus. Help me get this body inside. This isn't over."

They pulled the body into the kitchen, closed the door, and removed the mask. It was a woman — young, maybe twenty. She'd been shot through the chest three times, her blood smeared across the floor where they had just dragged her. Cody removed the comm device she wore and installed it on himself. He muted the mic, but would use the earpiece to listen to the enemy's transmissions.

"Jeremy, I need you to keep watching this door. Can you do that?"

"Yes, sir, Uncle Cody." He shook his head as if to clear the fog. "I—I never . . ."

"I know that, buddy. We'll deal with it later. Not easy to take a life. Sorry you had to find that out the hard way. Just keep focusing, okay?"

"I fooled her. Played dead. She just walked right in. She never made a sound. I mean it was —"

"Jeremy! Snap out of it. I said we'd talk about it later. Are you injured? Are you hit?"

"No, sir. Tell everybody I'm okay."

Cody relayed the message to the others by text. At that moment, he heard a scratchy transmission in the earpiece:

"Stand down, repeat stand down. We've lost Oscar 4 and we have unknown air traffic approaching. Abort. Expedite Alpha 1 to take out air traffic!"

Cody punched Shawn's number to warn him about the intercepted enemy transmission — the hostiles had broken off their attack on the house and would now focus on the approaching helicopters. But before he could reach Shawn, the back door came crashing down.

It was the last thing Cody had expected. The hostiles' previous transmission had set the trap, baiting Cody into lowering his defenses. They knew Cody had captured the headset. He had fallen right into their trap. Two hostiles now stood in the doorway armed with laser-equipped weapons. Cody and Jeremy had nowhere to go. Cody pushed Jeremy aside then dove the other direction. It seemed futile, but neither invader was able to get off a shot. When Cody looked up, the attackers were staggering a few feet outside the door, and within seconds both fell in the yard. What had happened?

Adrian came walking into view, his fiberglass bow in his left hand, his leather quiver on his back. "Ox!" he said. "Don't shoot!" He raised his hands. "The threat has ended."

Cody helped Jeremy to his feet. They walked out the door to examine the two intruders who now lay dead in the back yard. Both were men. Each had taken an arrow through the neck.

Adrian explained that these men were the same two he had spotted earlier. The circling pattern was a planned deception. The enemy gambled that after one attempt at the kitchen door, no one would expect a second at the same entry point. It almost worked.

Cody took no chances, immediately calling Captain Harris again. "Shawn, tell your crews to make an immediate one-eighty and get back on the ground. We have eliminated the ground threat for now, but I've intercepted a transmission that may or may not suggest an immediate threat to your aircraft.

Captain Harris recalled both helos but maintained his plan to send ground transportation for Cody's group and a medevac for Peaches. She was, after all, the star witness against Stanton.

Cody now refocused. He must find out what happened at Moon River. He pulled his cell from his pocket, took a deep breath to clear his lungs, and tightened his fist to stop his fingers from shaking. Before he could punch Baker's contact number, the phone rang. It was Baker.

Moon River had been attacked and ransacked, and there were at least five bodies in and around the barn, one of which was Marty's. Baker and Kenny were safe, but the SUV was not so fortunate.

"Also, brace yourself," Baker said. "The helo has vanished — vanished into thin air."

"*Vanished?*" Cody walked away from the others and lowered his voice. "What do you mean vanished? Who took it? How?"

Baker had no clue. "The helo is gone and the SUV is a smoking pile of rubble. We're gonna hide in the bushes for a few minutes and observe. If they put forensics guys in the SUV, we'll be made."

"Okay," Cody said. "You guys get outta sight. I'll call you back when I get a plan. There are always possibilities."

Cody's mind was racing. Where was the helo? Who had taken it, and would they try to blackmail him? What about the SUV? How many more times would they be shot at? What should he tell the others about Moon River?

"I won't be able to sleep here ever again," Brandi said. "I don't know how we'll ever make it up to the Lowe family. We can pay to repair the damages, but the death will remain."

"We gotta talk," Cody told Brandi alone. "Moon River is blown."

THE THIN LINE

Jeremy entered the parlor alone, closed the door, sat on the couch, and dimmed the lights. His head pounded and his shoulder throbbed again. He limped. He had emerged from the latest gun battle physically unscathed, but his previous afflictions from the helicopter incident were screaming at him again. In the faint light, he stared down at his hands. He had washed them twice, but had he removed all the blood?

Something wet ran down his left cheek. When he felt for it, he discovered that tears were streaming involuntarily from his left eye. Only then did he notice that his vision in both eyes was blurred by unwelcome teardrops. He wiped his face with his sleeve.

Knoxi came to the door and looked through the glass. Alex approached behind her. He waved both women away and put his shaking right hand over his eyes.

After a few minutes, Adrian came to the door and tapped lightly. Jeremy looked up and nodded. Adrian entered the room and closed the door.

"Here," Adrian said, opening his hand and offering him two red capsules. "I use these for the headaches. It's not an opiate. It won't disqualify you from playing baseball."

Jeremy decided to place his bets on the man who had saved his life. He swallowed the pills. "That was some shootin', ace. I see why they call you Silent Arrow."

"I never learned to shoot for the purpose of killing people. I learned for the challenge, for the sport, for hunting. My father was a great hunter with bow and arrow."

"My dad and great-grandfather played baseball. "I'm in the minor leagues hoping to make the bigs next year. I never had a call sign or special name like you and Sleeping Wolf."

"Maybe we'll call you Spider-Man," Adrian said. "I'm a huge fan."

"No way! A fan of which one? Me? My dad?"

"Spider-Man," Adrian grinned. "I'm a fan of Spider-Man."

Jeremy chuckled. "Dat's right. I walked right into that!"

Smiles faded quickly. Adrian drew a long face. Jeremy hardly knew the man, but it was obvious Adrian had not joined him in the dark room just to talk about sport hunting and Spider-Man.

"I killed my first human when I was twenty," Adrian said. "I was on my first tour in Iraq. Sometimes, soldiers make their first kill from several hundred meters away — too far away to see the eyes of their enemy. It may not sink in right away that you've just killed a man."

Jeremy's knee began to fidget.

"You and I were not so fortunate, little brother. We both got our first kill up close and personal. That's a lot tougher to handle."

Jeremy placed his hand over his eyes again.

"I had a friend from the rez. His name was Rat Killer, cuz he once killed a possum and thought it was an oversized rat. He was just twelve and got stuck with the name. He was good-natured about it. His real name was Johnny White Horse. We went through basic together and were in the same unit in Iraq."

He stopped to fill his lungs with a fresh breath. "We were watching a checkpoint from an elevated observation post and had been ordered to maintain that position until further orders. About 0900 a school bus pulled up. Two kids got out and walked up to the checkpoint. They looked like sister and brother. Tiny kids." He paused for several seconds.

"All-a-sudden, there was this big-ass flash of light. The concussion knocked us backward. We were only thirty meters away and we could see clearly down on the site. The two kids had been turned into red smoke, and five GIs had been blown to pieces. Some remains fell in front of our position.

"I looked away, but I could hear Johnny yelling. The bus emptied, and the frightened kids started running all directions. Johnny took off down the hill shooting the innocent kids who ran from the bus. No one knew what to do. Two of the scared GIs tried to approach Johnny, which was an absolute no-no. Johnny shot and killed one of them and wounded the other."

Adrian stopped for a deep breath again. "Captain Bradshaw stood on the road and fired his weapon at Johnny twice but missed. He looked up the hill and ordered me to fire. He knew I wouldn't miss. Before I knew what was happening, I raised my weapon and shot Johnny White Horse in the head."

Jeremy moaned, "You . . . had to kill your friend? Oh, man. I—I dunno what to say, man."

"No one knows what snapped in Johnny's head. Seven children dead. It cudda been worse. They promoted me. They said I saved lives. They said it was okay, that I had no choice. But . . . I mean, it'll never be okay. You just have to get past it. I've come to believe God didn't build us to be killers. We're not designed for it. If we ever reach the point that it doesn't bother us, we'd have to question if we're still human."

Jeremy wiped his face again. "I guess 'Thou shalt not kill' is a warning that you can wreck your own life."

"It's a thin line." Adrian cleared his throat. "A very thin line that separates an act of heroism from murder. A hero doesn't wanna hurt anybody, but sometimes has to. A murderer doesn't have to hurt anyone, but wants to."

"Yeah," Jeremy said. "I heard Cody say that once."

"The woman you killed fired at least fifty rounds into that kitchen in about eight seconds. I dunno how you survived, but if I could get past killin' Johnny White Horse, you can get past killin' a woman who tried to murder you fifty times."

I Don't Know

The slow passage of time while waiting for the Rangers to arrive was excruciating. Everyone wanted to vacate the hacienda ASAP.

Cody called a meeting in the parlor again. "Listen up, everyone. We believe the bad guys will *not* attack again tonight. They underestimated us before and lost three shooters. They know the Rangers are on their way. They won't be back. Where's Robbie? Anybody seen him?"

Brandi spoke up. "He's with Peaches. She's awake and doesn't want to be alone upstairs."

"Is Peaches able to be carried? I mean, maybe she could join us," Cody suggested. "Might take away some of her anxiety if she could meet everybody and be filled in. Is she decent?"

"Uh, Dad," Knoxi offered, "her clothes were all bloody when she got here and they were way too big. She's sort of just under the sheets right now. Maybe we can find something and help her get dressed. She'd love to know we want her included."

A few minutes later, Robbie walked in carrying his wife. Everyone seemed amazed at how beautiful she looked without the gray pallor and muddy hair from falling off the horse earlier. Alex cleared a spot for her on the small couch. Robbie sat next to her and introduced her to everyone.

Cody filled everyone in, relating the story about the FBI arrests of the sheriff and his men, and about the sniper attack which killed the sheriff and three of his deputies.

"Also," Cody said, clearing his throat, "the helicopter which . . . which some of you rode in has disappeared. We don't know who took it or where it is."

Knoxi caught her breath. Cody gave her a sharp glance, but she looked away and smothered a shallow grin.

Cody frowned and continued. "Captain Harris of the Texas Rangers said that Moon River was due to be inspected by law-enforcement agencies, but somehow the bad guys knew about it and got there first. The syndicate seems to know everything sooner than the authorities."

"Why is helicopter so important?" Alex asked Cody.

Because the forensics will point to us and that'll alert the wrong people. We could be in even more danger."

"Foren . . . forensits?" Alex didn't have a clue. "What does that mean?"

For the first time, Peaches opened her mouth. "Forensics: The use of science and technology to investigate and establish facts in criminal or civil courts of law."

It caught everyone off guard, as if this night couldn't have gotten any more bizarre.

"Uh, that's—that's right, Peaches. So, if authorities find the helo, forensics will lead to us, and we don't know who we can trust."

"When Baker and Kenny approached Moon River, they found the ranch under attack. Marty was killed. Baker and Kenny barely escaped with their lives, but the SUV was demolished by an RPG. They weren't hurt, but that vehicle will also have forensic evidence linking us to the event."

Knoxi jumped to her feet. "Excuse me, people. I have to talk to my father. Daddy, please come with me."

Knoxi ran from the meeting, galloped up the stairs and straight to her room. Cody followed her, closed the door, and sat down on the bed. He crossed his arms. "Well?"

"No time to explain. Do you have coordinates for the SUV?"

"What? No, I don't have any more details than I told you."

"Daddy, believe me, you should give me the coordinates."

"Not 'til you tell me what you're up to."

"I need to call Ryan. He . . . he moved the helo, but I had to promise to have dinner with him on campus next week."

"Ryan Maxwell? Sabre's son? Dinner? You promised to take him to dinner if he did what?"

"Dinner. He likes Taco Joint. I've seen him several times over the past six months since he quantumated those bullet fragments in your spine. We've been, uh . . . texting whenever we can. Sometimes he's so busy that he —"

"Are you telling me he —?" Cody stopped. His voice had gotten too loud, so he toned it down. "Are you telling me he somehow used the same technology on a Twin Ranger helicopter? From a distance? How? How can he do that?"

"I don't know, I don't know. He somehow triangulates on the coordinates with satellite and remotes everything so it can't be traced. Then he—he somehow zeroes-in on the quantum something-or-other of the seventh spacetime rainbow collider. He sent the helo to the bottom of the Gulf by defusing the eighth Joske frame with a time flattener. Yeah, I *think* that's what he said."

Cody yanked his phone from his pocket and punched in Baker's number. "I need the dimensions and coordinates of the SUV," he told Baker. "Make sure nobody goes near it."

Baker asked no questions. He gave Cody the numbers. "So far, no one's examined the SUV," Baker informed him. "I removed one of the plates. I couldn't find the other one. A thick fog has rolled in, so the feds and state troopers haven't started sifting through it yet. Probably waiting until dawn. The car's still smoking. The gas tank exploded after the RPG hit. There's scorched ground and debris everywhere. Nobody's going near it yet."

"You and Kenny stay out of sight," Cody said. "Move back a hundred yards and watch the vehicle. Tell me what happens." He pocketed his phone and looked at his daughter.

"Don't breathe a word of this, young lady. You hear me? What were you thinking? Why didn't you tell me what you were doing? Don't you realize Ryan works for the DOD? His research is still a secret."

He studied her face for a moment. The shifty-blue eyes, dimpled grin, the alpha, the sweet-n-tart — It wouldn't do for him to play the stern father. She was too much like her mother and *way too much* like him.

"So, lemme go over this again," he said. "You promised a Taco Joint fast meal to a guy who works at some hidden bunker in Colorado in return for sending a 1500-pound helicopter to another dimension? And he's flying all the way down here to collect the debt?"

"That's about it."

"Tell me that isn't as crazy as it sounds."

"Totally," she nodded. "Every bit as crazy."

He held out his arms and closed them around her. "I heard about the program at the Simmons Center. *Ha!* Cornered by Rolfe Sagan? I shudda been there. I had become too comfortable away from public life." He shook his head. "The crowds, they bother me. I was . . . I was hoping we could all move to the rez, but . . ."

"It's okay, Daddy. You had to deal with things most people could not even conceive. Your visit to Heaven? That sounds just as crazy to some people."

"It was real, baby girl. Real. That's why I was so depressed for a while."

"Depressed? Because of that?"

"Sure. I couldn't understand why God let me see the other side, then brought me back to this world. I didn't want to return. I see now how selfish I was. God has given me margin time. It's a gift."

Cody left her alone and went to join the others. Knoxi pulled out her phone and punched in the number. "Ryan, are we still on for Taco Joint?"

"Yep. Already got my tix."

"Okay," she said, "but I need another favor." She explained about the SUV and gave him the coordinates. He agreed, but he wanted a larger reward for his efforts.

"What?" she chirped. "What do you mean this ups the ante?"

"Frederico's Italian," he demanded.

"Are you kidding? Do you know how much Frederico's charges for a Bad Andy and a Calamansi smoothie?"

~   ~   ~

One hour later at Moon River, Baker and Kenny lost sight of the SUV. They moved closer, taking care to not be seen. The concussion hole was still in the ground, but the vehicle, all the rubble, every piece of debris which had been scattered within forty meters was gone.

Baker called and reported it to Cody. After the call, Baker and Kenny walked toward the highway five miles in the distance. They threw their weapons, including the launcher Kenny had confiscated, into a solid-waste pit at Sanford's Junkyard near the highway. Afterward, they caught Uber.

NOGALES

S tar and Hutch had been chasing daylight all afternoon, but by the time they finally approached Nogales, twilight was all that remained of the day. The trip from Lake Travis had taken fourteen hours.

They had been informed about the events at Lake Travis. Now, it was their turn. They had devised a plan for spying on the clothing factory across the Mexican border and hoped to launch their black drone, recall it, and be gone by the next morning. The quicker, the better.

Everything in Nogales was rugged. Everything was big. The dry, mountainous terrain and thirty-foot Saguaro cactus would remind one of the most romantic images of the wild, wild west. Even the name "Nogales" would have seemed the perfect title for a shoot-em-up western movie. As they approached the town from the north, they occasionally spotted mounted horsemen with badges and guns patrolling along the shoulders of US Highway 82.

In the remaining daylight, they could see several miles into Mexico. The border ran through the middle of town, separating the Mexican side from the Arizona side.

The beauty here was in the untamed — the pristine sky free of smog, the hills spiked with rattlesnakes and coyotes, the 120-degree afternoon heat, and the sudden monsoons which could drop five inches of rainfall in one hour and send summer temperatures plunging 45 degrees. Strong winds, dust devils, blowing grit, lightning strikes, flash floods, and wildfires were only a few of the hazards of this beautiful country.

Unlike Texas, which was bordered on the south by the Rio Grande River, Arizona had no such waterway to separate it from Mexico. The border was marked in some sections with an eight-foot wall, and in other places with virtually nothing. Large areas along the border were unprotected on any given night. Here, Mexican foot traffic could easily avoid detection.

Those who crossed illegally into the US were on the run; either running *away from* something or *toward* something. Only the desperate or the greedy would risk such hazards on foot.

The curse of this area seemed to be its active drug trade. Border Patrol agents focused heavily on trying to stop or slow it down. Drugs were big news and US agencies seemed more than willing to fund anti-drug programs.

But there was a dark presence here which rivaled or even surpassed the drug trade. It was the people trade. Human trafficking was rampant on the Mexico side, but much of the abuse and abduction activity happened in US border towns. Human traffickers made obscene amounts of money by "owning" sex slaves who could be rented several times per night to deviants who were willing to fork over the money.

Trafficking cartels south of the border operated "sweat shops" in which young women and children were forced to work with their hands during the day and with their bodies during the night. Many Mexican companies which exploited these unfortunate souls were subsidiaries of US corporations — the same US interests which owned leading news organizations. Some Mexican law enforcement officials took kickbacks from these unholy enterprises, and there was no shortage of US investors willing to sell their souls for a few extra million per year.

Star and Hutch pulled into the Modern Inn and Suites. It was the same hotel from which Robbie and Peaches had escaped a year earlier. It had not been "modern" since the 1960s and it wasn't very "suite." The odors of sweat, mildew, gunpowder and rotting flesh were covered up partially by room deodorizers and old cologne. The sleeping innkeeper could not understand English or Spanish and seemed oblivious. He probably had no sense of smell either. When our heroes finally entered their room on the ninth floor, they were so impressed with the Modern Inn and Suites that they curtly discussed the idea of blowing the place up before leaving town.

Their reasons for choosing this hotel were simple: It was just fifty meters to the border, it was attended by only one sleepwalking innkeeper, and their ninth-floor balcony was the perfect launching pad for Dracula the drone. The plan was to launch at 3 a.m. But things got complicated.

They made several trips to the car to bring up their equipment for operating the drone. Finally, they returned from their last trip and stepped off the elevator on the ninth floor. As they began walking down the corridor toward their suite, they heard voices coming from an open door ahead. When they passed by, Star glanced into the room just as a man holding a rope and a bottle slammed the door in his face.

"Did you see that?" Star sounded riled.

"All I saw was a guy holdin' a rope and a bottle," Hutch replied.

"There was a woman in the room," Star said. "I caught a glimpse. She was restrained. And there was another guy in the room."

"We can't get involved. Can't risk our mission." Hutch warned.

Star agreed. "We can't afford to get disovered. Understood."

When they entered their room and closed the door, they could faintly hear two men celebrating with devilish laughter. They also perceived a female voice sobbing, intermittently screaming. The sound was coming through the vents in the air conditioning system.

A cold chill burned in Hutch's chest. "You know," Hutch said, "I told you that my daughter Farah is a sophomore at A&M, right?"

"Of course. I remember that." Star dutifully slid a loaded magazine into his 9-millimeter handgun.

"I also told you she was rescued from a joint like this when she was seven before I adopted her."

"I remember that too." Star walked somberly toward the window and looked through the blinds. "Did you see the flagpole outside?"

"Yeah. Sort of bothers me. This is America. It needs a flag."

"Right on." Star released the blind. "That pole looks kinda' naked without a flag."

Both men armed themselves and walked briskly toward the room down the hallway.

Hutch banged on the door. "Senores! Pablo sent us! He said you would take our money. You can have your girl back when we get through."

The door opened immediately. "Get lost! Pablo don't even run this place no more. Find your own toys to play with."

Star blocked the door with his foot and held a knife to the man's throat. "We don't want somebody else's toy. We want yours."

The second individual in the room went scrambling for his cell phone which he had left in his jeans near the window. Hutch rushed into the room and tackled him before he could place the call, then choked off his windpipe until the individual passed out. When Hutch looked up, he saw *two* women on the bed, *not* just one.

Star, still holding the knife, forced his host into the room. No need to search these guys since their clothes were already lying in a heap. They tied up the men and put them in the corner, then turned their full attention to the women.

"Help me cut these ropes," Hutch said.

Both victims had suffered bruises, lacerations, and rope burns. Both appeared unconscious, incoherent, frail. The men hastily removed the ropes and covered both women with blankets.

One of them began to come around. She was thirtyish, dark with ebony eyes, brown skin stretched thinly over a boney frame, raven hair, and plenty to say. "Nice to see you boys again." She clutched the blanket to her chest, her voice weak and raspy. "Uh, I can't place you, but I know I met you somewhere. I'm glad you gentlemen happened along. I'm tired of playin' with these thugs. Wanna have some *real* fun? So, can you first help my friend? She's . . ." The dark-eyed woman ran short of words, tried to sit up, but couldn't find strength.

Star and Hutch thought they had seen it all, but this woman was a first. Despite being undernourished, humiliated, and in pain, she was gaming them, her eyes hiding the fear, undone yet unconquered.

"Uh, ma'am, I'm Hutchinson and this is Star. We gotta get you to a safe place."

An awakening of hope dawned on her face. "They'll be here soon, and we need to get this girl to a doctor," she said. "I'm Pearly Bishop. I've been held four months."

"I know who you are, ma'am. I've seen your picture. You're MIA. Your real name is Virginia Cutter, undercover DEA. Sorry we have to meet like this." Hutch helped her sit up. "You're a brave woman."

"They have orders to kill us. We weren't supposed to walk out of this room." She lost her air and struggled to gain another breath.

"Sorry, ma'am. We gotta move out. Your friend looks bad."

"This girl is Mica, my secretary. She wasn't trained for this."

"No one can prepare for this, Virginia. Lemme wrap you in this blanket. We can carry you both to our room and find you some clothes."

Agent Cutter clenched her teeth, her edgy voice terse and salty. "I can wrap myself, thank you very much. And nobody's gonna carry me." Her arms shook with fatigue as she struggled to surround herself with the blanket.

Mica was at least ten years younger, her auburn hair badly matted, eyes wide open as though she had seen the end of days. She was ice-cold and did not speak a word. Her only movement was the involuntary shivering.

Hutch brought along the prisoners while Star carried Mica. Virginia, strengthened by new hope, followed the men into their suite.

"We need to warm her up as soon as we can," Virginia said. "I fear for her life. Put her on this bed."

"What did those guys do to her?" Hutch laid Mica down and placed an additional blanket over her.

Virginia was panting from the walk. "A drug. Deadly. It drops the body temp. I've seen 'em use it before. Not pretty. After they had their way with her, they injected her. I was to be next."

"Do you know a doctor?" Star asked. "A hospital you can trust?"

"I only need a phone."

Star handed Virginia his phone. She glanced around and noticed the unassembled black drone lying on the floor, and the weapons cache and electronics components spread out on the bed. She stared inquisitively, then put the smartphone to her ear.

Cutter reached her agency but made no mention of how she had escaped. After the call, she collapsed into a chair. "Don't look at my feet," she said. "My toes skinny as pencils. My whole body's that way right now." She looked up and studied their suddenly-quiet faces. "But, of course, you smug heroes already know that, right?"

Hutch cleared his throat but couldn't string any words together.

Star knew exactly what to tell her. "I bet you'll fatten up nice!"

Virginia tightened her lower lip and narrowed her gaze. "I need some clothes," she rattled off. "You never want to walk into a hospital wearing a blanket that smells like King Kong puked on it. So, can you nice gentlemen get me something to put on, or do I have to wrestle you outta what you're wearing?"

Hutch snickered. "We have some disguises in the trunk. Who would you like to be, Oprah or Donald Trump?"

"On another night, gentlemen, that might be funny. You boys are loose gamers, caustic cowboys. From what I've seen, the less I know about you, the better. Can you watch my prisoners 'til I send someone from the agency to pick 'em up?"

"Don't worry 'bout your prisoners," Hutch said. "Ahd while you're waiting for your ride, here's a Hershey bar and bottled H2O. Help thyself."

"Use the shower," Star offered. "I'll go down and bring you back some clothes and a coupla' MREs. Any chance you can share your intel about Azteca Calientes? We plan to remodel the place."

She stared again at the weapons and drone parts. "I dunno what you're planning, but I tend to trust you for now. You charged into our trouble like a pair of pugilistic hammerheads. But, I mean, you showed us respect — rare by any measure. That's reason enough."

"You—you mean you were awake the whole time?"

"Look," she said. "I have intel on the drug lords, and more than enough evidence on the traffickers. It's just knowing who to give it to. Don't trust anybody when it comes to the kid-snatchers. Too many officials on the take and too many US news outlets protecting them. A story can be spun different ways, you know, and no one seems to have the stomach for a real fight."

"We work for a man who does," Star stated. "By the way, here's some ointment for your rope burns." He offered her the tube. "And, uh . . . if you need my help applying it, just say so." He grinned. "I'm not the least bit shy."

She yanked the tube from him. "Keep your big hands off me!" She turned her unyielding eyes away, but she could not conceal the amiable grin that now encroached upon her swollen lips. She pulled the blanket securely around her battered shoulders and made her way toward the bathroom, stepping carefully between the scattered drone components on the floor.

"Oh, I do hope you boys find a good shrink."

At daybreak, Star and Hutch loaded up and prepared for the drive back to Texas. Dracula had made its scheduled delivery over the Azteca Calientes clothing factory, and the "poop" which now spotted the roof was sending data to their waiting associate in Houston.

Virginia had been picked up by her agency and had taken Mica to a clinic. She revealed no details about her rescuers. Whatever laws they might be breaking, whatever game they were playing, she was alive because they had risked their lives and their own mission.

In her official report, which no one really believed, she was simply rescued by "good Samaritans."

Star occupied the passenger seat as he and Hutch drove away. "Those two bad guys will turn on their bosses. They'll prolly sing their guts out."

"Yep. After that, they'll qualify for witness protection."

"Well, at least they didn't get away scot-free. The flagpole looks better now, don't you think?"

Hutch looked through the back window one final time before turning onto the street. "Yep, all it needed was the right flag."

Six DEA agents stood around the flagpole staring up at two angry men hanging by their wrists from the top of the mast. Their britches were hoisted underneath them flapping in the morning breeze. Both offenders possessed rap sheets that would have made Saddam blush. No one seemed in a big hurry to get them down.

"So, you're single," Hutch said. "Wha' do ya' think of Virginia?"

"Diehard, compassionate, *baaadd!*" Star growled.

"Roger that with prejudice!"

"Hey!" Star said. "I just got a text. Check it out."

> *"I hear you boys decorated the flagpole. You guys are total morons. Dangerous, undisciplined. Too bad there aren't more like you. Love and kisses, Virginia."*

~   ~   ~

Back to Texas for Star and Hutch. The mission to gather intel had begun. The fake bird droppings would gather information for satellites and transfer it back to Houston. They hoped to acquire enough intelligence within a few weeks to plan a successful raid and learn who the major players were.

The Texas Rangers had successfully evacuated everyone from Lake Travis. Cody's group had stumbled into something much bigger than they could have imagined. So, what now?

Cody was determined to pick up the trail again and uproot the cartel. The Nogales factory was but a small pimple on a rotten potato. The real power came from much bigger Chessmen. Who were they? Could this be the reason he was brought back from the dead?

It was difficult for Robbie and Peaches to settle their nerves, having been on the run for many weeks. Robbie was determined to purchase a gun and learn to shoot like a professional. Cody had promised to help him. It wasn't so much that Cody was a good teacher as it was about Robbie's need for the stability of a father figure. Cody sensed as much.

The Cherokee brothers went back to Oklahoma and invited Robbie and Peaches to come as soon as Peaches could travel. After giving sworn testimonies they could enter witness protection, legally change their last name to Ahusaka, and disappear with the Cherokee for as long as they wanted. The proposal sounded good to Robbie.

Alex and Jeremy had become more than friends. The Muskets invited the couple to stay with them in separate guest rooms. Jeremy, in the shadow of the Lake Travis events, was not ready to go home and face his parents yet. Both he and Alex were adrift in their minds. Cody was like an uncle to Jeremy, and Alex needed Cody's and Brandi's parental-like guidance. Cody began to see more and more reasons why his life wasn't over.

With Lake Travis in the rearview mirror, Knoxi looked forward to college life, and especially toward her dinner date with Ryan Maxwell. They had seen each other several times over the previous few months, and Knoxi was unable to get him out of her head.

TEARS AND KISSES

Three weeks after Lake Travis

Austin-Bergstrom International Airport. It was a bright Friday morning in the Texas capital city of Austin. Knoxi stood near United Airlines Gate 25 awaiting the arrival of Flight #7705 from Denver.

She had seen Ryan Maxwell in person but a few times, beginning at Methodist Hospital in Houston nine months earlier. Cody had been pronounced dead from multiple gunshot wounds. Ryan had shown up with Secretary of Defense Amy Foster, along with a Secret Service escort, her Marine Corps detail, and a medical team from Bethesda. The events which had followed were still a closely-guarded secret.

When Ryan finally appeared with the other passengers coming through Gate 25, he was exactly as she had remembered — the eyes of an angel, the chin of a fighter, the genius of an ace. He approached Knoxi with arms open wide. Her heart raced when he embraced her. He was the absolute clone of his father, Sabre Maxwell, who had sacrificed his life twelve years earlier to save Knoxi and the other abducted children in Librador. Sabre had been a naval aviator before becoming a cutting-edge quantum research scientist in the Department of Defense. Ryan had since taken his father's technical genius to a new level.

Ryan's presence ignited Knoxi's senses more and more each time she saw him. She seemed translated, out of control but invigorated. He captivated her, like surfing at Ruggles where you're so scared your IQ goes to zero, all the while hoping the exhilaration will never end.

"It's good to see you, Ryan." Her greeting sounded formal. "I'm flattered that you wanted to fly down here this weekend to collect your dinner debt in person. Are we still on for Frederico's Italian?"

"Lemme just look at you a second, Knoxi. You have the most pyrogenic eyes I have ever seen."

"Uh, pyrogenic? My eyes? Should I have worn sunglasses?" She forced a chuckle. *Oh please, God, tell me I'm not blushing.*

Ryan grinned. "I apologize for the forward-sounding greeting. I—I actually rehearsed what I would say. Every time you text or call me, I try to picture you."

"Ryan, you rehearsed? I, uh . . . I mean, maybe we should start using social media and post our pics. Facetime maybe?"

"I have a better solution," he said. "Maybe we should meet in person more often." He put on his shades as they left the terminal building.

"What are you driving?" he asked while they boarded the tram to the parking area.

"I have a twenty-year-old Jaguar convertible. I paid only twelve-thousand US for it. Bought it off Craig's List." She installed her sunglasses.

After they arrived at her car they opened the doors, eased into the original leather seats, and drove through the exit.

When Knoxi turned onto the main road, Ryan inquired, "Do you still have security people following you around like Secret Service?"

"Yes, they keep close tabs. I have some new people. We've had a bit of a shakeup lately, but . . ."

"Shakeup? So are they keeping tabs right now?"

"I'm a student at UT. They don't follow me everywhere, but they aren't very far away either."

"Look, Knoxi, I'm not hungry right now. Maybe we could swing by my hotel and just have coffee or maybe sit around the pool and talk. We can do dinner tonight. Whatever you like. Even burgers and fries if you want."

"I gotta better idea, Ryan. Why don't we go to a place with privacy and a great view? Summa' the couples at UT rave about it. They say it's great for makin' out."

Ryan turned and looked out the passenger window.

"I'm sorry, Ryan," she laughed. "Sorry to make such a forward-sounding statement, as you said. Maybe *I* should've rehearsed."

"A great place to make out?" He rubbed his chin. "Sounds good to me."

"A great place for makin' out *at night*," she said. "*Not at noon.*"

He straightened his face. "I just wanna get to know you, Knoxi. That's why I wanted to come see you. That lab where I work under heavy security gets one-dimensional really fast. I love the work because it's fascinating. It captivates me, but I—I don't have a lotta friends, especially women."

Knoxi slowed down, made a right turn onto a narrow asphalt road, and drove slowly past a grove of trees to the edge of a white-rock cliff that overlooked a lake. She stopped underneath a giant cottonwood and killed the engine.

"This is it," she said. "Just so you know, I've never been here with anyone else."

He gazed into her blue eyes. "Knoxi, I—"

"Wait," she said. "Push this button right here on the console."

When he pushed the switch, the convertible top quietly rolled back and disappeared behind the rear seats. Without the roof overhead, nothing seemed to separate earth from heaven. The 70-degree temperature and light breeze were intoxicating beneath the high-noon shade of the burgeoning cottonwood.

"I need to say something first," Knoxi said. "Twelve years ago when I was six, I fell in love with your father. All us kids loved him. I cannot express the sorrow, the shock we all felt, and the pride we all experienced when he crashed the plane into that bridge so that we could escape. We came home. He didn't."

"I was a sixteen-year-old freshman at MIT when my father died," Ryan said. "We were given no details about his death. Things were so secretive with the Defense Department. We thought he had gone on some unauthorized mission in the line of duty. We assumed the government had covered it up. That's one reason I eventually took the DOD gig myself. I thought I could figure out what he was working on and learn what happened."

Knoxi reclined her seat slightly. "It would have been unauthorized even had our government known about it, Ryan. But Sabre trusted my father and joined the mission to rescue me. All of us owe our lives to your father's bravery and — You know, it takes a lotta love to do what your father did."

Ryan nodded, then exhaled with an upbeat. "When I learned about the technologies he was developing. was intrigued out of my mind. It all made such sense. I was born for this, Knoxi. I'm still discovering secrets that were hidden away in his mind."

Knoxi placed her hand on his cheek. "You are so sweet, Ryan. I haven't been able to get you out of my mind since that day I met you. I can't decide whether I'm in love with you, or if I'm in love only with the idea of loving Saber's son. I never forgot his face, never forgot how much he loved the children. He had this . . . this crazy green light bulb that would orbit around his head." She placed her hand over her lips and blinked back tears.

Ryan took her hand. "Knoxi, I have no such dilemma about why I see *your* face every day when I close my eyes. It's all about you. It's not about the idea . . . I mean, what I'm tryin' to say is . . ."

Knoxi waited. "Yes, Ryan?"

"I—I have a confession to make." He closed his eyes and winced. "I had to rehearse this too. Might as well just say it." He exhaled hard. "Knoxi, I lost the helicopter."

She caught her breath. "What? You *lost* the helicopter?"

"I sent it to the bottom of the Gulf of Mexico, but it isn't there. I have no idea where it went."

"Well, genius! Does that mean it could show up in Times Square? Baghdad? How long before it shows up somewhere?"

"Uh, well, maybe never. Maybe next week. Maybe twenty years from now. I have no idea."

"Ryan, what were you thinking?"

"I was thinking how much trouble I could get into by doing such a crazy, unauthorized thing, especially since you weren't forthcoming about why you needed the helo to disappear. I trusted you, and I believed that you would not have asked me had it not been a matter of life or death."

Knoxi pounded the top of the steering wheel once with her palm and then covered her face with both hands, soaking them with her tears. She tried to apologize but could not get the words started.

It caught Ryan off guard. "Hey, Supergirl." He gave her his handkerchief. "I didn't mean to . . . uh, I mean, like, I would never want to make you cry. Not ever. What did I say?"

"Oh, Ryan, you have no idea what we have been through for the past month. Thank you for trusting me. I am *so, so, sorry* I didn't tell you the details. I need to tell you everything. I need to tell *you*, of all people."

Over the next fifteen minutes, Knoxi tearfully told Ryan the situation she and the others were dealing with — the helicopter, the reasons why the SUV needed to disappear, Jeremy's heroism, Glorietta, Robbie and Peaches, arrows, guns, midnight escapes. "Daddy has a friend who is currently commanding the Texas Rangers," she said. "He sent an escort to get us out of there. They kept my name and others out of the news, but eventually it'll all come out. We're working to bring down the cartels before they figure out who they're really fighting against."

When she finished, her head rested on Ryan's left shoulder. After moments of silence, Ryan blurted, "I'm starving."

Knoxi raised her head. "Frederico's?"

"No," he said. "How 'bout Mike-n-Amy's Texas Burger?"

"*Oooh*, that sounds good. I'm sorry about your handkerchief. It's, like, soaking wet. You, uh . . . want it back?"

"Of course." He took it from her, rolled it up like a ball, and stuffed it in his pocket. "You're the only woman who's ever cried on it. I'm keeping it for sure."

Knoxi made a face. "Are you tryin' to be sweet or just plain gross?" She handed him the keys. "Here. You wanna drive?"

~   ~   ~

Sunday evening, three days later

Ryan and Knoxi had spent most of the weekend together. Saturday afternoon they had witnessed the Texas Longhorns football team defeat the TCU Horn Frogs at DKR Memorial Stadium. Saturday night they attended a party hosted by Coach Kristy Willis for her women's basketball team and guests. On Sunday morning they had attended University Fellowship Church and had dined afterward at Pappadeaux Seafood Kitchen.

After a late-afternoon basketball team meeting, Knoxi drove Ryan up the winding highway toward the secluded spot on the cliff again. They had agreed earlier to revisit the site at dusk prior to Ryan's evening airline departure. Knoxi's mind was swimming in emotion. Her short weekend of ecstasy was about to end in agony. In an hour, Ryan would be gone.

Sweet magnolia and evergreen on the hillside filled her senses as she drove her open-air convertible toward their sundown destination. Her soft, shoulder-length hair floated lightly on the evening breezes. She could feel Ryan's balmy, teddy-bear eyes trained on her face as they approached the turn-off. They had finally run out of words.

Knoxi turned from the main road onto the narrow asphalt path, drove slowly beyond the clump of trees, and eased the Jag into the same spot as before underneath the cottonwood tree. She killed the engine and set the brake. The sun slipped barely below the horizon.

"Well, here we are again." She smiled.

"Yep, here we are again," Ryan said awkwardly. "Uh . . . you know, from here that sunset looks a lot closer than it is."

"What do you mean by that?"

"Well, the light you're seeing departed from the sun eight minutes ago. Took it that long to travel ninety-three-million miles."

Knoxi sighed. "Do you always think like that? Science, quantum-whatever. Light-years? Light-minutes?"

She waited, but doubted he would answer in plain English. She chuckled at her own thoughts. *Oh, God, may he spare me the fourteen-letter words this time.*

She paused with a deep breath and gazed into the heavens. A rush filled her head. Suddenly, Heaven and earth were in perfect harmony, as though God had made this moment special just for her — soft cricket sounds in the bush, a twilight moon on the rise, a fiery orange sky in the deep west, and no other humans present.

"Knoxi, I gotta ask you something."

She leaned toward him, hoping he would turn his lips toward her. "What is it, Ryan? You can ask me anything."

"Do you think I'm playin' God?"

She frowned. "What? Of course not. Where did that come from?"

"Something Pastor Hayes spoke about in church this morning." He gazed toward the distant orange glow. "About how God created perfect sync — systems that maintain balance and harmony. About how man is the only creation with a choice to either be in harmony with God or go his own way."

"So how does that mean you're playing God?"

"I'm experimenting with technology that can move objects into different dimensions or to places unknown. I mean, just think about what could happen if the technology gets into the wrong hands. Things could easily go from balanced to unbalanced."

"Ryan, you gave my father a brand-new start. Trans-dimensional quantumation is *your* discovery and is soon to become a standard medical procedure. You're discovering secrets of creation that God put there for you to find. It isn't good or bad. It's how we use it that determines the virtue of it."

"Then I must make another confession."

"Another one? *Pleeese* tell me you didn't lose the SUV too."

Ryan reached into his briefcase and pulled up two large photos, each labeled: *Top Secret: US Dept. of Defense.*

"What're these?"

Ryan cleared his throat. "Uh, are you familiar with the space probe Voyager 2, launched by NASA in August 1977?"

"Ryan Maxwell, what are you saying?"

"Voyager has produced images of an asteroid large enough to destroy all life on Earth. I've computed that it will collide with Jupiter in about sixteen more years. The night I moved your SUV, its quantum signature became one with the asteroid. That wasn't supposed to happen, so I enhanced the asteroid photos using experimental technology. Take a look." He showed her the images.

Knoxi's jaw dropped. "You sent our SUV to an asteroid, millions of miles in space?" She chuckled, giggled, and screamed. "I'm gonna jump off the cliff!" She opened her door and dared him to chase her.

Knoxi squealed when he captured her before she could get near the edge. "You knew I'd catch you, right?" He turned her around.

"Watch out!" she warned. "I'm trained in three martial arts."

"I'm trained in four."

"Okay then." She raised her hands. "I surrender." Her eyes glimmered as the moonlight at dusk began to take effect.

"You? You surrender?"

"Ryan, even a crazy person couldn't make this stuff up! I mean, you lost a helicopter in some unknown dimension in the bottom of the sea, and sent our SUV into orbit around the sun! Do you know how insane that sounds? You're the most dangerous man alive!"

"So which is it?" he asked point blank. "Is it the *idea* of loving Sabre's son, or real love that keeps me on your mind?"

"Hmmm, good question. What do *you* think?"

"C'mon, Knoxi! No games. I want to kiss you *so* bad."

"Ryan, if you wanna kiss me, you don't have to ask."

"But what happens if you say no?"

She stared back a moment. "I won't."

Knoxi was always the one in charge, always in control. But before she could separate her mind from all the spinning turbulence of the past month, Ryan's arms surrounded her securely, strong as iron, soft as a down blanket. His lips pressing against hers were like the eager tides at Cocoa Beach that always took her strength away. For ten glorious seconds of helplessness, she was drowning in warmth. When she began to kiss him back, euphoria rekindled her strength only to see it followed by sadness when at last he spoke.

"I have to go, Knoxi. Plane to catch."

They walked silently back to her topless Jaguar. Knoxi drove him the remaining ten miles to the airport and pulled up to the terminal.

She gripped the wheel with both hands. "I don't want you to go."

"And I don't want to leave you, Knoxi, but I have algorithms and metrics to log, asteroids to track, helicopters to locate, and you have God's work to do."

"We're both doing God's work, Ryan Maxwell. Never forget it."

"Hey, lemme see you smile," he breathed quietly. "Please don't cry when I leave. Tonight we've found something worth waiting for."

Knoxi wiped tears from beneath her eyes. "I've heard that falling in love means your heart breaks in a good way. I'm feeling that now."

"Well," he said. "I guess it's real love then, right?"

"Absolutely real!" she affirmed with a breakout smile. "And next time, *you're* paying for the burgers!"

GROUNDS FOR LOVE

Six days later

Saturday morning. Fog, drizzle, temperatures in the 50s. Knoxi walked into Grounds for Love, a campus coffee shop situated on a corner a few blocks from her dormitory. The atmosphere here was quieter than most because it was a hangout for those who wanted to study. The sign inside the door said:

"If you wanna party, go down the street.
If you wanna study, have a seat!"

Knoxi loved parties, but this particular morning she was to meet her mother and Elena here, and she was looking for some quiet conversation. Elena had made a successful recovery from her gunshot wound and was getting around, albeit slowly.

Knoxi embraced Elena, who had already seated herself. "Elena, you are looking so good. I've missed you these last few weeks."

"I must say, Knoxi, you look good too. I mean . . . what I mean is, you look good too."

Something was up. Elena *never* giggled. Period. But today, both she and Brandi couldn't stop.

"What are y'all up to?" Knoxi wondered if either of them would answer. "What's all the snickering about?"

Brandi kept smiling. "How was your meeting with Ryan last weekend? I haven't heard a word. I thought you'd at least text me."

Knoxi squirmed and tried to camouflage her smile by reapplying her lipstick. "I'm sorry. What was it you asked?"

Elena swallowed her grin. "Star and Hutch are invading Azteca Calientes this morning." She looked at her watch. "It should be over in about thirty minutes."

Knoxi had a feverish chill. "I didn't realize they were going so soon." She walked to the counter and ordered tall caffeinated beverages for all three of them. When she returned, Elena explained the details of the planned raid.

"The guys collected the intel and devised their plan. They've recruited four Spanish-speaking professionals to assist. They will create a diversion and pose as federales. They'll evacuate the premises and drive the victims to the US side in vehicles marked as US Customs. If all goes right, they won't fire a shot."

Knoxi had only one question. "What about Pablo Cisneros and little Zorro?"

Elena was cautious. "Intel indicates that Cisneros and the little boy have disappeared. But if Cisneros shows up, they'll apprehend and drag him across the border and drop him off with the FBI who'll take credit for the collar. The little boy, of course, will be reunited with Alex. We'll have to get her new identity expedited. We'll also create the boy's paperwork."

Brandi sighed. "Does Alex know that Zorro may be gone?"

"Yes. Jeremy accompanied her to Nogales yesterday. They're hoping they will come back with Zorro. If not, I'm afraid Jeremy's gonna charge into Mexico determined to break some heads."

"Jeremy loves her, doesn't he?" Knoxi concluded. "That's so special."

"I take it your plans no longer include Jeremy?"

"Jeremy and I finally realized that we love each other as friends, but *only* as friends. I am so happy for him and for Alex."

All three women now quietly sipped their caffeinated brew, each waiting for someone else to speak.

Knoxi noticed her mother and Elena grinning again. She finally gave it up. "Does it really show that much?"

"Does it show, you asked?" Brandi folded her hands. "Honey, you're raising the temperature in this room more and more by the second."

Knoxi felt her cheeks with her palms. "How red is my face?"

"Oh, you wanna see?" Elena smirked and held up a mirror.

"I might as well tell you both. I totally can't handle this. I'm not in control right now. I feel . . . I mean, it feels like —"

"Like you can't decide whether to catch the wind and run with him, or say *bon voyage* and never see him again?"

"*Mama!* How could you say such a thing?" Knoxi gripped her cup with both hands and closed her eyes. "What I mean is . . . how did you know?"

Brandi and Elena each took another sip but remained quiet.

"Maybe I should not have let him kiss me." She lifted her cup to hide her wistful grin. "I mean I wasn't ready for that. I have plans for my life. Things I want to accomplish." She stopped to breathe. "But if I hadn't let him kiss me, he would have been *so* disappointed, and I—" She stopped short and attempted to shake off the grin. Her eyes glistened. "*Ohhh*, kissing him was the most thrilling thing you could ever imagine."

"Honey, how did you get so delicate all of a sudden?"

"Delicate? Mama, I've been shot at on a rooftop where I should never have been. I saw a man shot in the head after he had tried to choke me to death. I've ridden in a smoking helicopter in the middle of the night, and my best friend Jeremy is dealing with Post Traumatic Stress Disorder because he had to kill someone. Suddenly, I don't have all the answers.

"But I'm certain of one thing: I love Ryan Maxwell. I've never wanted to share everything about myself with any other man. But when I'm with him I can let myself laugh to tears, and I can cry and not feel uncomfortable."

"So, what kind of man is he? Gentle?"

"*Ha!* When he wants to be. But he's also . . . No, no, I mean he would never force me or ask me to do anything that . . ." She took a breath. "Oh, he's *so* good. He's just like his father."

"So, what's your hesitation?" Elena wanted to know. "Sounds like a cross between a superhero and a choir boy."

"His work is so secretive. He can't tell me what he's doing. And he works in some vault in the middle of some mountain in Colorado for weeks at a time. I mean, what kind of father would he be? What kind of husband?"

"You're asking the right questions," Brandi said, "but there are other things to consider. For example, is he complete without you?"

"I never thought of that. I—I don't really know how to answer. I'm sure he has needs like any man, but —"

"And faults like any man?" Elena asked.

"Well, of course. I mean, he's one of the most brilliant men in the world, but he doubts himself."

"How does he doubt himself?"

"He wonders if he's playing God. He's worried about upsetting the balance of creation. There. I've said it, as crazy as that sounds."

"So, did you share with him a perspective he had not considered?"

"Well." Knoxi thought for a minute. "Yes. I tried. I told him that he was discovering things God intended for him to find. I convinced him his work is good."

"Lots of highly-motivated men are self-doubters," Elena said. "Ironically, the most gifted sometimes doubt themselves the most. They find it lonely when going where no man has gone before, as the saying goes."

"You don't have his technical skills," Brandi said, "but yours is the voice of reason that could keep him focused on his destiny and not on his doubts."

Knoxi allowed a thin, dimpled smile to creep across her face.

"Sweetie, when I met your daddy, he was more than I ever deserved or expected, but he had little confidence in himself."

"My daddy? I can't imagine him having limited self-confidence."

Brandi doodled around the rim of her cup. "He told me outright that he trusted God but didn't trust himself. And there were other issues."

"So, you straightened him out?"

"Well, I wouldn't say I completely straightened him out, but—"

"Oh, yes, she did," Elena broke in. "I've been in this family long enough to know. Cody needed her as much as she needed him."

"But I have my education to finish," Knoxi said. "I've got my future to consider. I'm committed to play basketball. I wanna enter politics. I wanna change things. I have duties to consider."

"You don't want to melt yourself down for just *any* man, sweetie, and I'm not suggesting you give up your own plans just yet. But somebody once said, '*The glory of God is man fully alive.*'"

"A Saint Ireneas quote. I've heard it," Knoxi informed. "And that applies to *women* too," she smirked.

"So, which one makes you fully alive, sweetie? Blind duty or love?"

"Hmmm, tough choice."

"Yes. But what the world needs most is men and women who have come alive. I've lived all these years with the love of my life, and the two of us together have gone farther than either of us could have gone alone. I'm only saying don't rule out the possibility that God may have a better plan."

The conversation was interrupted when Elena's phone rang. It was Hutch. The raid on Azteca Calientes had gone beautifully. The bad guys had all run away at the first sign of trouble. No one had been killed, and thirty victims had been rescued. Planned Childhood and the Red Cross were set to receive the victims.

Unfortunately, Cisneros and Zorro were gone. They had disappeared into parts unknown prior to the raid.

Hutch wanted to know what to do with the evidence they had obtained from the sweatshop. "We have solid evidence, but who do we turn it over to? Some of the federales and local Mexican police are receiving kickbacks and the whole operation is protected by US interests. The minute we let go of evidence, we lose it."

"I have a few aces up my sleeve," Elena said. "You boys try to stay outta trouble. Good job."

When Elena ended the call, her face told the story. "It was a good mission," she reported. "Star and Hutch are a poor '60s act, but they're really good. Sorry we've lost Alex's child and can't bring Cisneros to justice. Maybe we could enlist Sam Black Hawk. He exposed that ideological cleansing group last year, remember?"

Brandi weighed in. "Black Hawk is trustworthy and popular, but we need a contact on the inside with roots in the syndicate."

"We need prosecutors with a spine," Elena said.

Knoxi perked up. "What if we were to use the whole world as our contact? What if we could release something on social media that would move the world? Maybe street-smart people, grass-roots people, would rise up and demand authorities do something. Maybe good people would join with us to save the victims and bring justice to the bad guys."

"In case you haven't noticed," Elena pointed out, "people mostly yawn at social media posts. They're willing to repost and retweet, but that's as far as it goes. It's mostly perceived as fake news, anyway."

"But," Knoxi said, "what if the most prominent news person in the world lowered the bricks on this whole operation?"

"You have someone in mind?"

Knoxi's eyes were dead-on. "I'm going to Baltimore as soon as I accumulate the intel."

"What?" Elena asked. "Baltimore?"

Brandi stared at her daughter incredulously. "You *must* be kidding!"

Beltway News Network

Baltimore, two weeks later

Knoxi thanked the Uber driver, stepped out of the car, and put her feet on the pavement in front of the massive building. The structure which had been erected in the early 1900s still stood proudly on Enterprise Boulevard in Colleyville, Maryland, a blue-collar suburb of Baltimore. The red brick building was a historic landmark and built like a fortress. It had been purchased and renovated by four major Wall Street banks twenty-five years ago. The banks had also purchased the company housed within its walls — a questionable, behind-the-back enterprise called Beltway News Network.

The new owners had soon transformed BNN from a vanishing tabloid into an emerging pace-setter in the multi-media news arena. Over the next two decades, BNN would become the most prominent news source on the planet, with studios and offices also located in New York and London.

Knoxi stood on the street corner staring up at the windows on the top floor. It was only seven stories high, but the massive structure covered a whole city block. The man she was scheduled to see occupied an office on the top level.

She entered through the glass turnstile and tried to picture Clark Kent entering on one side and emerging from the other as Superman. Her fantasy ended when she was immediately met by a host of security officers and receptionists, one of whom presented her with an ID badge. As she was escorted to the elevator, she marveled at the modern furnishings and contemporary ambiance. One would never suspect that the building was more than a century old.

The elevator, she was told, ascended only to the sixth floor. From there she must use a flight of stairs to reach the seventh level. She took the short elevator ride, stepped off, then found the stairs — a narrow staircase with a steep incline and an iron railing which reminded her of a fire-escape.

She climbed to the seventh floor, turned and walked until she came to a door at the end of the corridor. The message above the door made absolutely no sense. Had he placed it there just for her benefit?

— No Hostages Beyond This Point —

When she opened the door, the musty smell hit her harder than the appearance. She saw a room full of papers. Stacks and stacks of white, yellow and green documents were piled on abandoned desks whose days had long since gone. Creeky old wooden floors, individual light bulbs hanging down from the high ceiling, and a slowly-rotating suspended fan made this place look and smell like the rat-infested newsrooms of a previous era.

"Is that you, Knoxi?" The voice was familiar, but she saw no one.

"Yes, Rolfe, it's me. Little ol' me. Where are you?"

"Down here." He waved from the end of an aisle, then disappeared again. "Follow me," he said. "My desk is in here."

She followed the sound of his voice, walking slowly while taking in every detail — something she had learned from her father.

She wondered if the ancient typewriters sitting randomly throughout the room were still in use. Did anybody spit tobacco juice into the old-style spittoons which still sat along the outer walls?

Finally, she saw Rolfe Sagan at his desk, sitting behind a very old Underwood typewriter with a blank page installed in the roller. His Alcántara Dominican cigar was unlighted but well-chewed on both ends.

"To what do I owe this pleasure, Miss Musket?"

"Rolfe," she asked as she sat down, "why do you hide here in this cavernous relic of a newsroom? It smells like warmed-over yesterday."

"Well, it's like this, Knoxi: See, I don't like people much. Don't even like myself much. Up here, most people can't find me. I like it that way."

"You must have a low opinion of yourself, Rolfe. But still, when we locked horns at UT, you referred to yourself as 'the most prominent journalist in America.'"

Rolfe chuckled. "Did you come to gloat, or to just make a fool of yourself again? Should I have studied up on male reproductive anatomy before you came this morning? I had only a twenty-four-hour notice this time."

"Thanks for seeing me, Rolfe. I shouldn't even ask you about the *hostage* sign above your door. Is that to keep me from taking you hostage, or the other way around?" She waited while he mulled over her question. After an awkward moment, she said, "I suppose it doesn't matter as long as no one takes a hostage past that door, right?"

"Can't slip anything past you, can I, Knoxi? I enjoyed our conversation at UT. Lotta people there. Important people. In the three months since, my ratings have gone over the top. People love to see me lose. We should go on tour. I'll let you win every time. Sells a lot of papers and gets record page-views."

"So, you're just lookin' for an audience by any means? You don't really stand for anything?"

"I stand for things I can see, Knoxi, *not* what I can't see. Right now, I'm building a good portfolio. Money, money, money. The world is for the rich, the way I see it."

"I didn't come to debate, Rolfe. I came to ask for your help."

"Wait! Stop right there!" Rolfe tossed his chewed-up cigar into the trash and pulled out a box from his desk drawer. He opened the wooden container and pulled out a brand-new un-chewed Cuban

Cohiba and shoved it between his teeth. "Now, I'm ready to listen. This is monumental! The girl with all the answers needs my help?"

"Uh, Rolfe, seriously, you aren't gonna light that thing, are you?"

"This?" He pulled the cigar out of his mouth. "I never light these, child. I don't have any vices like smoking. I don't even chew tobacco."

"But you chew those cigars and they're tobacco."

"*Ha!* That's different. Do you have any idea how expensive these Cohibas are? Can't afford to chew them. What can I help you with?"

"First, about the anatomy thing at UT; you really pushed me into a corner. I had to come out swinging."

"Well, girl, you did a heluva job swinging. I gotta hand it to you. So, what's in the envelope? Lemme have a look."

"Not so fast, Rolfe. What I have here is an envelope with some . . . how shall I put it? Some photos and intelligence which were very hard to obtain, and represent sacrifice on the part of a lotta people. Did you hear about the big fire in Nogales a couple of weeks ago?"

"Yeah, yeah, some jeans factory. Prolly a meth lab."

"I have solid evidence otherwise. A meth lab explosion is the story they want everyone to believe. Someone rescued thirty women and children from that place and delivered them to Customs. The next day, the place exploded. Good way to get rid of damaging evidence."

"Knoxi, does your father know what you're doing? Do you know how dangerous this is? Where did you get your information? How do you manage to do this stuff without the public knowing? This and your college basketball career at the same time? Do you know how many powerful people would wanna ambush your pretty little white fanny if your personal vendetta became public knowledge?"

Knoxi sighed. "I'm part African American, you know."

"Yeah, yeah, I'm part Ethiopian and nobody can see that either."

"Rolfe, please don't change the subject. Please listen. The rich corporates are getting richer on the lives of helpless people. But you already know that, right?"

"Everyone has a conspiracy theory, Knoxi. Don't get carried away. People who stick their noses into conspiracy investigations often end up dead or missing. You're too nice a girl for that."

"Rolfe, do you consider yourself a decent person?"

"Of course not! You're decent, but *I'm* effective."

He placed his cigar on the desk. "Look, I turn a lot of people off, and I make a lotta people happy. This is a divided country. The more division I create, the more it pleases the people I work for 'cause that sells stories. It means money in the bank, and that means more money given to special charities every year, including the fight against human trafficking."

"Your math is as fuzzy as your reasoning, Rolfe, but look; you know how to stir people up. That's why I came to you. This story needs to be told by a prominent but unlikely source. You could blow the lid off a worldwide coalition of evil. This is what Pulitzers are made of. This is bigger than Watergate. Somebody needs to stir up the world for these kids!" She caught her breath, then snatched up the envelope and ripped it open.

"Look here!" Knoxi dumped pictures of children and young women on his desk. "These are real people!" She spread them out.

"Knoxi, Knoxi, your passion is admirable, but be a realist for a change. I can't publish your story. If I tried, I'd get my head bashed in and no one would publish it anyway. Everything today is fake. News reports are just entertainment. The media has an agenda. Corporate America owns the media, and they publish what benefits the elite. You can't fight these people."

Knoxi stood up and walked toward a stack of green papers, trying to clear her head. "So, what's your end game, Rolfe? Didn't you once want to be a *real* journalist?"

"A *real* journalist? What's that? I make my employers happy as long as I don't ask too many questions. I'm good at expressing the views of a few and affecting millions. I make my public believe the corporate line because that's the only thing that will preserve our culture. Good people like you talk sweet, but then you fail so miserably you come to me for help."

"So, you're the mouthpiece for the corporate elite? You help them stay above the law? Didn't you once tell me to think for myself? How does a brilliant man like you consider himself free?"

"Look, the corporate elites pay me big because they need a mouthpiece to tell their side. They call me their wiseguy. Some call it 'spin.' Doesn't bother me."

"Like the Nogales story? A meth lab? Was that 'spin' yours?"

"Like I said, Knoxi, don't be a fool. Just walk away." He leaned back, stuck the cigar between his teeth again, and crossed his arms. "So, aren't you gonna quote the Bible verse that says, 'What does it profit a man if he gains the whole world and loses his own soul?'"

"No, Rolfe. You already know that verse." She breathed the sigh of disappointment. "I'm leaving the pictures with you. You'll also find eyewitness statements implicating judges, politicians, and corporate contributors. If you change your mind, let me know."

She headed for the door, stopped, and looked back. "About the hostage sign, Rolfe; seems to me you're the one being held hostage. Frankly, I would rather be a fool for Jesus than a wiseguy for somebody else."

Knoxi left deflated. Why had she been so sure this would work? She stood on the same street corner again looking upward. The blue-velvet sky with cotton candy clouds reflected off the seventh-floor windows. One cloud formation resembled the face of God with His hand reaching toward the BNN building.

Her mind mulled over the events of the past three months. The helicopter, the well-planned raid by Star and Hutch on Azteca Calientes which freed thirty women, but which, unfortunately, did not recover little Zorro. Pablo Cisneros had vanished with the boy.

Alex finally had a new identity. Her new name was Annabelle Chapa. She and Jeremy were talking of marriage. Annabelle had not given up on someday finding Zorro. She dreamed of a reunion with her son whom she remembered sitting on her lap, his laughter the sweetest music she had ever heard.

Knoxi glanced up again at the clouds, then took one last peek at the seventh-floor windows. Could anything reach Rolfe? Would her life now be in danger? Her smartphone buzzed. It was a text from Rolfe — *Get back up here on the double!*

She rushed back inside, her heart racing. Moments later, out of breath, she reentered Rolfe Sagan's office. Something in the packet had moved him. His glazed, red eyes gave him away.

"Who is this woman? How old is she in this picture?" He showed her the sad face of Annabelle, formerly Alex, whose picture she had included with the package.

"Uh, that picture? She's one who escaped from the Nogales sweatshop before the cartel torched it. Do you recognize her?"

Rolfe stood up and turned his back to her. "Do you want some coffee? I ground the beans this morning. Fresh, good." He poured her a cup without waiting for her answer, then continued pouring while the coffee ran over the top, onto the cabinet, and down to the floor.

Knoxi rushed to the rescue. "Rolfe, Rolfe! Here, let me take the pot from you, okay?"

He let her take the coffee pot from his shaking hand, then looked for some towels. "Uh, sorry. I must have lost my concentration."

"What's going on, Rolfe? Do these lapses happen often? Here, lemme help you clean this up."

When they finally sat down again, he displayed a Halloween smile which reminded her of Joker in one of the old Batman movies.

"So, how do you like the brew?" he asked. "Colombian beans, fresh ground — *ahhh*, nothing else like it on the planet!"

Knoxi didn't answer, but she watched a sudden transformation take place. Rolfe's false smile melted. His complexion paled. He placed his index finger on the picture in front of him and pressed hard.

"Knoxi, where did you see this woman? How old is this picture?"

"How old? Just . . . just a few months. I'm not at liberty to tell you anything about her, Rolfe, because you're protecting the very people who nearly took her life. Now, what is this about?"

"Can you tell me how old she is?"

"She's . . . she's nearly eighteen. Why?"

"It's—it's her. After all these years," he shook his head.

"What do you mean? Who is she to you?"

Sagan stared at the photo for several seconds without breathing or blinking. Finally, his diaphragm moved again.

"Nineteen years ago, I was in Monterrey — just a rookie reporter lookin' for some fun. I went with a colleague to the Caballo Brasso on a Friday night. We were gonna get drunk and grab a couple of senoritas to keep us warm. That's when I first saw her. Most beautiful voice I ever heard. She was performing that night . . ." Rolfe faded, his eyes now cloudy and distant.

Knoxi leaned forward. "Rolfe, what happened?"

"I introduced myself. We talked all night 'til we were both drunk. My buddy, he had disappeared somewhere." Rolfe took a long sip of the Colombian fresh brew. "She took me to her room and I must have collapsed on the bed. When I awoke, she was gone."

"Is that all? Did you ever see her again?" Knoxi lifted her cup.

"Sure. That night she was performing again. We spent the next eight days together. She wanted me to marry her. Not sure why. But I would have done anything for her. The priest married us — *Ha!* the only time I've ever been to church."

"I take it the marriage didn't work out?"

"I had to come back to the States. She had one more week at the Caballo to finish her contract, then I was gonna come back for her. But . . . I got a big break, the big story I always wanted. I lost communication with her. It was like she had just vanished. When I finally went back later, she was gone."

"So you never saw her again?"

"Not 'til you showed me her picture today. That's her face I tell you. I've never forgotten. I gave up looking ten years ago."

"Uh, Rolfe, when you left, do you know if . . . I mean —"

"You wanna know if she was pregnant? I have no idea. If she was, I don't know who the father was. It could've been me. Could've been somebody else."

Knoxi fixed her gaze on his coffee cup. Rolfe responded, "Do you need a plastic bag for it?"

She met his eyes. "I can't slip anything past you, can I, Rolfe?"

He handed her a sealable clear plastic bag. She carefully covered his cup with a tissue, picked it up without leaving her prints, and sealed it inside the bag.

~   ~   ~

Days later, it was confirmed. DNA test results using Rolfe's coffee cup were 99% conclusive. Now, Knoxi was faced with new decisions. How much should she tell Rolfe? Could she trust him? After all, he had never shown himself to be a compassionate, caring person. But his reaction when he saw Annabelle's picture would have been nearly impossible to fake. The very fact he recognized her after all those years was strong evidence in his favor.

Should she tell Annabelle? Would she want to know her own father had been complicit in protecting large interests which harbored traffickers? She decided to start with Rolfe, then see how it goes before telling Annabelle.

She sent him a text — *DNA tests conclusive. Ur a father and u have a grandson missing in South America. Call me. Knoxi.*

But Rolfe Sagan never called. When she reached out to BNN, she was told he had resigned and had left no forward contact information.

On a Dime

Dodgers spring training camp
Four months later

"**K**eep your shoulder in, McNair! You're pullin' off the ball! Stop openin' up your front side! Stay back. You're lunging at the baseball!"

Jeremy stood in the batter's box sweating profusely. Dodgers' hitting coach Skip Johnson rode him hard, determined to make him live up to his enormous potential.

Major-league baseball teams began spring training every year in late February. Experienced veteran players, minor-league hopefuls, and a few long-shot invitees worked hard to train their bodies and hone their skills, all with the expectation of being among the elite who actually make it to a major-league roster.

In addition to training, teams played thirty exhibition games during the spring.

Camelback Ranch-Glendale, located in Phoenix, Arizona, is home to the Los Angeles Dodgers' training camp. With luxury suites, an on-site lake, multiple training fields, and a dazzling stadium, Camelback Ranch has been called the most intriguing place for spectators to watch Cactus League spring exhibition baseball.

"C'mon! C'mon, McNair! Keep your head down. Don't be lookin' off toward left field when the ball's in the zone. Stay through the ball!"

The coach knew just when to tone it back and slow down a little. "Look at me, son. Breathe a second. Smooth out your swing, stay back, throw your hands at the ball and the bat will find the pitch. Square it up."

Whack!

"That's it! That's it! That's what I'm talkin' about! Take it back up the middle. Stop tryin' to pull everything. You can make this team. I know you can."

Whack!

"Perfect! Perfect!"

Then a tender voice joined in. "C'mon Jeremy! Make hits! Make home run!" Jeremy's new bride Annabelle cheered him on from her seat behind home plate.

The hitting coach walked toward the box and handed Jeremy a towel. "Take a break, kid. Give your forearms a rest. I knew your ol' man. Played two years with him at Pittsburgh. Heckuva guy. Helluva hitter — reminded me of Aaron. He could take it deep on a line to all fields. Right field, left field, didn't matter. He could make either fielder think he was playin' the hot corner." He chuckled.

"Yeah, I remember," Jeremy grunted as he toweled off his face.

"I see the same talent in you, Jeremy. You're only twenty, and you could get the call this season. But, if you don't mind me sayin' so, you showed up at camp with a lotta anger ridin' you. It's none of my business, but . . . you know, to compete at this level, you gotta have maximum concentration." The coach glanced toward Annabelle sitting about fifty feet away. "I hope you can resolve any outside issues," he said quietly. "I'm always here to listen." He turned to leave, took a few steps, then looked back. "For what it's worth, I've learned that no matter how bad it gets, things can turn on a dime."

"This next one's goin' to right field," Jeremy scowled, picking up the bat again. The coach stepped back and motioned the pitcher to begin throwing once more.

Crack! The ball disappeared over the right field wall and bounded onto the golf course across the road.

"*Yay, Jeremy!*" Annabelle clapped her hands and stood. "You the best! You the best, honey!"

After sundown, Jeremy and Annabelle finally found themselves alone in their room. They had gone to dinner at a burger joint off Camelback Road and had decided to retire early. Jeremy was exhausted. This had been the third long day in a row since arriving at spring training.

Annabelle had met several of the other wives, but she did not feel comfortable with them. Her husband wasn't a household name, and most of the wives were older. Most players as young as Jeremy did not have wives. Some had girlfriends, and others departed after sundown to check out the Phoenix nightlife.

Jeremy was obviously troubled, but he would not talk about it. She was certain that the events at Lake Travis still haunted his nights. He had trouble resting, and several times he had called out the name "Zorro" in his sleep.

In another six days, the Cactus League exhibition games would begin. Jeremy felt pressured to perform like a star on the baseball field. The Dodgers had drafted him in the second round, placing high hopes on his future, their future. They were pushing him, hoping to successfully propel him to big-league success sooner rather than later.

Already Annabelle was getting her taste of big-league life. The extra batting practice, night sessions, early hours, fatigue, all wrapped together with the desire to succeed. Jeremy was preoccupied with all of it. She craved Jeremy's touch, but he had become uninterested in intimacy. Their marriage, three months old, seemed at a standstill.

Was he no longer the hero she had married? Had she displeased him? He was in pain. Even his batting coach had noticed. Why would he not talk about it? She, of all people, would understand. What would it be like if they moved to Los Angeles? Where would they live? How would they fare living in a large city where they knew no one? What would she do when Jeremy goes on the road with the team?

She was no longer Alexis. She was no longer Glorietta. She was Annabelle, a person she did not know. She had lost her son. She had lost herself. She could not bear to lose her husband.

Extra Innings Lodge, located on a back street a few blocks from camp, was moderately priced, but less than moderately comfortable. Jeremy left his clothes scattered on the floor on the way to the shower, then returned dripping wet, wearing a towel. He dropped the towel beside the bed and crashed head-first into his pillow.

Annabelle entered the shower. Jeremy had used most of the hot water so she didn't stay long. She briefly toweled off, then perfumed herself and slipped into a new lace floral lingerie which left little to the imagination. She seldom allowed Jeremy to see her scarred upper body. She was shy, and was afraid that her old wounds would only remind him of her sorrow. But tonight, she was desperate enough to use a different strategy. She walked toward the bed and eased onto the mattress. He was unresponsive.

She turned and cuddled next to him. "Jeremy, I know you awake. You can no fool me. Jeremy, why you not talk to me?"

He opened his eyes wide, turned and lay looking up at the ceiling fan. His scowl was the same one he had displayed in the batter's box that afternoon. Would nothing reach him?

She lay beside him on the mattress. "Jeremy, I know how much it hurt. *Por favor*, my husband, please notice me. Talk to me."

He closed his eyes as if to avoid looking at her. "You dunno nothin' about how I hurt. I saw her eyes when I shot her. She never made a sound. I don't wanna ever tell my parents. Don't want nobody to know. And I made you a promise that we'd get Zorro back, but he gone forever. I—I try to picture him. I dream about teachin' him to hit a baseball. I wanna take that Pablo guy apart. I hate him. I hate life. What kind of husband am I? I can't do this no more."

She rose up clutched his broad shoulders. "Look at me, Jeremy. I mean it. Look at me! You think I don't miss my son? You think I forget about dead women in pit? I still see them when I close my eyes at night — their faces, eyes open. You see these bite marks? They never go away. These scars on my skin from the whips? Look at me. I have to live with it always. My body ugly. You perfect. Big chest. Strong arms. Fast legs. You carry me to the helicopter. When I cried you comfort me. When I see your face I feel hope. But you have scars *inside.* No one can see but me. Now you hurt, I comfort you. Marriage work that way, no?"

Jeremy placed his forearm across his face. He could no longer restrain the tears that had been building for weeks. "You not ugly, li'l mama. You the mos' beautiful thing ever happen to me. I'm so ashamed I let you down."

"I not give up," she insisted. "I still believe Zorro will come back to me . . . *to us.* Sometime thing turn on the dimes, I hear coach say." She placed her head on his chest and held him until he fell asleep.

When morning came, Annabelle left Jeremy sleeping, slipped out of bed, got dressed, and went down the hall to get coffee for both of them. As she approached the breakfast room, she saw a man slightly-built with bulging pockets carrying a pipe wrench in his hand.

When the stranger saw her, he spoke. "Good morning, *señora. Cómo está esta mañana?"*

"My morning is fine, *gracias, señor.* Uh, do you speak English?"

"*Si, señora.* Ah, but not very good. I am plumber. I fix pipe."

"I not speak good English either, but want to speak like home-born American. My husband is American baseball player for Dodgers. He might get call this year!"

"If Dodgers need pipes fixed you call me, 'eh? I am Carlos Santana. I also preacher. Preach at small church and have misión center for the poor."

After their brief conversation, Annabelle bid her new friend farewell and returned to her room with Jeremy's coffee.

An hour later, the couple got into their pickup for the drive to Camelback Ranch. A mist was falling. Their truck wouldn't start.

Jeremy looked at his watch as heavy rain began to fall. "I gotta be ready to start workouts in an hour. I gotta find jumper cables now."

"Wait," Annabelle said. She opened the door and shouted, *"Señor Carlos!"* She waved. "Can you help us?"

Jeremy looked out and saw an early-nineties Ford pickup with bald tires and faded paint headed their direction. The driver was waving back at Annabelle.

"Who's that?" Jeremy wanted to know.

"Carlos Santana, the man God send us to start truck," she said.

"Uh, how do you know that?"

Carlos pulled behind Jeremy's truck, raised his jacket over his head, and ran to Jeremy's window. "You baseball player? You need help, señor?"

Jeremy stared at the stranger standing in the rain. He wore a sweat-rimmed ball cap, worn-out dungarees, and tennis shoes with duct tape holding the soles together. Jeremy, by contrast, wore designer jeans over his Dodger boxers, a brand-new Dodger batting practice jersey custom-fitted with his name highlighted across the back, and a game-issue cap. His antique Chevy lowrider truck, for which he had just paid twenty thousand cash, was due to enter a restoration facility in Houston after spring training was concluded. And yet, here was this fortuneless individual offering his help.

Jeremy opened the back door. "Here, amigo, hop in the back seat. Let's wait 'till it stops raining. I'm Jeremy. I take it you've met my wife Annie already?"

"Yes sir, I meet her in coffee room."

"It's Annabelle," she giggled, "but my husband call me Annie."

"I am plumber, also preacher in small Mexican church on Indian School Road. We very poor, but money from fixing pipes help feed poor children at street mission. Every day I ask God for one person I can help. So, today God bring you to me. How I help you?"

Jeremy fidgeted, suddenly admonished about the three-million-dollar signing bonus the Dodgers had given him — money he had refused to touch pending a rainy day.

"We—we doin' okay, brotha'. How long you been doin' this?"

"Five years. But my wife, she take my two girls. They leave for Mexico two years ago. She not want to be poor anymore. Last month, I fall from second-floor window, injure my neck, hurt my hip. I lose my voice. Cannot walk, cannot speak. I think my life over."

"So what happen, Carlos?" Annabelle asked. "Please. Tell us!"

"God ask me go back to church and preach."

Jeremy looked back at him. "How you know He ask you dat?"

"I just knew. God speak to us if we listen and we anxious to please Him. I only know He ask me. I walk into church, my leg no longer stiff. I speak. Voice strong. Many people repent. Some crying. My wife call from Mexico. My girls miss me. Wife miss me. She want me to forgive her. Church take up offering to send her bus money."

Annie and Jeremy had no words. They had faced the darkest of humanity, but now were moved to tears by this man whose wealth seemed endless because his desires were selfless.

Annie wanted to tell him about little Zorro, but she and Jeremy couldn't break their silence. It was part of the new identity agreement.

Carlos stared quietly for a moment. He knew the look — their eyes reflecting the pain of quiet desperation, faces begging for answers. He had seen it before.

"Señior Jeremy, Señora Annie, sometimes we are like truck; dead battery, need jump start. Never lose your hope. I tell you my favorite American word — *things can turn on a dime.*"

Carlos opened his door. "Rain stop. I get jumper cables now."

As Carlos moved his truck into position for the jump start, Annie and Jeremy rummaged through their pockets and searched every compartment in the vehicle. They managed to come up with just over $1400 cash which they stuffed into a brown envelope — enough for airline tickets. No long bus rides today for the Santana women.

DTC GLOBAL

One day later, Chicago

How do you walk into the office of a self-proclaimed "worlds most-powerful CEO" and tell him he has a not-so-hidden aperture in his armor? How do you tell him he's a bald-faced liar? Franki Bell was about to find out.

For two decades she had walked down the same hallway. Her twenty-fifth-floor office suite in the DTC Global building was a feather in her cap, as it were, for an African American woman who had risen from the projects to become one of the most powerful executives in the DTC worldwide consortium. It would have been a triumph for anyone, male or female, but today she was having doubts about herself. Sleepless nights will have that effect.

She was witty, beautiful, aggressive, and as heartless as needed in order to get her way. She usually did. Her boss, Derek Townsend Carasco, the president of DTC Global, Inc., *always* had his way. Only a few had opposed him over the years, and they had disappeared by one means or another.

She never asked questions. After all, she had it pretty good. She had learned how to stave off his blatant sexual advances, and that had even worked to her advantage. *So far.*

But today, her knees were numb as she approached his office just down the hallway from hers. Her five-inch heels made her an inch taller than her boss, and that had always boosted her confidence, but not this morning. Beginning to lose her nerve, she paused in the hallway outside his office suite, turned to her right, and walked through a door to a narrow outdoor balcony. It was a favorite spot for underlings who liked to take their smoke breaks overlooking the north side of the city.

The traffic jam on the streets below was the norm for 8:25 a.m. in Chicago, but she wasn't thinking about the morning traffic. Her hazel eyes focused instead on the veranda nearby which could be accessed only from Carasco's office — the same terrace from which a close friend and associate, Tera Hoffman, had "jumped" to her death only one month earlier. But was it really suicide?

The chilly wind off Lake Michigan made Franki Bell shiver. Could she charm her boss one more time? Perhaps she should wait until another day.

"Don't tell me you're getting cold feet about the merger." Carrasco had followed her onto the balcony.

It startled her, but she covered by giving him the sly lip. "My gosh, DC, you shouldn't sneak up on a girl like that unless you wanna feel a boot heel in places where the light never shines!"

"I saw you come out here," he croaked. "This is not the time to develop feelings, Franki, not unless you wanna spend those feelings on me."

"Well, sugar, you should know my feelings aren't for sale."

"Come into my office. It's cold out here. I have a million ways to warm you up."

"Don't count on it, Sharkey," she murmured. "It's all business 'tween you and me unless you like it rough. I mean *really* rough!"

He grinned like the hungry hound. "That's what I like about you, Franki. You got no limits."

They walked into his private office and sat down. "So, what's on your mind? This is our biggest merger ever. After this, we own mankind. As usual, I'm expecting you to cover all bases. Gerald is in the Falklands right now. This merger is gonna happen. Worldwide, baby, worldwide!"

Franki laid out the situation. "You wanna hear my suggestion? As your chief legal counsel, I advise you to sell out. Get out while you still can."

Carasco stood up. "What're you talkin' about? The missing reporter?"

"It's not just that, lover. It's those people who got captured in Texas. They're gonna sing like little birdies in the tree."

"Ha! You mean that twit, Stanton? He's been in custody six months and hasn't told 'em anything. Besides, who's gonna believe that perv?"

"Well, what about that lieutenant in the Chicago PD still askin' questions about Tera Hoffman? He doesn't believe she jumped on her own from *your* balcony."

"I told you a hundred times how much I miss Tera. She was a trusted friend. I got news for you. She slipped, okay? It was during that ice storm, remember? Besides, why would I want to kill her?"

"Honey, it isn't what I think that counts. Look. Here are some photos and figures I think you should see. You said you were gonna divest the company of these Mexican enterprises. You lied to me. I have proof. We're all going down."

She handed him a binder filled with evidence linking DTC to massive cover-ups, accounting irregularities, illegal guns and narcotics, international sex slavery, and trafficking of children.

Carasco tossed the binder onto the desk. "Where'd you get this?"

"An internal whistleblower in Madrid. She probably thought the leadership of the corporation would wanna know about it. You can't hide this forever."

"Yeah, yeah, Sadie Sanchez — delusional, psychotic. Nobody took her seriously. The company had her committed and then she killed herself. Her so-called evidence was supposed to never see the light of day, so how did you get it?"

"C'mon, boss, another suicide? That theme isn't gonna work forever. If I was able to find this evidence, someone else can find it.

And, stud, I remind you the missing reporter is Rolfe Sagan, and he ain't no lightweight. We have reason to believe he's snooping around in South America. Look at this photo from Buenos Aires four days ago. Please tell me he's working for you. Otherwise, we got a problem."

"It's not Sagan," he stated flatly. "Sagan's dead."

"How do you know?"

Carasco's frivy smile made a fast exit. "Now, you listen to me. I don't know how you got this picture and I don't care. Drop this. Those Mexican shops are legitimate, profitable businesses. They have police on patrol twenty-four-seven. Nobody's gonna find anything there because there's nothing to find."

"Nothing to find? What about that factory in Nogales, Mexico? It was raided, then torched. Who raided it? Was it torched to cover up evidence left behind? And Tera's hard drive was stolen right after she fell twenty-five floors off this building. Who has the drive? Is someone blackmailing you?"

Carasco grinned arrogantly. "Do you think anyone has a big enough pair to blackmail me?"

"Look," she said, "We have subsidiaries in fifty-five countries. Are you aware what these companies do?"

Carasco's temples bulged. "This conversation is over." He motioned for her to leave.

Franki Bell left Carasco's office shaken, but she was good at hiding it. She was in trouble. If Carasco went down, she would fall with him, and if she hung around any longer, she would probably have an accident. She had worn out her welcome. So, after twenty years, she decided to leave Chicago in the rearview mirror.

The news about Rolfe Sagan had stunned her. She had secretly known him for twenty years, and Rolfe was the only male on the planet she trusted. He was as cold as she was, creatively wicked, and a master at spinning facts. Franki could always enlist his help by doing him "sweet favors" as he called it. If he were alive now, he could make this go away.

Carasco watched her leave his office. He buried his head in the documents Franki had left behind, then looked up to see a suave male associate standing in the doorway wearing a cold smile and a brown suit. Carasco nodded. The man in the suit got the message. He left immediately.

Franki crammed her 5-inch alligator heels into her purse and hit the street running, having already identified the tail behind her. She was now a target. She zigzagged across 8th Avenue several times, crouching and moving alongside slow vehicles for cover, but the dapper individual in the brown suit matched her every move. She moved onto the sidewalk, raced down a stairway to sub-street level, pushed through the front door of Loose Deuces Tavern, and found the ladies room.

Crouching in one of the stalls, she pulled out her smartphone and sent a text with files attached to Rolfe Sagan, hoping against hope that he was still alive somewhere in the world.

Franki removed her blazer and pulled off her white lace blouse, revealing a toned upper body wearing a tight-fitted black sports bra. She gathered her raven hair into a ponytail, pulled off her Lady Cat designer jeans, amputated them below the knees with her small utility knife, stepped back into the jeans, and wore them as cutoffs.

She hoped to disguise herself as a crazy, cold-weather jogger long enough to give her pursuer the slip. Bare feet on the cold concrete sidewalks would suck, but the alligator heels would be a dead giveaway. This wasn't her first girl-chase.

She stuffed her discarded clothing into the bottom of the trash, then looped the shoulder strap of her purse around her neck and walked onto the street as if she had not a care in the world. As she started to jog, two suits with strong arms ended her last hopes, snatching her off the windy street and forcing her into a waiting car. They motored a path directly to DTC Global.

The men gave her an overcoat, walked her into the building as if everything were peachy, and escorted her back to the twenty-fifth-floor balcony.

Dark morning clouds now swirled overhead, propelled by a strengthening north wind which howled through the steel railings like angry hornets. "Gimme the coat," demanded the man in the brown suit.

"Are you kiddin' Joker? It's cold out here."

"Look, Franki, this can be easy or hard, your choice."

She handed back the coat and wrapped her arms around herself. "Is this the same deal you gave Tera?"

"Same deal, sweetheart. You can either jump, or we'll take you to the sand works at mud springs and leave you. It'll take about eighteen hours for the chemicals to suffocate you with your guts on fire. If you jump now, at least someone'll find your body. Tera made the smart decision. She gave us her hard drive, then we let her jump on her own. Saved her a lotta pain."

"Now, it's your turn," the other man said. "We'll even help you get up on the rail, provided you give us your phone first. We wanna know who you've contacted in the last twelve hours."

"Nobody's gonna believe I jumped."

"Ohh, it won't be hard to convince everyone, not when we tell how despondent you've been these last weeks since your friend jumped. You just decided to join her, that's all."

Franki refused to go without a fight. She smiled, held up her phone, and charged headlong into both of them, resulting in all three sliding across the slippery floor. One of the men seized her by the ankle, but she twisted free and pushed him against the rail and attempted to throw him off the building, all while clutching the phone in her left hand.

The suave assassin in the brown suit pulled his handgun and shot Franki through the neck, but she had enough strength to lift herself over the rail and disappear before they could take her phone. They watched her fall, but the two men shuddered to see her punching buttons on her smartphone as she descended twenty-five stories and smashed onto the concrete below.

"She outsmarted us."

"How do you figure that?"

"She knew if I put a bullet in her we would have to bribe the coroner to rule it suicide. She also destroyed the phone. I have no idea if we can retrieve the data."

"You think she had time to send somebody a text on the way down?"

"Better hope not."

THE MESSAGE

Five days later, Austin

Knoxi heard a buzzing sound. It persisted. Finally, she awakened and realized her cell phone was coming alive and about to vibrate off the nightstand. The caller ID told her it was Ryan.

She threw off the covers and reached across the table, knocking her bottle of *Clear Eyes* to the floor and tipping over her Pecos Stone table lamp. Her roommate, Sarafina Cameroon, extended her big hand just in time to catch the lamp before it hit the rug.

Knoxi fumbled for the phone as if it were the only oxygen source in the room. Sarafina, an All-Big Twelve Conference forward for the Lady Longhorns, smiled, knowing how emotional Knoxi became on the rare occasions when Ryan would call. She waved bye-bye and turned toward the door. Knoxi waved to her six-foot-six roommate as she left the room.

"What a surprise!" she said to Ryan. "What's the occasion this time? Did they decide to let you out of your dungeon to breathe real air for five minutes?"

She waited. "What? You have ten days off starting when?" She listened, then gasped. "Ryan, Ryan, honey, listen to me. Sorry to interrupt. If you have ten days off starting in three weeks, let's do it then! Spring break fits right in there. We could get married. We— we'd have plenty of time! We talked about June, but that's too long. Please, honey." She waited.

Ryan was cautious. "Are you sure you wanna move that fast? I mean we've only known each other since —"

"You call this fast? My mom and dad got married after just eight days. They didn't turn out so bad."

"I was ready six months ago, Knoxi."

"*Oh! Yes! I love you so much! I am so excited!* Oh, sweetie, wait. Please don't go yet." She paused for a deep breath and tried to settle her feelings. "I—I have another favor to ask. It's . . . the technical kind."

"Let me guess," Ryan said. "You want me to beam myself to the campus?"

"What? Can you actually do that?"

"*Ha!* Not if I don't wanna end up on some asteroid. These favors are becoming intergalactic. I still don't know what happened to the helo."

"No, no Ryan. It's not a helicopter this time. *Ha-ha!* Been there, done that!" She composed herself. "I've been getting these recurring signals on my phone for the past five days. It's some sort of prank or whatever and it's on a loop. It arrives exactly every sixteen hours. It's untraceable."

"Did you ask your service provider about it?"

"Sure. They don't have a clue. That's why I've been tryin' to call you. It's starting to scare me. I mean, it's glimpses of faces with a coded or encrypted message of some kind."

"So, it's a text with pics?"

"No, it's not a text. It doesn't show up as a message. It takes over the whole phone for about fifteen seconds and nothing else works. I can't access my apps or settings when the signal hits. Everything else goes silent. These creepy faces come up, this scrambled message takes over the whole screen, then it's gone."

"Okay," Ryan breathed heavily. "Somebody's trying to send you a message and doesn't want to be found. It's like an emergency weather broadcast or Amber Alert that preempts all other programs, but this takes it another giant step forward with Thialitic coding, a crypted clivical with quantification devoid of program graphics, and an underhaul with NASA filters and robot anti-lite coangularity. An easier description would be remote singulation with antispacial warps, probably quadlusive microscale jetrix with —"

"Ryan, you are the scariest person ever! Have you thought of rebooting yourself? I mean, what happens when your brain runs out of storage?"

"A'right, a'right, I get it. Look, this person is well-connected to have this rare technology. The signal cannot be intercepted. It's unstoppable and untraceable if it's what I think it is."

"So, what can I do?"

"I can stop it and I can trace it. But don't you wanna know what it's trying to tell you? The message or whatever?"

"Of course. How?"

"I'm gonna link your phone directly to my corbopathic tricosifter. I built it myself. Next time you get the signal I'll analyze it. This could be significant. You said the trail went cold on some of the leads you were following a while back? Maybe it isn't so cold anymore. In fifteen seconds, I want you to type in five-two-zero."

"Okay," she said, counting the seconds. "Five-two-zero. Got it!"

He waited a moment. "We're linked. It worked. How long before the signal's due again, assuming sixteen hours from the last episode?"

"Uh, four hours, twenty-two minutes and five seconds on my mark," she said. "*Ready . . . mark!*"

"Okay, I'll let you know what I find. Go kick some butt on the court today. And one more thing; ever since I met you back in Houston when Cody was in the hospital, I thought if I stayed busy I could keep you out of my mind. It never worked then, and it doesn't work now."

"Really, Ryan?" She hugged her phone with both hands. "I—I gotta tell you, school and basketball don't help me either." She waited a moment. "Ryan? Ryan, honey? Are you still there?" No response.

It suddenly dawned on her that she had committed to marry a man she still barely knew. But, remembering how she had felt when he kissed her, it couldn't be a bad thing, right? She wrapped a robe around herself, stepped into some flip-flops, and ran down the dormitory residence hallway shouting her good news: She and Ryan were getting married at spring break!

Senior team captain Laurie Madison reminded her the Lady Horns were due to play against West Virginia on national television in just four hours. "You better get your head in the game, girl."

The other players looked at Laurie and frowned.

Laurie raised her hands. "Okay, okay, I get the message." She planted her hand on Knoxi's shoulder. "Congrats, li'l sister. We're happy for you."

"Now we're ready to party!" Sarafina shouted. "But not 'til after we kick some tail against West Virginia today!"

~   ~   ~

The next day

"So, how much time do we have?" Brandi complained to her daughter. "You have no idea how much work it is to plan a wedding. When I talked to you about coming alive, I didn't mean in one month!"

It was Sunday. Cody and Brandi had arrived on the campus early. Knoxi had called the night before to give them news of her accelerated wedding plans. They met in a deserted study room at her dorm.

"I—I'm not sure of the date. We just wanna do it near the beginning of spring break. We still have to decide the day."

"You know, Knoxi, we still hardly know Ryan," Brandi said. "Have you talked to him about reserving time for family after you're married?"

Cody jumped in. "I don't know Ryan at all. I know he's twenty-eight, and you just turned nineteen. I trust him because I knew his dad. We'll be proud to call him our son-in-law."

"You're not much help," Brandi mumbled under her breath.

"Thank you, Daddy. I phone or text him every chance I get. Sometimes he's unreachable for a week or more. But I don't worry. He's an unassuming person with gigantic accomplishments. He's like the big fish who swims so quietly you never know he's there until you feel the energy in his wake."

Suddenly the quiet conversation was interrupted by her phone ringing. Everyone jumped. The caller ID told Knoxi it was Ryan. "Hi, sweetie! Uh, Mama and Daddy are here. I hadn't expected to hear from you so soon. The phone startled us."

She arose with a troubled expression, walked into the hallway, and looked both ways to make certain no one was listening. "What do you mean it's dangerous?" She whispered. "Did you figure out the coded Thialitic encrypted clivical with the lowhaul and anti something-or-other, whatever you said? What about those gross images I'm seeing?"

"It's underhaul, *not lowhaul*. A simple explanation is —"

"Ryan! Never mind. Just get to the point."

As Knoxi concentrated on Ryan's words, she looked back at Cody and Brandi who were now on the edge of their seats.

Then she caught her breath. "What? You're coming here today? How did you —? I mean, a jet? Marine detail? Texas Rangers? Ryan, why do we need all that?"

After her call ended, she slowly walked back into the library looking wrung out. Two couples had shown up to study. She suggested that her parents accompany her to the sun deck on the roof. Hopefully, they could talk privately there.

They walked onto the roof and found it deserted, then sat down at a table. She explained about the dark images and coded message she had been receiving every sixteen hours. Ryan had already decoded enough to know that it didn't make any sense without more information from Knoxi.

He demanded to know specifically what she had been working on. Ryan had never sounded more serious. He would be landing at Austin in less than four hours, arriving by military jet transport, and accompanied by four armed US Marines. Texas Rangers would drive Ryan and his Marine escort to the campus in unmarked vehicles.

Knoxi elaborated. "He thinks I'm in immediate danger because the technology to mask such a message from all tracking, including satellite, is very complex. He thinks it's from some heavy-hitter who wants to turn over classified or stolen intelligence to me."

Brandi looked confused. "You're right, that makes no sense."

"Listen, Fort Knox, if there's something you aren't telling us, this would be a good time."

"Daddy, you haven't called me 'Fort Knox' in years." She tried to smile. "Believe me, if I knew what this was about, I would tell you everything."

Cody leaned back and crossed his arms. "I believe you. We shouldn't speculate on it 'til we talk with Ryan. There could be a reasonable explanation."

Knoxi shook her hands to jettison the surging anxiety. When she was little, her daddy seemed so big. He was even bigger now. She fought the urge to sit in his lap and collapse into his big arms just one last time. But after all, she was nineteen.

Cody shifted the focus. "I got a disturbing call from Sly last night. The Dodgers have moved Jeremy up to Triple-A Oklahoma City this season. They think he might make the Dodgers big-league club sometime this summer. He's playing center field this spring."

"Oh, that sounds good, doesn't it?" Knoxi smiled guardedly. "Jeremy's been a little . . . a little secretive with me about things since he married Annabelle. I hope they're happy. He had his first spring exhibition game last night, but I haven't heard how he did."

"He was one for two with a strikeout and a throwing error, but the club is still high on his talent. Sly texted me immediately, of course. But it's not baseball that his dad's concerned about."

"So—so what is it, then?"

"Same thing you said. Jeremy won't talk, not even to his parents. He's gotten secretive. Would you believe that Jeremy has never taken Annabelle to meet his family? They were married in Vegas at a wedding chapel. He informed Sly and Julia after the fact. They're flying to Arizona as we speak to meet Annabelle today. Jeremy doesn't even know they're coming."

"I think Jeremy was more shaken up after Lake Travis than he let on," Brandi said. "He needs to spend time with his dad, and they need to meet Annabelle."

Knoxi had another comment. "I haven't given up on little Zorro. We'll find him. I pray that every day. We'll get him back. I know it doesn't seem like it now, but . . ." She shook her head. "He's not even three yet." Knoxi forced herself to smile. This was no time for tears. Ryan would be arriving within hours.

~   ~   ~

Meanwhile, in the Mountain Time Zone, the sun was just rising in Arizona. Jeremy was up at dawn because the Dodgers were going to Goodyear Park on the west side of Phoenix for an afternoon game against the Cincinnati Reds. In three hours, he would be on the bus with the team and Annie would follow in the truck. They walked to the breakfast room and ran into Carlos Santana. He was repairing another leak.

When they told him Jeremy was going to Goodyear to play ball, Carlos offered to pray for him at the breakfast table. In his broken English, he asked God to give Jeremy clarity and help him to be his best mentally and physically to display the talents God had given him. "Make Dodgers happy for Jeremy come through in clutch. Amen."

Jeremy had played well the night before in his first exhibition game. He had made an error in the third inning but had made up for it with an RBI double in the fifth. His and Annabelle's perspective had changed since meeting Carlos on that rainy morning seven days ago. Annie had become slightly more comfortable with her new identity, but she lived under an increasingly dark shadow of grief over losing her only son. The pain went away occasionally, but always returned.

Jeremy struggled to leave his baseball emotions on the field, but had a long way to go. When he was younger, he had watched his father arrive home so psyched after playing baseball that he would be unable to sleep. Mistakes, failures on the field would haunt him for hours, and the good things — the victories, personal successes — would leave him so high he'd be wild-eyed until the wee hours. Father and son both loved the game, but each understood how much the game could get you down. Or up. The secret was learning how to command your own feelings and be ready to play with full intensity the next day.

Jeremy had become more conversational lately, but he still didn't talk to Annie much. It seemed to her that he preferred talking to his buddies and coaches more, since he would become quite chatty when he hung with them.

They returned to the room. Jeremy plopped down on the bed. "I gotta close my eyes just a second."

"Jeremy, you no can go to sleep." She tried to get his attention, but he began to snore.

As she watched him, she prayed a silent prayer. "Oh, God, por favor, I know how to be Alex, I know how to be Glorietta, but I donno how to be Annie."

She shook Jeremy's shoulders. "Wake up, stud! Get yo butt outta dis bed!"

Jeremy popped his eyes open wide.

She cracked a tiny smile. "I learn to speak English good, no?"

Someone knocked on the door. "See who dat is," Jeremy said. "It's prolly Carlos. I gotta find my shoes. We ain't got much time."

When Annie opened the door, she caught her breath and threw both hands over her mouth. Standing before her was a middle-forties African-American couple whom she had never seen, yet she knew immediately who they were. The man was tall, athletic, with large forearms and biceps, barrel-chested with intense brown eyes. His facial expression, identical to Jeremy's, was a dead giveaway. The woman was stately, beautiful, with a smooth bronze complexion and eyes so soft they probably never needed sleep.

As Annie stared, the woman in front of her, a complete stranger, became tearful and held out her arms. Without thinking, Annie stepped forward into a silent embrace.

"Dad? Mom?" Jeremy choked. "What are you doing here? I—I mean when . . . when did you —" Jeremy and Tanner stared at each other, trying to ignore the two emotional women locked in an embrace.

Tanner broke the silence. "I—I cum to see my boy." He struggled. "And . . . I, uh, I wanted to meet my daughter-in-law, that's all."

Finally, Annie turned around. "Jeremy, invite 'em in, dude, they ain't got no time fo' wastin', you feel me?"

Julia tried to string some thoughts together. "I'm so sorry. I—I know we should've called. It's just — Well, I certainly hope you are Annabelle," she chuckled.

"Oh, yes ma'am. I ain't speak no good English much. Jeremy, he's teachin' me."

"Ain't that the truth!" Julia embraced her son then turned back to Annie. "Baby, Jeremy is an amazing person, but he completely obliterates the English language."

Annie's eyes beamed huge. "Oh, señora! I—I mean Jeremy amaze everybody! He ain't afraid. He big, big hero. He run through bullets, carry me to helicopter, jump off building and catch plane with one hand — smooth move, cool as a mule, baby!"

Sly squinted, not as one staring into a bright light, but rather as one asking if he were in the wrong place. Julia stepped up. "So, you are learning English by listening to Jeremy when he talks to you?"

"Oh, no. He never talk to me. He talk to ballplayers. He talk to coaches. I listen, learn to talk like American."

"Uh, Mom, Dad, we weren't expecting you. I mean, we got a lot to tell you."

"You got that right, son. Now we gittin' somewhere. So why haven't we — I mean why haven't you answered our calls. What are you thinking, marryin' someone who, uh, I mean —"

"What your father means is, we'd like to know your wife. We're disappointed we haven't met this lovely woman earlier."

"Uh, yeah, yeah, dat's right," Tanner said. "We—we'd like to know how you met. Uh, what about your wife's family, and —"

"Dad, her name's Annabelle. I think she prefers Annie. And about how we met? About her family? That's . . . complicated."

"Well," Julia chimed in. "So, the part about the helicopter? Jumping off the building? That part sounds especially complicated." She waited but got no response. "Jeremy?"

Jeremy squirmed. "So, like, the helicopter wasn't goin' all that fast at the time."

Annie jumped back in. "Jeremy ain't no coward. He fight brave. He like crazy man. Indian from Oklahoma name Adrian save his life. Sheeese! Very close call!"

Tanner dropped his hat on the bed. "Do you mind if I sit?"

"Uh, no, no, of course not, make yourself at home." Jeremy dropped his backside onto the couch.

For a few awkward moments, no one could think of anything to say. Finally, Jeremy's eyes glazed over. "Look, these last few months have been the hardest . . ." He ran out of words and placed his hand over his face to hide hot tears that rolled down his unshaven cheeks.

"Dad, Mom, I shudda called you. I just couldn't figure how I was gonna tell you. I mean, I had to shoot somebody. And that's not all that's happened."

Annie scooted to Jeremy and put her small hands on his shoulder. Julia sat down on the edge of the bed with her hands in her lap.

Tanner softened. "Uh, obviously, you kids have seen trouble. We—we family. I mean, you're stuck wid us. Don't be tryin' to do dis by yourself."

Annie buried her head against Jeremy's shoulder, shedding tears upon his trendy Dodger game jersey. Julia's soft eyes glistened at the sight of her son and his new bride weeping together on the couch.

Annie raised her head and wiped her eyes. "I pray this morning before you come because I donno who Annie is. Now I have whole new family."

"Look here." Tanner stood, stepped forward, and spoke with animated hands as much as with words. "It don't matter none. Wha'chu done been through we can hear 'bout later. We family. Right now, ain't nothin' else matter." He looked at his watch. "We got a game today! Son, you got to catch a bus. You reckon they's room for a ol' washed-up right fielder to ride along?"

Jeremy put his big right arm around Annie and reached his left hand toward his father. "Dad, that'd be the mos' greatest thing I could think of. We'll make room on na' bus. The skipper and all the guys know my ol' man's a hall-of-famer. They been askin' when you comin."

"Cool as jello, man. I could ride wit' you, and you're mama can ride wit' you're wife in na' truck."

"Perfect for me," Julia said, glancing at Annabelle. "If that's cool with you, Annie."

"Me? Of course! Uh, one question I wanna know. Why Mr. Musket call your husband 'Sly?' What means Sly?"

"*Ha-ha!* Sweet child, if you haven't figured that out already, you will!" Julia crossed her arms. "And, baby, if you wanna learn to speak good English, pick somebody better to learn from than these two king studs. C'mon, I'll drive. We can take our rental car."

The trip to Goodyear Park was supposed to last only fifteen minutes. Traffic was light on Sunday. Annie's nerves calmed as she buckled her safety belt. Her stormy three-month marriage to Julia's son had left her as one gasping at times for oxygen. Julia's soft-spoken words seemed to breathe tranquility into Annie's world. It was obvious that Jeremy had his father's game face and strong will, but Annie had also seen his compassionate side, and Julia's presence now gave her new hope.

"Jeremy tell me you win beauty contest."

"*Ha-ha!* That was a long time ago when I was a sophomore at Maryland University. I was runner-up in the Miss Black USA Pageant."

"You so pretty."

"So are you, precious child. Now, tell me what you meant when you said you don't know who Annie is?"

Annie folded her hands in her lap. "I tell you my story, but you will cry. You must drive. Maybe we wait 'til later?"

"How do you know I'll cry? It couldn't be that bad."

"I know you will cry," Annie said. "I know because you have much love. Much love make you cry if you hear my story."

Julia stopped at a traffic light. "I have to tell you something first, Annie. When I saw you standing in the doorway of my son's room this morning, I felt — You see, I lost a daughter when Jeremy was just two years old. She was stillborn. Tanner doesn't ever talk about it. Jeremy doesn't remember. But when I laid eyes on you, I somehow saw you as the daughter I was never allowed to raise. I—I know it must seem sentimental, but —"

"I lose child," Annie blurted out. "He maybe alive. Maybe not."

Julia waited silently until the light changed, then pulled into a deserted parking lot in front of a bank. She turned off the motor. "I want to hear your story. No one can bear that pain alone."

Annie shared her dreadful tale with her new mother-in-law. It became obvious they would not finish the drive in fifteen minutes. Annie told about Nogales, little Zorro, the pit, the faces of the decaying women. She revealed the events which had happened at Austin and shared about meeting Jeremy and falling in love with him at first sight. She bragged how Jeremy had cradled her in his big arms despite his injuries and carried her when she was so broken she could not get off the floor the first time she told her story.

By then, Julia's eyes were red and swollen. Annie, determined to shed no tears this time, apologized.

"I knew you would cry because Jeremy cry when he hear story first time. He love little Zorro when he never even seen my son." She turned her face away. "I promised I not cry this time."

Julia reached across and held Annie's shoulder. "Jeremy loves little Zorro because he knows how much *you* love little Zorro, and I love Zorro for the same reason."

"I not want to embarrass Jeremy in front of all the men. I not speak good. I not sound smart."

"Are you kidding me?" Julia chuckled. "Embarrass? Sweet thing, you have street smarts beyond your years."

"They beat me, treat me worse than mad dog. I not want to be that person anymore."

"Sweetie, you aren't *that* person. You're the woman who outsmarted them all. You survived. You won! You're still the woman who rushed onto the stage in a torn dress and walked off the stage a star. You refused to die when there was no reason to live. You're still Glorietta, every man's brightest hope."

"You think I can make Jeremy bright hope?"

"Oh, honey, I saw the way he looked at you. I saw the way my husband adored you. He wanted to hug you but he didn't wanna lose it in front of Jeremy."

"You husband play baseball too. Maybe I learn from you how to be good baseball wife."

"*Ha!* The secret to keeping heavyweights like Tanner and Jeremy focused is to be smarter and stronger than they are without letting them know it, and you're already pretty good at that!"

"So, Señora McNair, what means *sly* in English?"

"Call me Julia, precious. And *sly* means tricky, scheming, always looking for an angle. And when Sly finds out he has a grandson, you haven't seen the end of scheming. He'll devise at least a hundred ways to find that boy, and he would trade his two batting titles and World Series ring in one second if it would help."

"I not give up. We find Zorro so he can meet his *real* father and family."

~   ~   ~

UT Campus, Sunday afternoon

Knoxi received her awaited text from Ryan. He had just landed in Austin. He requested they meet at Grounds for Love on the UT campus at 3 p.m.

When they arrived, the coffee shop was closed. A clean-shaven individual wearing civilian clothing approached the three Muskets, identified himself as a Texas Ranger, and showed his badge. "Captain Harris sends his regards, Mr. Musket." The ranger nodded to Knoxi and Brandi. "Follow me please. Mr. Maxwell is waiting this way." He directed the three of them to the back door.

Ryan was sitting alone in a back corner. All the shades were pulled, the room dimly-lit by a single low-output lamp.

He stood up and shook hands with Cody. "I haven't seen you since Methodist Hospital, sir. I congratulate you on not getting shot lately," he chuckled. "And ma'am," he said to Brandi, "you look as gorgeous as ever. Easy to see where the love of my life gets her beauty."

"You're quite a charmer, Ryan. My daughter is quite taken with you."

"Oh, Mama!"

"Actually, ma'am, I'm the one taken with her. She's the most important thing in my life, and I have reason to believe she may be in danger if I further my investigation of these strange one-way electronic communiques she's receiving. I need to know more before proceeding."

They sat down. "Here's what I have been able to decode. I'll spare you the technical drivel. Just watch this replay with the decoded text."

Ryan pulled a tablet from his briefcase and started the fifteen-second presentation. The faces of two men filled the nine-inch screen, followed by the image of a woman's face covered in blood, stressed, wind-blown, falling. Her eyes barely open, she appeared at the point of death. Then an email address flashed onto the screen, followed by more encrypted files.

Knoxi seemed sickened, but did not recognize the faces.

"That's what I figured," Ryan said. "I did a facial recognition on the bloody-faced woman. She was Francine Bell of DTC Global. People there knew her as Franki. She supposedly committed suicide a week ago — jumped from twenty-five floors up. She fell from the same platform as this woman, Tera Hoffman, one month earlier." He showed them Tera's picture. "Both cases were ruled suicide. The same deputy coroner named Terrence Baldwin presided over both cases and signed them off."

Cody spoke up. "Okay, so what we're seeing is a woman known as Franki Bell taking a selfie while bleeding to death and falling twenty-five floors? Unimaginable." He shook his head. "I've seen bad stuff, but . . ."

"Well, if someone's gonna commit suicide by jumping, they wouldn't bloody their own face first," Knoxi said. "So, what's going on?"

"Maybe this helps." Ryan played the footage again and stopped it when the email address showed up. "Do you recognize this email?"

Knoxi expanded the screen view and looked closely. "Hmmm, rs@hostagepoint.net? Can you get into the email itself?"

"Already a step ahead," Ryan said, pulling a seventeen-inch laptop from his case. He logged into the email. "Check it out. RS received several emails from franki@btcglobal.com. One was sent two hours prior to her death. Read the content."

Knoxi read out loud. "Baby, I'm in deep trouble. It's all comin' down. I confronted DC this AM. Thought he'd understand. You were right. I should have listened. Make this go away. What should I do with the files? I'll end up like Tera."

Knoxi looked up. "So, Franki, the dead woman, sent an email to rs@hostagepoint.net asking for help just before she died?"

"Correct, a couple of hours prior to her death," Ryan said. "She was desperate for help after confronting DC. Those are the initials of Derek Carasco, her boss, the head of DTC Global."

Brandi joined the discussion. "What files is she talking about?"

Ryan had already accessed the files. "Franki attached these files she mentioned. I've glanced at them. Documents implicating DTC Global in everything from child trafficking to gun smuggling. The company is attempting a merger that would make them the most powerful corporation in North America. Derek Carasco is the kingpin."

"But I have no connection to Franki Bell," Knoxi pointed out. "I've never even heard of her."

"That's just it, Fort Knox, these messages didn't come to you directly from Franki. RS is the one sending the looped message to you. And get this: the signal originates from Buenos Aires." Ryan turned to Cody. "Sir, I hope you don't mind my calling your daughter Fort Knox. She said you're the only one who calls her that, but —"

"It's okay, Ryan. So why is this character sending Knoxi stuff from South America? Who is RS? Why these spooky, cloaked messages? Why not just send a text or normal email?"

"Probably because RS, whoever that is, doesn't want to be found. He or she could be anywhere using a remote sending tower, anything to reflect a signal. The real question is how did they get hold of such technology?"

Knoxi gasped and covered her mouth with both hands. She stood up and walked across the room. "Of course! Hostage point! The sign over his office door. RS — Rolfe Sagan! It's Rolfe. He's alive!"

"When were you in Sagan's office?" Brandi crossed her arms.

"He's trying to contact me while staying hidden." Knoxi put both hands on her forehead. "Oh! I wonder . . . I wonder if he's looking for Zorro." She turned around with glistening eyes and a flushed face. "I told him about Alex, but I didn't reveal to him her new identity. I mean, he has a grandson. Maybe he's searching for him. Maybe he's found him."

"Knoxi, Knoxi, slow down." Ryan walked toward her. "Breathe. You're gonna hyperventilate." He offered his hand for support.

"Oh, no I'm not! No need to tell me when to breathe!" She pushed past him and sat down again.

Ryan looked at Cody, who returned a blank stare and a "good luck with that one" shrug.

Brandi's light came on. "Knoxi, are you saying —?"

Knoxi popped a grin. "Yes, Mama. Annabelle is Rolfe's daughter and little Zorro is his grandson."

"Excuse me?" Ryan raised his hand like a first-grader. "Can someone fill me in? Who's Rolfe?"

"Rolfe Sagan," Brandi said. "The guy your fiancée melted like cheese toast in the meeting at UT."

"Uh, you mean *the* Rolfe Sagan? The BNN guy who is MIA?"

"Right," Knoxi said. "But I didn't exactly make toast out of him."

"That's not what I heard," Ryan threw in.

"*Ohh-hoo, believe it!*" Brandi said. "It was God's handiwork."

"Sorry to burst your airship, Mama, but Rolfe was just acting. He gets more downloads and page views that way."

Ryan crossed his arms and frowned. "Rolfe Sagan is the reporter who wrote an ugly piece about my dad when he disappeared. He said my father had gotten all sorts of special privileges from the Navy and the DOD because he was black, and he even accused him of espionage — of stealing technology then disappearing with it."

"I didn't know that," Knoxi said. "I was only six then. Rolfe's an opportunist, a spin doctor. He never cared about anybody until —"

"So how do you know he isn't acting now?" Ryan asked. "What if this whole thing blows up in your face? *Our face!*"

"We have DNA confirmation. Annabelle is Rolfe's daughter."

Cody placed his fist on the table. "Okay, does Annabelle know?"

"No, Daddy. Would Annabelle really want to know a father who was complicit with corporations who invest in trafficking? Rolfe didn't know about her until I went to his office and tried to turn him."

"What?" Cody bristled up. "Why didn't you talk to me first?"

"This is all your fault, Cody," Ryan said as he came around and stood behind Knoxi. "She's just like you." He reached his arms around her. "And I love her even more for it. Isn't it poetic that my father gave his life to save fifty kids twelve years ago, and one of them would turn out to be the only woman I will ever love?"

Cody and Brandi breathed a collective sigh as they watched their only daughter stand up, turn around and passionately embrace the son of Sabre. It was difficult to tell who was kissing whom, but Ryan was clearly his own man, and from that moment forward, his sonship in the Musket family would be forever forged.

PIRATES OF THE CARIBBEAN

O n the following morning, Knoxi's phone received another coded message. This one was different. It was the face of a child, sad, pale, and thin, followed by more coded files. She called Ryan.

"I'm on it," Ryan said. "Meet me at the coffee shop ASAP."

Knoxi walked with her parents into Grounds for Love and waited a few moments until Ryan came walking in. He was followed by four US Marines who positioned themselves on the other side of the room.

Ryan and the Muskets sat down. "Okay, here's what I have." Ryan reached across and took Knoxi's hand. "Brace yourself." Then he made eye contact with Brandi and Cody individually. "Not sure I'm ready for this, but here goes."

They stared down at the notes Ryan was holding.

"I can show you the decoded documents later, but for simplicity, I've made an outline. The boy's face is described as "the object of my search." He's at a lat/long coordinate in the northeast corner of Haiti."

"Haiti?" Cody tightened. "All you have is a lat/long? What's there? A village? A building?"

"We don't know what's there. Nothing shows on satellite. All we have is a coordinate."

"Then let's go. We'll find out what's there when we arrive," Knoxi stated strongly. "What's the problem?"

"The problem? Pirates. That corner of the country has been taken over by that pirate group that's been raiding ships and setting off bombs in airports. Nobody has been able to stop them. This character Pablo, who originally laid claim to the boy, sold him to these pirates."

"So, Pablo abandoned him?" Brandi intensified. "So now this child is owned by *Pirates of the Caribbean*?"

"Yes, ma'am. But this is not a movie. In the last six months, this den of pirates has attacked a children's school and—"

"Yes, sweetie," Knoxi interrupted. "We don't need to hear those horrible stories again."

"Okay, understood." Ryan peeked at his notes again. "Here's the part that gets dicey. Your contact, RS, presumably Sagan, says that if you can deliver the boy safely to his mother, he'll release a factual report on social media that will change the world. RS is tired of being held hostage and says you would know what that means."

Knoxi caught a long, deep breath. "It's Rolfe! It's definitely him! He's found Zorro!" She looked at Ryan. "How do we get this done?"

Knoxi caught a long, deep breath. "It's Rolfe! It's definitely him!" She looked up at Ryan. "How do we get this done?"

Ryan hesitated, frowned again, and placed his elbows on the table. "Okay, here's the part I can't wrap my head around." He rubbed his chin as one who brings bad tidings.

"Come on, sweetie, speak up." Knoxi waited. "Ryan?"

"On twenty-nine March . . ." Ryan hesitated, still rubbing his chin, "the child will be at these coordinates in the northeast corner of Haiti, near the Dominican border." He showed them a map with the lat/long position circled. "It's in the middle of nowhere, 'bout thirty miles from the border, no town, no building, nothing on the map or satellite photos. Mountainous terrain. No tellin' what's there."

"March twenty-ninth? That's still three weeks away," Knoxi said. "Why can't we go now?"

"It gets worse," Ryan responded. "You're gonna have to go yourself, Fort Knox."

"No way!" Cody grumbled. "There are options available — other people who are more qualified for this. What's this guy's real reason for punching Knoxi's number? What game is he playing? Did he say he wouldn't play ball unless Knoxi went on the mission?"

"Knoxi's the only one who knows the password," Ryan said.

"What? What password?" Brandi was fuming by this time.

"Well, ma'am, I —"

"Oh, Ryan! Stop calling me, *ma'am!* Call me Brandi, or Mom, or, or anything but ma'am!"

"Uh, okay, uh, Brandi . . . or that is, Mama Brandi, or just Brandi."

"Okay, okay, Ryan. Brandi it is," Cody said. "Explain to me why this clown says my daughter has to go."

"When she arrives at the lat/long, she'll be asked for the password. March 29th is the only day that will work. Rolfe won't play ball otherwise. He must have his reasons, but I don't like it either. I suggest we handcuff her to a chair, lock her in a room, and lose the key 'til the mission's over."

Brandi's mouth gaped open.

Cody held up his arms and flashed a noble grin. "You learn fast, Ryan. We both know chains and handcuffs won't stop her."

Ryan nodded reluctantly.

"Well! I never heard a more foolish proposal!" Brandi stood up. "Knoxi isn't trained for this kind of danger." She gathered her purse and walked toward the door. "I need some air. Don't follow me." She left through the side door.

Knoxi glanced toward three coeds who were sipping coffee near the front of the store. Thankfully, they had been too busy drooling over the four Marines to notice her mother's animated exit.

Cody arose and walked toward the door. "You kids excuse me. My wife wants me to follow her." His face managed to force a grin as he disappeared through the exit.

"I'm sorry about Mama, but I can't say I blame her."

Ryan chuckled it off. "I'm glad we got past the formal greetings and stuff. Now, it's like family."

"March twenty-ninth is two days after spring break begins, so I guess we'll have to wait 'til after Haiti to plan our wedding."

Ryan enveloped her in a somber embrace. "No time for wedding plans when you have a mission like this to prepare. Nobody can know what we're planning, not even the mother of the child. Nobody."

"I know," Knoxi shrank back. "I wouldn't get Annabelle's hopes up anyway, not until Zorro is safe."

~   ~   ~

Three weeks later
One day before the mission

Knoxi sat alone at Grounds for Love reading over the mission plan put together by her father and his associates. Officially, the spring break had begun this day, thus the campus was largely deserted. It was late afternoon.

Cody remained uneasy. Rolfe was the only individual who knew what would be waiting at the designated coordinates in Eastern Haiti. Tomorrow they would leave for the Dominican Republic, the country that borders Haiti on its eastern side. The following day, Knoxi would be flown across the border in a small aircraft to receive Zorro and return under cover of darkness.

How much danger would his daughter be in? Rolfe Sagan had spent his life preying on the weak, seeking dollars more than truth, and making faithful people doubt. Should they now offer him their blind faith in return for his promise to expose a hidden underworld — a legion of death and debauchery of which he had been a part? It was a grind on Cody's nerves.

Knoxi somehow believed Rolfe's heart was in the right place. She could not forget his eyes when he looked at Annabelle's picture — that bizarre blend of exhilaration and sorrow. The eyes seldom lie.

How did Rolfe know she would have access to technology that could decipher his secret messages? Did he know about Ryan? What else did he know? He had promised to fill in some of the blanks after she arrived in the Dominican Republic.

She and Ryan had planned to marry at spring break. Now, all bets were off. Would they ever get the chance? She had feared that Ryan's work would often disrupt their family life, but now she was the one whose duty kept them apart. No one, not even her teammates, must know about this event. It was a journey from which she might not return, but the fate of so many was in the balance.

Did she just want the glory? Was that it? On the court, with her team trailing by two points and just five seconds remaining, she would want the ball. But with a world at stake, was she really the one to take that shot?

Deep in thought, Knoxi sensed someone standing behind her. She had not expected company. When she turned around, her grandparents, Ray and Whitney Barnes, stood ready to embrace her.

"Grandpa! Grandma! What are y'all doing here? Do Mama and Daddy know you're here?"

"We came to, uh, see you off in the morning." Ray's voice was tentative but strong.

Whitney jumped in. "And we want to meet Ryan, your wonderman. We didn't get to thank him for saving your dad's life in Houston."

Whitney glanced at her husband the way she always did when he wanted the floor. "Go ahead, Grandpa, tell her."

Ray cleared his throat as he sat down across from his granddaughter. "I read your eyes, baby girl. I've always been able to."

"I know, Grandpa. I'm already about to cry. Somehow, I knew you'd come. I—I'm afraid to go, but I'm afraid not to go. It's hard to weigh everything. Too many things to consider. I don't know how to be certain. I'm not used to playing with such high stakes."

"Well, let me clear things up a little," Ray began. "You can walk away from this. Just don't go. No one will blame you. No one will get hurt, and everything will remain like it is now. In two days, everyone will wake up to the same life they had today. Same future. No change. If you're happy with that arrangement, just sit this one out."

Knoxi's head dropped into her hands. "Grandpa, Grandma . . ." She paused, searching for the right words, then stared at Ray and Whitney with eyes red and misty.

Ray acknowledged with a difficult smile and silent nod.

Whitney's voice wavered. "And we can't wait to see that little boy when you get back."

"If you don't go, baby girl, you'll always wonder, and that won't do for you." Ray folded his hands. "Some opportunities never come again."

"Grandpa, do you believe people like Rolfe Sagan can change?"

"Not for a minute." He reached across the table and took her hands. "But I've seen it happen."

Suddenly, the door opened and beautiful people began streaming into the shop. Knoxi recognized her teammates even though she was not accustomed to seeing them dressed for a party — heels, designer evening wear, curls, locks, trimmed and manicured head to toe.

Sarafina Camaroon, her roommate, explained. "Hi, little sis. Spring break started this morning but, hey, we got invited to this gig, so we stayed on campus one more day. We were told someone's gonna party here tonight! Have you heard anything about that?"

Knoxi looked around. She was the only player on the team who had not been informed. Something was up. Cody and Brandi came through the door walking hand-in-hand, looking totally innocent.

"What are all you kids up to?" Cody asked.

The room was silenced. Most of the women and their male guests had never met the famous Cody Musket. Here he was in the flesh. Everyone smiled, but no one said a word.

Brandi took over. "I want to thank you all for coming," she said. "I want to tell you a love story." Everyone clapped and some whistled.

"A few years back, a very troubled and lonely single mom was walking alone on a rainy night to a movie. She was assaulted by three men in ski masks who had in mind to end her life." Everyone booed loudly.

Brandi held up her hands. "But it just so happened that an unknown rookie baseball player was following this woman because he had fallen hard for her at first sight, and yet was too scared to introduce himself." Now the team cheered.

"The three men had no idea that this ballplayer was a highly-sensitive US Marine who had a very fast fuse. And if it hadn't been for . . ." She stopped to settle her wavering voice. "If God hadn't put this man in that theater on that Friday night, I wouldn't be standing here this evening, and Knoxi wouldn't have a daddy." The team and their guests erupted with loud applause.

"But the story doesn't end there. You see, just eight nights later, I put together a surprise party for this man after the ballgame. It was sort of like this party, except that I invited the preacher along and . . . well, the rest is history." Everyone whooped like beasts of the wild.

"Now," Brandi concluded, "I wanna bring your coach into this." She looked toward the front door. "Coach Willis! Are you out there?"

When the door opened, Kristy Willis was escorted by two men. On her right walked the groom, Ryan Maxwell, and on her left Reverend Phil Tutor, the Muskets' pastor in Houston.

Knoxi pressed her hands against her red-hot face. Was this for real? Had her mother and grandmother moved heaven and earth to see her dream come true like a fairy tale that very night?"

Now the party was on. Knoxi bolted into Ryan's arms and everyone was treated to a long kissing scene.

Amidst the cheers, Pastor Tutor spoke up. "Hey, you're supposed to save that for the end!"

Calls for, "*More! More!*" punctuated the laughter.

After the ceremony and another thrilling kiss, everyone enjoyed the cake and other refreshments. Knoxi finally found a few words. "Well, I have to say, I was *really* surprised! I don't know whether Ryan was involved in the conspiracy, but I plan on interrogating him later tonight!" Laughter shook the tables again and rode on every sound wave.

"I also want to say that my grandmother and my mom are the two greatest females on the planet." More applause. "I know they are the ones behind this. It has their handwriting all over it. They did this tonight because . . ." She put her hand over her lips and glanced at Brandi. "I mean it makes this night soooo special. Thank you, Mama. Thank you, Grandma."

Knoxi couldn't stop. "I hear so many women say, 'I wish I had a good man in my life.' Well, in my life I have three of the greatest men who have ever walked the face of the earth: my grandfather, Captain Ray Barnes, USMC retired, my father, USMC retired, and my husband who makes popsicles in Colorado." This time, the roof came down.

Sarafina stepped in. "Quiet, everyone! Geez, I never knew a popsicle maker before, 'specially one who arrives in a military special envoy aircraft. But your husband can deliver as many popsicles as he wants. I won't complain, long as he brings his US Marine escort with him every time!"

Soon the laughter died down.

"I love you all," Knoxi said. "Now, my mom just handed my husband this key." She pulled the key from Ryan's hand and waved it around. "So, y'all party here as long as you like. We're holdin' our own private party for two at the Hilton tonight!"

DOING GOD'S WORK?

The morning after

The new day had come way too early for Knoxi and Ryan. The flight to Puerto Plata Airport in the Dominican Republic would take four hours. They had chartered a *private* jet because, after all, they were not on official business. They were simply a happy couple on a honeymoon vacation.

Officially, Ryan had been given a three-day leave of absence. He suspected that his immediate superiors knew more than they revealed and that they were monitoring his activities closely.

As the charter lifted off, Knoxi tried desperately to hold on to thoughts of last night, to savor every moment until the last second. She and Ryan must now transition from one world to another — from the marital bliss of joy by surprise to a cloak and dagger game where the hopes of thousands would seem to ride on the dubious promises of one Rolfe Sagan. Is this what it means to do God's work, as Ryan had once told her? Today it felt more like the valley of shadows mentioned in Psalm 23.

The plan called for the group to stay the night in Puerto Plata, the Dominican port of entry on the shores of the North Atlantic. Ryan, however, would spend his night setting up mission headquarters on a mountaintop at the Haitian border from where he would monitor and direct the mission.

Knoxi must sleep alone tonight. Tomorrow, she would board a small single-engine aircraft which would carry her into pirate-controlled territory in Eastern Haiti.

As their charter flight departed Austin airspace and leveled off at thirty-one-thousand feet, Knoxi turned her head away from Ryan. She could not bear to let him see the apprehension on her face. Where was her faith? Strangely, her concern wasn't because of the danger, but rather because of what was at stake. Through it all, she determined that no one, not even her husband, would see her cry until this job was finished.

Ryan reached over and found her hand. "Popsicle maker? Couldn't you think of something funny instead?" Knoxi shut her eyes and never budged. He leaned close to her. "I feel it too, you know."

She acknowledged with a wistful glance and glistening eyes. "No one sees me cry today." She clenched her fist. "No one."

He delicately eased her head onto his shoulder and shielded her face with his hand. Her warm teardrops rolled between his fingers, but with her face hidden no one else would know.

He thought to enhearten her with a spontaneous prayer. "Oh, God," he whispered reverently, "I cannot think of a better honeymoon. I mean, doing God's work? For the children? Like, I swear before all heaven and earth I love this woman with all my soul. I'd rather take her place tomorrow, but You seem to think the best man for this job is a woman."

Knoxi smothered a snicker.

Ryan continued. "Lord, I don't believe you've brought us this far to leave us on our own. So . . . uh, yeah, amen."

"I'm sorry, Ryan," Knoxi chuckled. "I couldn't help myself. The best man for the job is a woman? I've heard that said before, but never so apropos." She blotted her eyes. "I didn't want you to see me cry. I'm declaring a no-cry zone for the next twenty-four hours."

"Hey, I couldn't see anything. Did you cry?"

They became quiet. Finally, she broke the silence with a question. "Ryan, do you think God ever laughs?"

"Of course. Just wait 'til we bring smiles back to the faces of a jillion kids. I mean, that's why we're going to Haiti. I know God is smiling on us right now. Like, can't you feel it? This is His work we're doing."

When they landed at the city of Puerto Plata, they were met by Dominican armed border guards and customs agents. As planned, Hutch accompanied Knoxi to her small hotel unit and situated himself in the adjacent room. Star went with Ryan to help set up his mountain post near the Haitian border. Cody and Brandi would stay near their daughter and accompany her the next day to meet the aircraft that would carry her away.

Cody had hired twenty trusted and trained operatives to infiltrate the countryside around the rendezvous point and make certain no one would get near Knoxi. The only details missing were the ones Rolfe had agreed to provide.

Knoxi opened the door to her room. It smelled fresh. The windows were open, and sheer curtains were lazily reacting to the light cross-breeze. Hutch inspected the room before letting Knoxi enter. "Clear," he said. "I'm next door. Your parents should be here as soon as they fill out the rest of the customs stuff."

Knoxi saw a brown envelope on the bed with two words scribbled on the flap — Hostage Point.

"Hutch, look! It's from Sagan." She sat down, tore open the envelope, and read the hand-typed letter. . .

> "Hello, Knoxi. You came. I knew you would. Sorry for all the secret crap. Read this carefully then destroy it. (I always wanted to say that.) The reason you have to go get the child yourself? You're the only one I would trust.

"At the specified coordinates sits a church carved into the side of a mountain. That's why it doesn't show up on satellite. The church is called Maria de Dios. It's run by a Mother Francesca. The last Wednesday afternoon of each month, a nun is flown from Puerto Plata airport to the isolated church. The plane lands in a field about 50 yards away. The nun enters the church, stays a few minutes, then carries a package out containing precious metals donated by local miners. After that, she flies back to Puerto Plata.

"Tomorrow, you'll be that nun. The habit you'll wear is already in your closet. A team of commandos sent to get the boy would be cut down before they could even reach the door, but they shouldn't suspect a nun who comes regularly.

"There is a legend that the church is protected by Saint Maria. She will show up tomorrow wearing a dark frock. She'll protect you. Everyone is superstitious. That's why the pirates let the nun pass. It's the only way to get the boy out without him being killed.

"Remember, you'd rather be a fool for Jesus than a wiseguy for somebody else."

"Lemme see that letter," Hutch said. "You think it's genuine?"

"Totally. What puzzles me is —"

"Wait! Lemme guess." Hutch chuckled. "The dark-frocked woman? Saint something?"

"Saint Maria. How do you figure? I mean, Rolfe hardly believes in God. Why would he believe in some earth-roaming saint?"

Hutch had another question. "And where'd he get that one-liner about bein' a fool for Jesus?"

Knoxi shook her head and folded her arms. "Hard to tell whether he thinks he's the fool or thinks I am."

~   ~   ~

The next morning dragged by slowly. Knoxi awoke at 7 a.m. She pulled the pillow over her head and closed her eyes again, then drifted off to sleep and awakened suddenly when a mysterious female figure with a dark complexion and black frock invaded her dream. She rolled out of bed. The clock had moved only four minutes.

Knoxi was not supposed to meet the pilot until 3 p.m. What would she do with herself for seven more hours? Before another moment passed, she heard a knock. She looked through the peep-hole and then threw open the door.

"Ryan! I didn't expect to see you until I returned tonight with little Zorro." What she failed to notice was Cody and Brandi standing behind him. They all walked into her small room and sat on the bed.

"I only have a few minutes, Fort Knox," Ryan said. "I need to put this device on you and give you some last-minute instructions."

"Uh, okay, where do I wear that? Looks like a knitting needle."

"*Ha!* No. This monitors all your vitals. It also allows me to see what you're seeing; picks up your visual images from the frequency of your optic nerve. I can also hear everything you hear, only better."

"Let me guess," she said. "You invented this?"

"Yep. You wear this right next to your heart. That's it. You just gotta let me tape it on you."

"*Ooo-hoo!* I—I mean we should go in the other room and you can, uh, fix me right up."

"Okay, but I have only a few minutes. We still have work to do at the border post."

When Knoxi disappeared into the other room with Ryan, Cody and Brandi knew it was time to step out for some air. Five minutes later Knoxi and Ryan opened the door and joined them. They decided to get breakfast and began moving toward the café.

Cody walked beside his daughter. "I still don't trust Sagan. I don't buy the reasoning that you're the only one he trusts to get this done. Some other woman with field training should be the one putting her life — I mean putting herself in that spot."

"I don't like it either," Ryan asserted. "Not even a little."

"It is what it is, gentlemen," Knoxi said. "After what that man's seen, I can't blame him for not trusting anyone."

Cody weighed in on Sagan's character. "Untrustworthy people usually *don't* trust anyone. I get that. I get that really well."

Brandi broke her silence and grasped Cody's hand. "Your daughter couldn't walk away from this any more than you could have walked away and left me on the floor of that theater with three men on top of me. One thing I've learned: When you're in a necessary battle you didn't choose, you're doing God's work."

At 3 p.m. Cody and Brandi stood at a distance while they watched Ryan escort "Sister Theresa" toward the small yellow Super Cub. Ryan had left after breakfast to check on his command post, then had returned in time to see his wife board the plane. Knoxi was now wearing the nun's habit.

"Ryan, how can I leave without kissing you?"

"Just imagine how we can make up for it later." Ryan kept his eyes forward as they walked.

"Sweetie, how did you convince your boss to let you come on this mission? Isn't your work top secret?"

"My direct superiors know what I do, but most of the personnel up there think I'm just a clown. They don't believe anything I'm workin' on is ever gonna amount to anything. They all laugh behind my back."

"You must be kidding. You better hope I don't ever come up there. I'll set 'em all straight."

"No. It's good cover. If they think I'm incompetent, it protects against espionage. I mean, if there's nothing of value, there's nothing to steal."

"Well," she resolved, "if you're doing something that'll change the world and you don't care who gets credit, you must be doing God's work."

He kept his voice down. "When you get back, the first thing I wanna do is get you out of this habit you're wearing and debrief you."

"*Ohhhh,* that should take at least a week, right?"

Saint María

Knoxi said goodbye to Ryan as they approached the aircraft which would carry her across the border. "Thank you, sir," she said formally. No kiss. Only a handshake.

The Super Cub is a rugged single-engine aircraft well-suited for mountain and bush flying. It features only two seats installed one behind the other and can be flown from either seat. It is known as a taildragger because it appears to drag its tail when not in flight — two full-size landing gears in front and a small wheel underneath the tail. The wing rests overhead.

"Goodbye, Sister." Ryan shook her hand. "Have a nice flight."

The pilot wore a broad smile as she waited alongside the bright yellow Super Cub. She was mid-twenties with red hair, freckles, and quick metabolism, as revealed by her rapidly-moving jaws while stuffing an even bigger wad of bubble gum into her grinders.

In between chewing, she greeted her passenger. "Good afternoon, Sister Theresa. Ever been in one of these planes before? Is that your boyfriend?"

"Uh, no . . . no, my dear. No to both questions. Have you?"

"Have I?" the pilot asked. "You mean do I have a boyfriend?"

"No, no. I mean have you ever been in one of these planes before?"

"*Ha-haa!* That was a good one, Sister! Yes, ma'am, this is gonna be a fun ride. I'm glad you speak English. Glad you like to joke around. I'm from Cincinnati. Go Cincinnati Reds!"

"So, what's your name, my child?" Knoxi wondered if it was proper for a nun to say "my child" to someone obviously older.

"I'm Jenny. I love baseball and I love flying. Got my license when I was sixteen! Let me get this seatbelt around you." Jenny made certain her backseat passenger was comfortable and secured. "There ya' go, Sister. That should do it."

The pilot jumped into the front seat, closed the side door and yelled, "Clear the prop!" She started the engine.

As they began to taxi, Knoxi donned a headset which she found hanging next to her seat. She wanted to listen to ATC communications. While it was true she had never flown in a Super Cub, she had sat at the controls of similar aircraft. She was instrument-rated with nearly 200 hours of flying experience, but Jenny didn't need to know that.

The aircraft was barely large enough for two. The tandem seating, fore and aft, was cramped. The plan was for her to hold three-year-old Zorro on her lap during the return flight.

She had a yoke and flight instruments at her fingertips. She looked forward over her pilot's shoulder and realized the front control panel was additionally equipped with a state-of-the-art GPS system — weather and terrain avoidance, direct navigation to any point on earth, instrument-landing capabilities, and communications.

They climbed to 9,000 feet. The afternoon countryside was beautiful with green rolling hills. The sky was dotted with scattered cumulonimbus clouds which produced an occasional light shower. These clouds would likely grow in size as the cooler evening approached. The sun was low in the sky as they crossed the border into Haiti. It would be dark before the mission was over.

They passed over a mountain peak, then descended rapidly. Soon, the aircraft began to circle. Jenny had been relatively quiet after becoming airborne, her only communication with traffic controllers. Knoxi figured out that this monthly flight to the church was a special arrangement that did not require a mandatory landing first at an official Haitian port of entry. But, where would they land?

"I don't see an airport," Knoxi said. "I don't even see a field large enough to set this plane down. We're getting really low."

"Don't worry, Sister. I make this trip every month. Scary at first. But just remember, this plane can come in over sixty-foot trees, then do a full-stall descent and land on a field just four-hundred-fifty feet long. When I'm ready to leave, I always take off toward the west cuz the field is downhill that direction. *Ha! I love this!*"

Jenny made a sharp turn back toward the east and chopped the power. The aircraft descended like a fast elevator, coming out of the sky like a lead balloon. The ground came up faster than Knoxi was prepared for, but when Jenny flared the aircraft back, the ship touched down softer than a kiss. The ground was bumpy as the aircraft rolled out and finally came to rest in the shadow of the mountain.

They climbed out of the plane. Knoxi's eyes searched intently in the direction she expected to see the church.

"Can you find it, ma'am? The church? It's right in front of us about fifty yards. See it?"

The light was rapidly fading. Sunset was still forty minutes away, but the mountain and the scattered clouds shadowed everything. Knoxi stared for several minutes before she realized she was already looking at the church. Hidden from the untrained eye but in plain view, the stunning magnificence of Maria de Dios, the church carved into the mountainside, transported her thoughts to another reality. It was like a doorway to eternity, so natural, yet made with human hands.

She quickly came back to herself and glanced around again, gathering intel in a 360-degree radius — an old habit Cody had taught her.

"Are you lookin' for her, ma'am?"

"Uh, looking for whom?"

"Saint Maria. Everybody looks when they get here. Some claim to have seen her, especially with night approaching."

"It's going to be dark when I get back from the church," Knoxi pointed out. "Will you be able to take off and get out of here with no runway lights, no published IFR departure, and no ATC giving you vectors?"

Jenny grinned. "I thought you didn't know anything about flying. Who are you really? You don't act like no sister."

"Believe me," Knoxi assured, "I'm here doing God's work."

"Like I said, ma'am, I take off downhill toward the west, then climb to forty-six-hundred MSL, make a left forty-five-degree bank, pick up a heading of zero-niner-zero and haul ass. Climb at five-hundred feet per minute for ten minutes and you'll clear that mountain we flew over earlier. No sweat."

"Okay, okay, I—I trust you, Jenny. I'll be back here as soon as I can. You'll be ready, won't you?"

"Of course. I'll stand with the plane 'til you come back."

Knoxi walked rapidly toward the entrance of the church, her sandals crunching noisily upon the rocky earth below her feet. She heard the call of a hawk somewhere in the distance but detected no other living sounds.

Suddenly, cold fear slowed her steps. What about a password? She would not know what to say when she reached the door. Why had Rolfe never given her the password? And why had Jenny felt the need to school her on the procedures for flying back across the border under darkness? Jenny was a talker, that was for sure. Knoxi turned her head and looked back, but Jenny was no longer standing near the Super Cub. Where had her pilot gone? Had she decided to catch some winks inside the plane?

Knoxi forced herself to move forward again — too late and too close to turn back now. As she stepped onto the stone portico in front of the door, she heard murmuring voices at her distant six. She turned around but saw no one. Had she imagined the voices? It was getting dark. It was time to complete this. She raised her trembling fist, but before she could knock, a voice inside the door spoke to her. It was gruff, grinding, female, speaking English. "I'd rather be a fool for Jesus . . ."

Knoxi swallowed hard. The voice inside awaited her response — *the password.*

Her heart pounded as she spoke the completed sentence. "I'd rather be a fool for Jesus than a wiseguy for somebody else."

She waited, then moved her ear next to the door. She heard not a sound. How quickly her thoughts unraveled. A fool for Jesus? Of course! This was all a cruel hoax from the sick mind of Rolfe Sagan. He wanted to see how far she would go. She burned from head to toe, stepped back, and looked toward the plane. Still no one standing near the yellow Super Cub.

When the door clicked open, it sounded like someone cocking a gun. Knoxi jumped and used both hands to prevent all her breath from escaping through her mouth. Mother Francesca, the elderly matron, stood in the doorway holding a small boy. His cheeks were rosier than in the picture Rolfe had sent earlier, and Knoxi could now see the facial resemblance she was looking for. The eyes never lie.

"Go quickly, my daughter. This one carries hope for many, but you must decide." She offered Knoxi the child.

But Knoxi's hands wouldn't move. They seemed frozen to her burning cheeks. She could avoid being a target if she simply walked away without the boy. He was obviously sedated, his eyes barely open. He wore a pair of cargo pants and a little workout shirt with a slogan on the chest — *Grandpas need hugs too.*

Knoxi's pledge to not cry was growing more difficult by the moment. She took little Zorro into her hands, wrapped him in a blanket the matron had provided, and turned back toward the plane. As she traversed the crunchy ground again with the child in her arms, she caught sight of a shadowy figure within her peripheral vision. Someone was mirroring her movements. She ran, praying she would not trip over a rock before she reached the aircraft.

"Jenny! Jenny! Start the engine! Jenny? Do you hear me?"

She spotted three bandidos closing on her right. They began shouting, demanding she stop or be shot. Knoxi clutched the child tightly and stopped. "Okay," she whispered to herself, panting. "Don't let 'em see you cry, and never let 'em see you sweat."

Three more bandits showed up, making the total six, all with assault weapons and big ammo belts. Two carried machetes, giving new meaning to the term "hackers" in this region. With handguns for backup, this bunch was truly dressed to kill. Their faces seemed to blend with the night; not so much skin color as darkness of deep soul — bloodthirst, greed. Pirates.

Was Ryan watching this? She used her thumb to make sure the needle-like device was still attached to her chest. Her only chance was to delay things long enough for Ryan and her father to send in their guys who were supposed to be watching. She heard two of the late-arriving rogues discussing the possibility that Saint Maria might be near. She decided to play a card from Elena's bag of tricks — she would pretend not to understand the language.

The leader was soft-spoken at first with cunning eyes. *"Hermana, no queremos hacerte daño. Solo queremos el chico. Eh?"*

"Uh, pardon me, señor. I don't understand. Are you asking me if I need an escort to the plane? How nice of you! I hear there are pirates in this region." She had promised herself to not let them see her cry or sweat. She had made no such promises about telling a lie. "And by the way," she rused, "do you gentlemen like baseball?"

"Eh? Baseball, Sister?" He grinned at his compadres. *"Beisbol?"* They all nodded and smiled back. "Si, we all love baseball. Eh, but why do you ask? We have other important matters to discuss first."

"Well, nothing could be more important right now than getting this little one back to his father in America. He is a famous baseball player for the Dodgers."

"The Dodgers? *Ha-ha!* No. You see, we already buy this boy, so he is our property. We don't want to hurt you, Sister, because you are doing the work of God for the church. But my affection for you only goes so far. You give him to us, we all leave happy. Eh?"

"Not so fast there, amigo. I know two people who won't be happy. One is the *real* father who is willing to pay you to help get his son back, and the other is Saint Maria who is watching right now. If I am not in the air in five minutes with this boy in that plane, you will never see the end of your sorrows."

This created a buzz among the bandits who stared at each other with eyes fully-dilated and glowing red in each pupil.

But the English-speaking leader wasn't fooled. His wry smile stretched his face again. "I tell you what we do, Sister. We will wait for Saint Maria. If she is not here in . . . say . . . five seconds, we shoot you and take the boy. Eh?"

Knoxi had run out of words. Why hadn't they already shot her? Was it because of the nun's habit she was wearing? She counted off the seconds while gripping little Zorro snugly. She felt his body next to her, warm, trusting, tender.

All six pirates moved within five feet of her. She would die regardless. What choice did she have but to hand him over? Choice? Was this what the matron meant? She must choose? She hugged the boy tighter.

Bang! Bang! Bang! Gunshots suddenly split the night air like claps of thunder. Bright flashes, fury, ringing ears, echoes from the nearness of the mountain. She froze again, still standing with the boy.

She tried to close her eyes but could not. Her vision was glued to the shocked face of the sleazy spokesman standing before her gripping his ears, then slumping to the ground, and spitting out his blood at her feet.

The other bandidos began discharging their weapons in every direction, frantically shouting and firing at shadows. Something struck Knoxi in the left heel, causing her to lose balance and fall to the ground with the boy in her arms. The bullets continued ricocheting every direction while Knoxi frantically crawled toward the aircraft.

She slid underneath the fuselage for cover, bumped into something which did not belong there, and shielded the boy as best she could.

When the shooting stopped, she raised her head and peered from beneath the belly of the plane. The fearless leader was lying motionless where he had fallen, two others were crawling away without their weapons, and the other three were gone. Then she realized she was lying against a body, still warm. It was Jenny, her throat cut. She finally shut her eyes. She could still see the flashes underneath her closed eyelids, and the ringing in her ears was deafening.

Still holding Zorro and lying beside Jenny's body, she looked up again and saw someone approaching slowly, deliberately. It was a woman emerging from the dark shadows wearing a black frock and sandals. She carried a gun and walked with a limp. Knoxi had expected to see friendly commandos storming over the field, but they were nowhere in sight.

Whoever this woman was, she was a friend. Knoxi crawled from beneath the aircraft, picked up the drowsy child, then tried to stand, but her left heel could not take the weight and she fell again. She looked down and realized the heel on her left sandal had been completely destroyed by a bullet and the impact had left a dark bruise on the side of her foot. She removed the sandal and limped toward the woman. Rolfe had told her Saint Maria would show up, but who was this person?

"You need . . . you need to take the child and go," the stranger said. "They'll be back. Your own people got delayed on the other side of the hill. They were . . . am . . . ambushed." The woman collapsed.

The cloud cover broke momentarily, allowing the rising moon to make its first appearance. Knoxi could now see that the woman in the dark frock was bleeding. "You're hurt. Let me look at your wounds."

"No, no, Knoxi. I'm done. I've been shot enough to . . . to know. Take the child. Get outta here."

"Oh, please, maybe I can squeeze you in the plane."

"No. By the time you'd reach . . . reach the border, you'd be carrying a corpse. Go now. Take my sandal. I won't be needing it."

"At least tell me your name. Do you have any family?"

"Honey, I'm just a pistol in the wind. It's all I've ever been."

"No, no. Jesus knows who you are —"

"Child, I know that. Me and Jesus, I mean, I already, uh..." She coughed. "It's settled. Star, Star said — Uh, do you know S . . . Starsky and . . . Hutch?"

"Of course. But how —?"

She brightened momentarily, then faded. "Tell that crackshot Star he's still the handsomest man I ever saw." She struggled to get a breath. "Tell him . . . tell him not to be decorating any flagpoles in this country. Too . . . too dangerous . . . yeah . . . too dangerous here." She closed her eyes and took her last breath.

Knoxi quickly pulled off the dead woman's left sandal and installed in on her own foot. Her left heel and ankle were screaming, but she struggled to her feet and moved toward the Super Cub. She would have no time to study the flight manuals or logs. She was already on borrowed time.

She strapped little Zorro into the back seat securely, then climbed into the forward cockpit and sat down. She turned on the master power switch, primed the engine, adjusted the mixture, and placed her fingers on the ignition. But prior to starting the engine, something told her to turn on the forward landing light. When she flipped the light switch, she was mortified to see a woman's face looking at her through the front windshield. The forlorn woman was mumbling something in Spanish. She had zombie-like sunken eyes, a partially bald head, and a contorted, tearful expression. From the pilot seat, Knoxi could see only her face. Had the engine started, the woman would have been cut to shreds by the propeller.

Knoxi leaned out through the open window on the left side of the cockpit intending to tell the woman to move back, but the spectacle before her eyes shattered her already-stretched nerves.

She could now see clearly that the woman's clothing was literally rotting off her body. She carried an infant in her exhausted arms, a baby boy who could have been perhaps six months old, but who looked barely human. She had seen pictures of starving people before, but pictures alone had never revealed the depth of pain as seen face to face. Shades of Mozambique flashed through her mind again.

Knoxi was stunned, and when she listened to the woman's mumbling Spanish, she could no longer hold back tears she had promised to not cry. The woman sobbed, stumbling, begging. She was a picture of indignity and humiliation, pleading not for herself, but for her child.

"*Por favor, toma mi bebé. Llévalo contigo a América. Por favor. No tenemos comida, no tenemos refugio. No tengo leche. Por favor, no lo dejes morir. Por favor, no dejen que mi bebé muera.*" ("Please, take my baby. Take him with you to America. Please. We have no food, no shelter. I have no milk. Please don't let him die. Please, don't let my baby die.")

Then Knoxi heard another voice — a second woman approaching the aircraft from behind. Then a third mother carrying twins emerged from a clump of scrubby bushes. In the shadowy moonlight it was a horror film, but worse. This was real. She had no more room in the plane.

"I can't take your babies. I have no room. Please. I can't take them. Please let me save the one I have in the seat already." She explained it in both languages as she stepped out of the plane, having forgotten she was wearing the nun's habit. She reached out her arms. The women stepped back.

Now the words of Mother Francesca replayed in her mind again. Was this another choice she was to make? Deciding which child lived and which ones would die?

"Oh, God, no. No, no, no. How can I leave them?"

After a moment, the women came closer and let Knoxi extend her arms around them. Maybe it was her own sobbing and prayers that made the women trust her.

Knoxi spoke softly, "*Por favor. Tengo que ir ahora. Te conseguiré ayuda. Lo prometo. Lo siento, lo siento mucho.*" (Please. I have to go. I will bring help. I promise. I'm so sorry. I'm so, so, sorry."

The women wandered away aimlessly and disappeared into the shadows.

Knoxi had forgotten about her left foot. The pain. But the burning and aching returned as she watched the women leave.

She managed to climb aboard, start the engine, and taxi into position for a take off. She couldn't fly and cry at the same time, so she paused to wipe her eyes, then shoved the throttle forward and accelerated toward the line of trees at the western boundary of the clearing. Knoxi lifted off the ground knowing she must be airborne soon enough to clear the sixty-foot treetops, but another unexpected obstacle came first.

She saw muzzle flashes in the distance and heard bullets hitting the aircraft broadside, tearing through the fuselage. She turned left, away from the gunfire, to make the aircraft a smaller target. The bullet sounds stopped, but now she was outside the perimeter of the departure procedure described by Jenny. Seconds later when she entered a cloud bank she lost sight of everything.

With this development, she decided to resume climbing toward the west, heading 270 degrees. This would keep her close to Jenny's departure route. Upon reaching the altitude of 4600 feet, she executed a steep, climbing left turn to a heading of 90 degrees, due east, and continued to climb through the clouds until she broke out on top at 9000 feet.

Now the brilliant moonlight seemed to slow down the pounding in her head, but it did nothing for her shaking hands or her throbbing foot. With the aircraft on automatic pilot, she programmed the GPS.

"Ryan, honey. Ryan? Daddy? I know you're listening to me. I'm still taped. Uh, look, I don't wanna go back to Puerto Plata airport. I turned off the transponder so that no one can track me. We can't let 'em know where I'm taking little Zorro. They knew we were coming."

Suddenly, the engine coughed. She jumped out of her skin. Checking her instruments, she beheld the fuel-pressure needle bouncing up and down like a basketball. The engine was obviously starving for fuel. The pressure indicator returned to normal for a moment before finally falling to zero. The fuel gauges indicated that the right-side fuel tank was now empty.

Looking out the right window, she could see that a gunshot had grazed the underside of the wing, leaving a crease in the fuel tank. It must have happened as she was departing. She switched the fuel-selector to the auxiliary tank located behind the rear seat, but that did nothing to restore fuel pressure. Finally, she switched to the left tank which indicted only half full. The engine started again.

"Ryan, I have an emergency. Gotta recompute my range and then decide where I'm gonna land this thing."

After doing the quick math, she estimated fuel remaining to be only 35 minutes — not enough range to reach any public airport.

"Ryan, Daddy, my aux fuel is inop. The port-side tank is less than half full, and that's all I've got. GPS shows only one airport within my range, but it has no lights. It's a private strip called Rancho Sanchez Aquas, twenty-seven nautical miles from my position. I'm turning to one-one-zero degrees and beginning my descent."

Tracking directly to the small airport by instruments, Knoxi descended into the clouds. No more moon. No stars. No sense of movement. The only scenery was the inside of a cloud. In a few minutes she would break below the ragged cloud cover, but tonight, according to the forecast, that would put her only 600 feet above the ground. Without runway lights and with no moonlight, would she be able to find the landing strip?

Valley of The Shadow

Cody, Brandi, and Ryan remained at the makeshift mission command center at the top of the mountain. Brandi had gone outside to look overhead for the Super Cub, hoping to catch a glimpse should it fly within visual range. She was still looking when she heard Cody's frantic voice.

"Let's go! We have her destination and ETA!"

"Okay. Where's Ryan? Is he going with us?" Brandi opened the passenger door and jumped into the car.

Cody sped away. "No! Ryan's staying here. He practically ordered me outta there. He said he needs to stay and monitor. Told me to take you and go pick Knoxi up."

"What? He ordered you?"

"Don't start. Ryan knows what he's doing. We're better off leaving him alone. Knoxi's in real danger."

Brandi lamented. "She's been in real danger all day. What were we thinking? We're all responsible. It's as much my fault as anyone's."

They sat quietly, then Cody broke the void. "We—we also have a private ambulance on the way."

"How did things get so out of hand?" She wrung her hands.

"We gotta pray she'll have light enough to land," Cody said. "She's never flown one of those little —"

"She'll do fine, she'll do fine! I just wish . . . I wish I could talk to her. *Ohhh*, Cody, she must be so scared! And that poor little boy. *Ohhh*. And after what that child has been through!"

"Stop it!" Cody said, as he spun the squealing tires around a steep curve. "Knoxi invented a new term today, remember? We're in a *No Cry Zone* until further notice."

She covered her face and acknowledged with a nod, blotting her eyes on her sleeve.

~   ~   ~

Knoxi's left foot was about to explode. The pain now extended from her heel down to her toes and all the way up to her left hip. The bullet had not broken the skin, but somehow the force of impact on her sandal heel had traumatized her entire leg.

She tried to move her toes but could not. The sandal was way too tight. She wanted to remove it from her swollen foot but the sandal might provide foot protection should she be forced to crash-land.

When she broke below the clouds, she was still on course for Rancho Sanchez Aguas, but without moonlight it was almost impossible to identify objects on the ground. Her GPS readout indicated she was six miles from the runway which was situated near a reservoir. She decided to look for the body of water first since it might be easier to spot.

The three-year-old boy began to cry. She forced herself to ignore him even as his volume increased. Soon, he was screaming. His sedative had worn off. It was all she could do to not scream with him.

After three minutes, the GPS indicated she was just 1.2 miles from the runway. So far, so good. But now the unthinkable happened. Her engine quit running, creating a strange and terrifying silence. The child even stopped crying. The only remaining sound was the eerie, lonely howling of the wind whistling past the lame-duck aircraft. Time had run out for Knoxi and Zorro.

The reservoir was nowhere in sight, her altitude less than 300 feet. They were going to crash. As the reality took her, she heard familiar words in her mind: "*Though I walk through the valley of the shadow of death, I will fear no evil, for You are with me.*"

"Oh, God. This is not a good night to die. For the children, for the little one on board, for the sake of —"

Suddenly, a deep male voice interrupted her thoughts. "A little crowded in here, isn't it?"

She jumped and swiveled her head right and left but saw nothing. Where had the voice come from? *I imagined it, right?*

"Don't be afraid of me," the voice said. "Turn left to heading zero-two-zero."

"Ryan? Oh, sweetie." She calmed herself. "Ryan, did you hear that? Should I turn left?" She made a sharp left turn to the prescribed heading and kept her eyes peeled, but had no clue what to look for. "Calm down," she whispered to herself. "Hallucinatory stress. You're just imagining things."

She continued on that heading for a few seconds and saw nothing, but it was too late to do anything else. Then, a bright moon peeked out from an opening in the clouds and lit up a shining body of water at twelve o'clock. The crystal-clear image of the moon reflecting in the water shone like a beacon straight ahead less than 100 meters away. She caught her breath — *the reservoir!*

"We aren't dead yet!" she barked. "This is still a no-cry zone!"

One glance at her altimeter told her she was now just 200 feet above the ground — not enough altitude to reach the runway. But in the partly-cloudy moonlight, she spotted a concrete levee which bordered the near side of the reservoir. The levee was barely within range, unlighted, narrow. It would be dicey but it was her only shot.

She lowered the flaps and slowed her approach speed. When the Super Cub touched down on the scant concrete surface, the left tire collapsed, spinning the small plane out of control. The tail swung upward and the aircraft flipped onto its spine and slid at an angle down a steep embankment, finally coming to rest on the muddy slope.

Knoxi heard no sounds and saw nothing but blackness. She tried to open her eyes but they were too heavy. Gradually, she came to her senses. A child was crying. She smelled smoke and began to fidget. The air was hot. Finally, she opened her eyes but the world was upside down. The flames outside her window were coming from above and flowing toward the ground which didn't make sense.

The baby screamed again. The cobwebs broke away when she realized the wings were on fire and that she and her precious passenger were hanging upside down in an inverted aircraft.

When she released her safety belt, she eased onto the ceiling beneath her, crawled through the tight opening between the front and back seats, lay down on the ceiling under little Zorro, and freed him from his restraints. She then kicked open the side door which had been damaged.

When she rolled onto the ground beside the plane holding the boy, it became apparent their fight for survival was not over. The Cub was burning and was in danger of a larger explosion. She saw fuel leaking from the auxiliary tank behind the rear seat.

Her facial skin and hands were hot. Her leg and hip hardly moved with the effort. In order to escape the flames, she would have to carry the boy up the incline to the top of the levy.

She tried to scramble up the hill, but her feet slipped on the muddy ground. Again and again she pushed herself but could manage only a few feet. She finally stopped when her body wouldn't work anymore, gradually slipping downwards toward the burning aircraft.

~   ~   ~

Cody and Brandi arrived at the ranch to find it deserted — no lights, no people. They had to cut through chains to open the gate. They found the intended runway but were surprised to see a long line of diesel trucks parked down the middle of it.

Ryan called to say that Knoxi had touched down a mile short of the runway at the opposite end of the reservoir.

"This runway's unusable," Cody said. "It's a good thing she didn't try to land on it. Uh, Ryan, is the aircraft in one piece? Did she make it? I mean, is she —" Silence, as Cody tried to hide his concern from Brandi. "So, so are you still getting vitals?" Silence again.

Brandi pulled on Cody's arm trying to listen. He finally ended the call. "Ryan isn't sure yet. He's getting only intermittent readings from the neuro-insular cortex sensor he placed on her chest. There is a levee at the far end of the reservoir. That's where she tried to land. C'mon, let's get over there."

The road to the levee was chained off with signs warning to stay away. Again, they had to cut through. As Cody swung the gate open, they saw a gigantic flash of light in the vicinity of the levee. He ran back to the automobile, jumped in, and gunned the engine, spinning the tires again.

Brandi was at a tipping point. "Did you see that flash? Cody, how could she land in this darkness? The levee isn't lighted, and I heard Ryan say ATC wasn't expecting any breaks in the cloud cover for moonlight."

Cody was quiet for a moment before he spoke. "I checked the sigmets and airmets. They forecasted solid stratus up to seven thousand feet. I haven't seen a stitch of moonlight all night. But that doesn't mean they didn't make it. She has instincts. She won't panic. And besides —"

"Oh, Cody. I have the same feeling as when we approached that tavern in Librador years ago. Remember?" Brandi placed her stressed left hand on his knee as he gunned the motor. "I couldn't wait to see if Knoxi was inside that tavern, but I was so afraid to look."

Cody placed his right hand on hers, stared ahead and never flinched.

The flames grew less intense as they approached the site. Cody stopped the car, took Brandi's hand and gently pulled her from the vehicle. "C'mon, let's go find our girl and meet Zorro."

They rushed to the top of the levee. From the high vantage point, they spotted something burning in a distant field. Could have been a pile of rubble. Could have been a crashed airplane. They listened for sounds and heard a child crying nearby. Cody aimed his flashlight down the hill.

"Look!" He said. "Down there!" The child was standing at the bottom of the incline on level ground. They slipped and slid down the 40-foot embankment toward the boy. On their way down, they came upon Knoxi lying motionless in the mud.

Cody knelt beside his daughter and placed his hand along the side of her neck to check for pulse. She grabbed his hand and looked at him but said nothing.

"Fort Knox? Are you still open for business?"

"Hi, Daddy," she whispered. "Where's Mama? Where's Zorro?"

Brandi knelt down holding the child. "We're right here, baby girl. You did a good job."

Cody scanned the gritty slope with his flashlight — long skid marks, scorched ground, broken Plexiglas and yellow paint scrapings on the muddy gravel. He smelled 100 octane avgas, but there was no aircraft.

"What happened here?"

"I — I was slipping toward the flames with Zorro. I couldn't move. I must've passed out."

"So, what happened to the Super Cub?"

"Daddy, do you really have to ask?"

DEBRIEFING

K noxi chose to not ride in the ambulance which met them at the ranch. She had inhaled some smoke but wanted to go directly to the hotel. They obtained a portable oxygen system for her. Little Zorro went to the private hospital for observation and a medical evaluation. Hutch went with him for security.

At 1:15 a.m. Ryan Maxwell carried his wife over the threshold of the Capitan's Suite at Diamante de Dominica Hotel in Puerto Plata. He had reserved this magnificent lodging at one of the finest hotels in the Caribbean to provide Knoxi every comfort after her harrowing and heroic mission — an event for which she would never receive the international accolades she deserved.

The cloud cover had finally cleared at midnight, unveiling a brilliant, high moon over the North Atlantic, its beams shimmering across the breakers near the beach. The light of the moon also bathed their ninth-floor chambers with a soft glow. Ryan mentioned the moon, but Knoxi did not respond.

Knoxi had shed the nun's habit and returned wearing the yellow dress she had left behind that morning. Her aching foot and leg seemed paralyzed. She could not move them and the pain was nearly unbearable. Having endured the traumatic events of the long day, she was bereft of spirit and weak bodily. Ryan now wondered if they should have taken her to the private hospital along with Zorro.

Ryan laid her on a gigantic king bed covered with a thousand scattered rose petals. It was his idea. She may have stormed the gates of Hell, but he knew she was still a pink-rose girl.

"Is it okay if I get you out of these clothes and dunk you in the sauna?"

Knoxi didn't answer. She lay still on the bed, looking up at the ceiling and blinking only occasionally.

Ryan tried again. "Uh, okay. I need to at least look at your leg. Gotta see what's going on. You weren't able to walk earlier. Did the pain meds help any? Your dad is bringing Dr. Graves in from Houston tomorrow."

Knoxi spoke with slurred speech, a languid smile, and drooping eyes. "Good thing you brought your bag of tricks to the party." She cleared her throat. "At least you didn't lose the plane this time."

"I used a retrogenic geoterra remoter and routed the coordinates through my HQ in Colorado." He examined the dark masses underneath the skin on her left foot and ankle.

"Ouch. That's tender."

"At least you have feeling in your foot. We—we thought we had lost you when it happened. I mean, like, we heard all these shots, then you went down. But your eyes musta' been shut because we couldn't see anything. We didn't even know where you were hit."

"The heel. The heel of . . . Uh, did you see her? The woman?"

"The one who showed up when our guys got delayed?" he asked. "She mentioned Star and Hutch. Star said he didn't know she was going to be there. She had told him goodbye a month ago. Said she was fatally ill. Some disease. He had lost track of her."

"I—I don't know her name. She just . . . just came from nowhere like the legend — Saint Maria. Rolfe told me she would show up. But how? I mean, did he know her? How much more does Rolfe know?"

"She gave you her sandal. That's when we knew your foot had been injured in some way."

"Oh, that feels good. Whatever you're doing to my foot, keep doing it."

"So, Fort Knox, do you feel like listening to some good news?"

"Good news?" she mumbled, closing her eyes completely.

"Sagan released his media bomb early, *before* you reached Haiti, *not after* the mission. He probably thought the broadcast would create a diversion so the pirates wouldn't notice you. It was a smokescreen. Too bad it didn't work. Somebody knew you were coming."

Knoxi seemed oblivious, her mind elsewhere, her face devoid of expression. Long teardrops now streamed downward over her cheeks. These weren't the tears Ryan had expected — not tears of joy or relief, but rather of deep sorrow.

"Hey, Supergirl, it's over. We won. This is good news, right?"

"I saw his face." She writhed. "I saw his face, Ryan."

"Whose face?"

"He wasn't what I expected." She sat up. "I mean, there was no stained glass. No choir . . . no angels . . ." Her voice faded like a whisper. "And there was no room."

"What face?"

"It was Jesus. I tell you I saw Him. But He didn't look like the pictures I've seen. He was a child with infected eyes . . . tired, hungry, dying. He was a woman with shriveled breasts. Faces with no hope . . . no future. How could I choose between them?"

Tearful and overcome, Knoxi folded herself into Ryan's arms. "I told them I had no room. I told them *all* I had no room, don't you see?"

"*Shhhh.* We'll talk about it later." Ryan cradled his weeping beauty and carried her slowly toward the garden bath. He had pressed the remote earlier, filling the sauna and programming the water temp and bubbles.

As they approached the bathroom door, he soothed her bruised soul with quiet words. "Rolfe Sagan's revelations have broken the back of the underground. The mega merger had been thirty years in the making. Now, it's coming unraveled in just one night."

When they entered the room, the tub was filled to the brim with crystal-clear water and bubbles overflowing.

"Bubbles? Ryan, you went to so much trouble. I'm sorry I'm not up for the debriefing you were expecting."

He helped Knoxi remove her yellow dress, then carefully lowered her into the bubbling water. "I have no complaints," he assured. "We have the rest of our lives for debriefing. Tonight, you have faced down dark principalities, and you've put a smile back on God's lips."

"Ryan," she sniffled, "If that's true, why am I crying? I can't stop, and my leg doesn't work anymore."

"These tears have been trapped inside you all day. You gotta let 'em out. Tonight, tears are better than words. Words can be used over and over. Words can get old, but tears can be used only one time, and they're always fresh, always new."

"That sounded sweet but made absolutely no sense." She slipped her face underneath the bubbles and reemerged. "*Ohhh*, sweetie," she sighed. "I didn't know you were *such* an accomplished masseur. I can wiggle my toes already."

Your dad told me about this Marine Corps student pilot trying to earn his wings, who had an emergency one night, and —"

"Yeah, I know, I know," she interrupted. "When he landed they had to pry his fingers off the yoke 'cause he was so scared."

"Yep. It was a month before the kid regained use of his arm."

"A week," she said. "It was only a week."

"Well, there you go." He chuckled.

Ryan picked up the remote and dimmed the bath lights. He reached across and opened the window shade, allowing the full moon to have its way with them.

"When the gunshot to your heel took you down, it probably saved your life. There were so many bullets flying through the air, but none of 'em could find you."

She slipped beneath the water again and came back up. "Oh, Ryan." She touched his cheek. "You've seen me cry more than once, but I've never seen a tear in your eye until this moment."

Ryan's face straightened. In the soft moonlight, his big eyes were warmer than roasted chestnuts in winter. Knoxi shut her eyelids and reveled in the moment.

Ryan leaned in and kissed her on the cheek. "Your choice was never about choosing between the starving kids," he whispered. "It was about standing on that porch and deciding whether to take Annie's son into your hands and become a target, or leave him behind and run for your life." He shut his eyes tightly. "When God asks you to make a choice, it means He knows you'll make the right one, and that you'll find His strength to live with it."

~   ~   ~

At daybreak, a new era had begun. Rolfe Sagan was back, if only for one final play. By mid-morning, his sensational revelations had stunned the corporate world. Three suicides had been reported among prominent CEOs, and one major news corporation had filed for protection under federal bankruptcy laws. The Dow Jones Industrials fell 1700 points in the first trading hour, and business news channels struggled to assemble enough people in their studios after prominent network gurus had been named as co-conspirators.

Ryan and Knoxi slept until late morning. Ryan had wanted Knoxi to rest in bed for at least twenty-four hours, but at precisely 11:00 a.m. they were awakened when the landline rang. Ryan fumbled for the receiver.

Knoxi arose and retreated to the walk-in closet in the next room to get dressed. Meanwhile, Cody and Brandi knocked on the door.

Ryan's call ended as he unlocked the door to receive the Muskets. "Knoxi went to the other room while I was on the phone," Ryan told them. "She's prolly getting dressed. She was walking better."

"Whew, that's a relief." Cody breathed a sigh. "I wrangled with it all night. I arranged a specialist from Houston to examine her today, but his flight here has been delayed."

Just then Knoxi came back into the room walking with a slight limp. "I feel . . . well, I'm not sure how I feel."

Ryan had the floor. "Everybody, let's go to the patio. I have some news. The call I just received was a total surprise. We need to discuss it." They headed toward the open-air patio.

Their ninth-floor veranda provided a hawkeye view of the Dominican Silver Coast. It was crawling with spring tourists. The sight of ocean-going vessels on the sun-splashed North Atlantic in the distance — luxury liners, tankers, yachts, sailboats — gave proof that life and commerce would go on, at least for some. Slow-drifting cumulus clouds overhead and gentle sea breezes created the perfect setting for a celebration, but there would be no victory dance this morning. They gathered the chairs around the table and sat down.

Ryan began. "I just got a call from General Ty Mason's aide. The general is here for a summit with Caribbean leaders about piracy issues. He says I am being invited — and I use that word loosely — to a conference in his aircraft this afternoon at 1500 hours. He specifically requested that Knoxi be there, and he suggested we not be late."

Knoxi seemed tuned out. "Uh, piracy issues? Yeah, I agree it's an issue, but —"

"Fort Knox?" Ryan snapped his fingers in front of her face. "Hey! Did you hear?"

Knoxi hardly blinked. "Yes. I've . . . I mean we've been asked to come to the airport?"

Brandi seemed alarmed as she reached across the table toward her daughter. "Knoxi, General Mason, the Chairman of the Joint Chiefs, has asked you to come to his plane this afternoon for a meeting. Are you aware of what that might mean?"

Knoxi frowned. "They must already know everything. Or, they're gonna question me. What do I tell them? How many laws have we broken? I mean, we've initiated a paramilitary incursion into a sovereign nation directed by an employee of the US Department of Defense."

"The general's trip has been scheduled for several weeks," Ryan said. "It might be just a courtesy call. We covered our tracks. I don't believe anyone could connect us to last night."

"What about the crashed plane? Don't you think my DNA and fingerprints are gonna be everywhere? What about the Dominican news? Aren't they all over this?"

"Uh, not exactly," Ryan answered. "Rolfe's social media revelations are grabbing everyone's attention."

"It doesn't matter," Knoxi resigned herself. "I'm still tryin' to wrap my head around it. I don't wanna think about any more crises. Just whatever happens will happen. I'll take the blame for all of it."

Ryan's concern was easy to read. Knoxi had lost her will to fight. "I wanna know what you think, Cody. You're the only one among us with any combat experience. Say something. Please, sir."

Cody flashed a pleasing smile. "I suggest we get breakfast. There's a buffet at the restaurant downstairs. Let's not jump to conclusions 'til we hear what the general has to say."

After the meeting broke, Cody caught his daughter's hand and asked her to stay with him for a few minutes.

"Hey," he began. "Remember that stupid poem I wrote you when you were little? I called it 'Hey There, Beautiful.'"

"Daddy, that wasn't stupid. It still makes Mama cry when she reads it. She saved that crinkled-up paper you wrote it on."

Cody dropped his eyes. "Sometimes, baby girl, things don't make sense. Like last night. I mean, have you had time —?"

"Have I had time to sort it out? Or time to cry? Is that what you're asking?" She walked a few steps to the rail and looked down at the tiny people below. "I can still *smell* those men. I see them. I still see those women when I close my eyes. How can I go back to playing basketball after last night? That would be meaningless now. I should be happy today. Why do I feel so . . . so wounded?"

"Because last night you came face to face with the lowest of humanity. It will always leave you shaking your head, feeling angry, feeling guilty because you can't save everyone."

She turned around and faced him. "Daddy, I promised those women I would help them."

Cody pocketed his hands. "Our guys were delayed getting to you, but they located the woman with the twins and delivered them to the Red Cross today. She was saved because you drew her into the open."

"What about the other two women?"

He shook his head. "We didn't want to tell you. I'm sorry." He exhaled slowly. "You don't need to hear any more about that."

She turned away again and stared down at the street traffic.

Cody moved close behind her and held her shoulders. "It's always about the people we couldn't save," he confided softly. "Those are the ones that haunt us."

She nodded. "I understand it wasn't my fault, but that doesn't help. And the experience has left me terrified. Daddy, I was *so* scared. I don't believe I could do this again."

"What you did goes beyond bravery," Cody said. "It was compassion that drove you. Everyone's scared, but your pain from seeing the suffering in your world is greater than your fear of doing something about it. That's why you would do it again, Fort Knox."

She turned and hugged his neck. "Daddy, for a man who pretends to be ordinary, you can be so profound. When does it ever get easier? I mean, the pain you mentioned; it's still there. And the future I had planned doesn't motivate me anymore. None of it seems important after this."

He stared into her eyes and put his arms around her waist. "No warrior returns unwounded. A piece of us never comes home. God sends people into our lives to fill in the missing pieces. Your mother was there for me, and you have a life with Ryan to go back to."

"You mean if General Mason doesn't bring charges against us?" She folded her arms and leaned back against the railing. "Daddy, Ryan will make such a good father. But when will I ever see him? I mean, like, tomorrow he's off to Colorado again to work in that glorified deep-freeze. *Ohh*, I dread being without him right now."

Knoxi's voice was now quivering. Cody waited. She needed a moment.

"I'm not going to cry," she said. "I promise. But sometimes . . . sometimes it seems God isn't paying attention. I mean, the evil, those poor women, the suffering babies."

Cody hung his thumbs on his front pockets. "When your mother and I met, you were almost two years old. When we were attacked for the second time that week, I had to kill two men. I totally shut down. I gave up. Your mom, she—she hardly knew me, but she risked her life to approach me and she threw her love around me like a blanket."

"Daddy, you've told me this story before."

"Yeah, I know, I know. But here's what I didn't tell you. I was savin' it for the right moment. See, later that night, you still wouldn't stop crying. Finally, I picked you up. You were the purest, most innocent thing I had ever touched. You stopped crying and grinned at me as big as the sky. When I felt your heart beating, I could feel mine beating again. I had seen those kids burn to death in Afghanistan, but you fixed broken places in me that even your mom couldn't reach."

"I remember only bits and pieces of that night," she said "I still hear the sounds of the shooting, my ringing ears. I was so scared until you picked me up, but I don't remember much else."

Cody smiled. "You looked straight at me and said, 'You never know,' just as plain as sunrise. Until then, you had never spoken a word in your whole life. We all knew it was a miracle. After the horrible things we had seen, we figured it was God's way of telling us He was paying attention after all."

"Daddy, I—I need to ask you something else." She turned and put her hands on the railing again and gazed far out to sea. "Did you see any angels when you went to Heaven?"

"I did. They were different than I had pictured. They're created with different personalities, different sizes, colors — same as people. He sends 'em to protect and fight for us sometimes. Why do you ask?"

"So, last night . . . last night I was three hundred AGL when the engine starved out. I was trackin' direct to the ranch, but I didn't have enough altitude to make it. Then, this . . . this voice that sounded like the Jolly Green Giant spoke to me. He made some crack about how cramped he felt inside the plane, then told me to pick up a heading of twenty degrees. He told me not to be afraid. *Ha!* I was petrified outta my mind."

"So that's how you ended up at the levee?"

"Exactly. I mean, it all worked out, but couldn't it have been just an acute hallucinatory psychosis? Like, I mean, stress can do crazy things to your mind, right?"

"What about the visibility?"

"It was the moon. It lit up the reservoir like a heads-up display."

"Baby girl, there was no moon last night. Not for anyone else, that is."

WHERE'S THE GENERAL?

Hours seemed like days as Knoxi counted off the time until their meeting with General Mason. Several times she walked back onto the patio and stared in the direction of the airport, hoping to see the general's plane departing the island early. Meeting General Mason today was the last thing she and Ryan wanted to do.

Hispaniola, the island which was divided into two countries — Haiti and the Dominican Republic — had been a favorite hangout of pirates for centuries. The modern pirate was equipped with technology and fueled by the unrest of masses. Piracy was once considered romantic, even honorable by some, but no more. The revenue losses to shipping lines and the trafficking of people, a deplorable enterprise, had taken the romance and honor out of the equation, enough to draw General Mason to the scene.

At last, their ride showed up. It was time. Ryan and Knoxi were taken by Hummer to the airport, then passed through security and escorted by US Marines to the aircraft. The boarding platform had too many steps to count. Knoxi's left foot began to cramp as she climbed the stairs toward the forward entry door.

When they entered the airplane, two Secret Service agents met them. One wore a smirkish grin. "This way, sir, ma'am."

They were led toward the meeting room at the rear of the aircraft. Ryan and Knoxi could see the door where they were headed. The leather seats on both sides of the aisle were worn, stained, torn in places. Perhaps five-star generals didn't rate.

Knoxi breathed hard as the door opened. The general was nowhere in sight. Sitting at a small conference table in the cramped compartment was a woman with a familiar face — Secretary of Defense Amy Foster.

"Hello, Ryan." The secretary stood up. "And hello to you, Knoxi. How does it feel to be married to this Casanova?"

Knoxi's mouth gaped open. "Madame Secretary? What a . . . what a surprise."

"Hello, Madame Secretary," Ryan said. "We didn't know you were coming."

"Neither did anyone else," she grinned flatly. "Make sure we keep it that way." She invited them to sit. "Want some coffee?"

"Any time the SecDef arrives unannounced, something's up," Ryan said. "So, if you don't mind my asking —"

"It was a last-minute decision. We got wind of some strange happenings in this area last night." She picked up the glass coffee pot. "Some satellite images made no sense. A small aircraft crashed, then reappeared in a different location, then totally disappeared altogether." She poured them each a cup. "You kids know anything about that?"

Knoxi stared at Ryan, but he did not return her glance. "Uh, what type of plane was it, ma'am?" Ryan asked.

"Oh, that's what I figured; neither of you would know anything. It was my job to ask. Infrared imaging on this island is spooky anyway. A plane is missing along with the pilot, a small boy, and a Sister Theresa that no one has heard of."

Knoxi leaned forward. "Uh, Madame Secretary, you say the plane moved, then disappeared? So . . . where do you think it is?" She turned and tossed Ryan a confused expression.

Secretary Foster took a sip of coffee. "How's your honeymoon so far, dear?"

Knoxi swallowed hard. "Uh, the honeymoon? It's . . . ."

"You and Ryan will have adjustments to make, but that can be glorious, right?" The secretary took another sip. "By the way, I'm sure you've heard about the reemergence and the subsequent demise of

Rolfe Sagan last night. He didn't last long. His body has been found in Buenos Aires — death confirmed, so I hear."

Ryan sounded surprised. "Sagan dead?"

"Affirmative. But we have only begun to research his findings. If they're legit, what do you think turned him? We've been investigating him for years, but he was too smart and too popular."

"Well, ma'am," Ryan responded, "you never know. I'm sure you've heard about the confrontation Knoxi had with him at the University of Texas."

"Of course. But Ryan, my dear, Rolfe was just playing with Knoxi. Playing games was his favorite thing. He corrupted many, but others counted him a hero. We've been handed a goldmine of damaging information on what may be the largest underground attempt to profiteer from slavery in our lifetime. Maybe it doesn't matter why Sagan turned."

"That's . . . good news," Ryan said. "But I, uh —"

Knoxi stood up. "Madame Secretary, I need to —"

"I hate to interrupt." The secretary raised her hands. "Ryan, could you give us the room, please? I think we women have a couple of things to discuss alone if you have no objection."

Ryan had no objection. After all, she was the Secretary of Defense and his boss. He smiled, nodded, and excused himself, kissing Knoxi on the cheek as he departed.

The secretary stood and walked to the refreshment bar, then turned around. "Knoxi, honey, I know your mother, but I don't know you very well. I remember the day we met at Methodist Hospital when your father was . . . well, you know."

"Yes, ma'am. I was younger then."

"Oh, it wasn't that long ago. Barely over a year. I never forgot those eyes of yours. Honey, they were more than beautiful. They had a confidence and wisdom beyond your years, even in that difficult circumstance. I thought I was in charge that day until I met you. But today, I don't see that same fire. I noticed it the moment you walked through the door."

Knoxi fought tears again. Her eyes burned, but she said not a word.

"Child, what are you going to do with the rest of your life?"

"I'm not sure." Knoxi blotted her eyes. "I just can't —"

"By the way, did you hear about your friend Jeremy?"

"Jeremy? I—I'm not sure."

"Do you know he made the Dodgers? Spring training broke yesterday and Jeremy McNair will be in center field tomorrow for Dodgers Opening Night in LA."

"*Ohhh*, of course. Opening Night. That's wonderful."

"Well then, you also know that he and his wife Annabelle have been trying to adopt a three-year-old boy from, uh . . . let me find those adoption papers. Here they are! He's from San Antonio! Here is all the paperwork, his complete file."

"Uh, paperwork? You mean —"

"I know you must be happy for them. Wait until you hear what I want you and Ryan to do. See, we have arranged a brief, private presentation to be held in the Dodgers' clubhouse before the game, so that all Jeremy's teammates can congratulate the couple. I cannot think of a more appropriate person to deliver the child to his new parents than you, Knoxi Maxwell."

"Madame Secretary, I am so honored, but why me?"

"Now, listen up. We work our tails off every day trying to make a difference, and what we see in return is mostly crap. Especially from the guys at Justice. Too many good guys get their hands slapped, while too many bad guys can't be touched. But this morning . . . what I mean is, sometimes we need to see the good, feel it, experience it. Sometimes we need to hold something beautiful in our own two arms. Ryan will accompany you. After that, both of you get lost for a while."

"Uh, get lost? I thought Ryan had to be at work."

"*Ha-haa!* Are you kidding me? Nobody up there takes him seriously. He never accomplishes a thing. Don't you know that?"

"Oh, totally! Ryan has told me again and again how lazy and incompetent he is!"

"Right. It's those scholars in Congress who really make the wheels turn. I mean, right now they're working hard on a bill to have the American raw peanut declared an endangered species."

"Yep!" Knoxi grinned. "That's progress!"

The secretary sighed. "It's easy to get in over your head, Knoxi. Take some time. You and Ryan are better as a team than either of you alone. Establish your relationship, your home. And remember, some of the most world-changing acts in history are performed by those no one ever hears about."

~   ~   ~

Dodger Stadium
Opening Night

It was the first official game of the season. Fans had been lining up for several hours outside Dodger Stadium expending nervous energy while waiting for the gates to open. Ryan and Knoxi arrived just after they had opened those gates, and the lines of people were still streaming up the hill at Chavez Ravine, the site of the ballpark.

Ryan looked at his watch. "It's still an hour and a half 'til game time. The driver'll take us directly to the players' gate and we'll be ushered into the Dodgers clubhouse from there."

They rode in a VIP limo with Julian Carroll, the director of an adoption agency in San Antonio, Texas. His presence put the public stamp of authenticity on the event which was about to unfold.

Knoxi, who had been fighting tears since landing at LAX, held little Zorro on her lap. He was fidgety, cranky. It had been a long week for the small, dark-eyed youngster who had no home, no parents, and no country.

"Oh, I hope they were able to get Annie into the clubhouse. All those rich professional athletes; how cooperative will they be? I can see this becoming a huge disaster."

Ryan flashed a chipper grin "Hey, what's not to like about this?"

"Well, for one thing, this little guy hasn't spoken a word since I picked him up, and right now he isn't in a good mood."

The car stopped in front of the gate. Stadium security and two LA cops escorted them into the Dodgers' clubhouse. The ballplayers were loud. Knoxi and Ryan could hear them long before reaching the door to the meeting room. Opening-night jitters coupled with the presence of Jeremy's beautiful young wife in the clubhouse had everyone hyped. Team members were perspiring heavily, having just come off the playing field from pregame workouts. Jeremy, the youngest player on the team, stood with Annie who looked somewhat out of place.

After Director Carroll appeared in the doorway, Dodgers' Manager Jim Morisey took center stage. "Alright, listen up, guys. I know this is unusual, but we get so few special moments, you know, and, uh, you know, we should be reminded again, you know, how great this country is. I wanna bring on Mr. Carroll Julian to make a presentation . . . uh, wait." He installed his spectacles. "I misread that name. It's Mr. Julian Carroll — sorry about that. Opening game jitters, you know. He's gunna make a, uh, you know, make a presentation to our rookie center fielder and his wife, uh . . . Annabelle."

The room quieted down. Secretary Foster's offices had arranged the pregame meeting, but had revealed no specific details. When Annie and Jeremy saw Knoxi enter the room with a small boy, Jeremy's game-face scowl disappeared and Annie's cheeks became as pallid as the last ghost rider. Mr. Carroll froze with the sudden realization that something bigger was happening than his remarks were prepared for.

Knoxi walked into the room with the small child resting his head on her shoulder. She giggled, then cried, then giggled again as she slowly moved toward Annie, whose shaking hands had latched onto Jeremy's big right arm.

Annie's inquisitive eyes were answered by Knoxi's assuring and tearful nod. As Annie reached out, the room became so still the players could almost hear their own tears hitting the floor. This was no ordinary adoption. Something here transcended baseball. ~~They had no idea.~~

Mother and son beheld each other for the first time in over two years. Annie delicately dropped to her knees with the boy in her arms, looked up, and invited Jeremy to join her. Jeremy never would have favored losing the moment in front of his teammates, but he knelt beside Annie, giving thanks to God, unashamed of the tears streaming down his sweaty cheeks. As the liberated child met his father for the first time, forty ballplayers, coaches and team officials removed their hats and huddled close.

Ryan and Knoxi had decided in advance that this moment should belong only to the McNairs, little Zorro, and their baseball family. They turned silently and walked hand-in-hand toward the exit, leaving behind perhaps the quietest opening-night clubhouse in the history of baseball. As they departed, they heard behind them what Annie had once described as "the purest music God ever made" — *the laughter of a child.*

Extra Innings Lodge

Six days later

Phoenix, Arizona. The day began like any other for Carlos Santana, the sometimes plumber, sometimes preacher, and friend to Jeremy and Annie McNair. It had been a week since the Dodgers had broken training camp and departed for Los Angeles.

Carlos' wife Diana had returned from Mexico with their two daughters after a two-year separation, and the Santanas had begun to put their lives back together. On this particular morning, Carlos had driven to Extra Innings Lodge, as usual, to do his daily maintenance and make his rounds. The management had given him more and more responsibilities, and life had begun to blossom for his family on several fronts.

During spring training, the Santanas had become close friends with Jeremy and Annie. Diana Santana had been an English teacher in Mexico, and she hoped to be employed in the coming year by a local high school. Meanwhile, she began to spend many weekly hours helping Annie improve her English while Jeremy was with the team.

Jeremy and Annie had also become regular attendees at Carlos' small Spanish-speaking church on Indian School Road. Annie translated Carlos' sermons for Jeremy, whispering them into his ear as they were delivered. When it was announced that Jeremy had made the Dodgers' opening day roster, the church gave the tall rookie outfielder a small going away present — a Dodgers game jersey with the words "Honorary Mexican" written across the back shoulders. Jeremy promised he would wear it to charity events and news conferences, and that when anyone asked about it he would reply by telling of Carlos' little church, their work with the poor, and the encouraging words which had helped shape his life — "Things can turn on a dime."

Now that spring training was over, the Santanas watched the Dodger games on cable in the hotel lobby each night. On the Dodgers' opening night, after going hitless in his first three plate appearances, Jeremy stepped into the batter's box in the bottom of the ninth inning and hit a game-winning home run, delighting 50,000 delirious fans, bringing them victory in his first game, just as his father had done.

Carlos, Diana, and their two girls called for everyone to gather around the TV when they saw Jeremy come onto the screen for an interview after the contest. They cried when Jeremy surprised the world by introducing his wife, a beaming and tearful Annie, and their handsome son Zorro. They had been praying and waiting, Jeremy said, for the child to join them, but things had looked impossible. They had no idea their prayers had been answered until one hour before game time.

Now, six days later, Carlos had finished his rounds and was anxious to go home and prepare his next sermon. He threw his toolbox into the bed of his old truck, opened the door and slid into the driver's seat, being careful not to snag his britches on the exposed springs. He started the engine and drove forward a few feet, but when he attempted second gear, the shift wouldn't budge and the vehicle began to smoke. He wasn't going anywhere. He shut off the engine.

As he stood beside his smoking vehicle, he heard a commotion near the front entrance of the lodge. A small crowd had gathered to watch two men unload a vehicle from a flatbed truck. Carlos walked slowly toward the curious crowd, wondering if someone might offer to take him home.

One of the bystanders saw him approaching and motioned to him. "Hey Carlos, come over here quick! This is for you! Come sign your name to receive it."

Carlos stood still and just stared. It was a vehicle. Any fool could tell that. It was wrapped in a form-fitting, padded covering and shaped like a truck. This must be a mistake. As he came near, the delivery driver handed him a form to sign and passed him a letter. He tore open the envelope.

Dear Carlos, Diana, Maria, and Lucia:

We miss you guys. Can't wait for you to meet our son. Here's a few pics.

I suppose you heard about my opening night home run. The first in my career. I'm sending you the ball I hit out of Dodger Stadium that night. You'll find it in the glove compartment.

In the off-season, Annie and I want to get involved with your street mission for the homeless.

I hope you like the way I had the truck restored. It's yours.

Jeremy, Annie, and Zorro

Carlos pulled the cover off the vehicle. It had been Jeremy's low-rider; the same truck which had needed jumper cables when he had first met the couple. It was now a shimmering dark blue metallic with spirited silver flames on the hood, a new engine, impact sound with satellite radio, and custom interior. When Carlos opened the door, he leaned over the plush leather seat and opened the glove compartment.

The home-run baseball had been mounted in a nifty display case crowned with the Dodgers' logo on the top. Clearly visible on the surface of the ball were these words in Jeremy's handwriting:

"With God, things can turn on a dime." – Jeremy McNair

THE CHOPPER

Fifteen years later
South Miami Beach

How much farther? I need to stretch my legs. My foot's acting up again."

Ryan looked at his watch. "With this traffic, about fifteen more minutes to the resort."

"I wouldn't miss this for the world," Knoxi said. "It's too bad Rolfe Sagan didn't live to see how prominent his grandson has become. They're expecting a hundred-thousand fans to show up."

Ryan nodded. "Yep. You know, with all the knowledge and information Sagan had and the technology he was able to access, why didn't he try to rule the world himself? He was content to remain in the shadows and help someone else get all the credit for the evil he unleashed. That's kind of paradoxical isn't it?"

"Paradoxical?"

"Sure. He had this in-your-face arrogance coupled with the humility to let someone else take credit. He always stayed in the shadows while others basked in the limelight. Why didn't he just manipulate himself to the top of the food chain?"

"I don't believe Rolfe wanted to rule the world. His favorite game was to make fools of everyone around him, letting them believe they were powerful, then laughing at them behind their backs. That's what he craved more than anything."

"Until he learned he had a daughter and grandchild," Ryan said. "Something changed in him."

"I'm not sure," Knoxi answered. "I think he just wanted to see if he could manipulate something good for a change. His grandest achievement was manipulating me to pose as a nun and do something I was never qualified to do. I still have no idea how he managed to find little Zorro."

"Like I said, with all his capabilities, he could've been the most powerful man in the world. Instead, he was only as powerful as he needed to be to get what he wanted. You and Virginia Cutter were the only two individuals in the whole world he trusted."

"Hey, Dad, Professor Ross says Rolf Sagan saved the world and paid for it with his life.

"Yeah, Dad, Professor Ross says Rolfe Sagan saved the world and paid for it with his life."

Ryan kept his eyes on the road. "We shudda named our twins Pete and Repete."

"Mom, how come you know so many famous people like Rolfe Sagan? We don't know any famous people."

"Yeah, Mom, we don't know any famous people."

"Well, your Grandpa Cody is pretty famous and Zorro's famous."

"They aren't famous. We've known them forever."

"Mom! Why can't we go swimming? It's a perfect day. I mean we brought our boards and everything."

"Yeah, Mom. Why can't we go swimming? It's a perfect day. We brought our boards and everything."

"I told you already," Knoxi reminded them, "it's about the helicopter. Ever since it showed up on the sand last week, this place has been infested with sharks." She turned and looked at her sons in the back seat. "It isn't safe and it's like this all the way down to the Keys."

"Well, can't Dad just make all the sharks disappear?"

"What? Disappear?"

"Sure, Mom, like on Oahu last September. I mean, I've never seen anything like it."

"I told you, that was just a rumor. Don't believe everything you hear. Your dad? Make sharks disappear? C'mon, guys."

"So how come he promised to show us how to do it someday?"

Knoxi looked at Ryan. "You promised to show your sons how to make sharks disappear?"

"Uh, well, not in so many words, but . . ." He twiddled his fingers on the steering wheel.

"It's okay, Mom. I mean we can still have fun. Remember when we went to Zorro's gig at Albert Hall in London? I told those little kids my name was Albert and my twin brother's name was Hall. The next day we told the same kids I was Hall and he was Albert. They couldn't even remember which one of us was white and which was black."

"I didn't know about that. You boys are twelve! You're practically grown men." She poked Ryan. "Did you hear that? They've been hanging around Star and Hutch too much, now that they're retired."

"Star and Hutch are cool as cake, Mom."

"Yeah, Mom, Star and Hutch are cool as cake."

"Listen to that!" Knoxi ruminated. "I mean, these are your own sons — Uh, sweetie, what are you looking at?"

Ryan was focused on a special news bulletin just arriving over the *PhaseScreen*. "Hey, take a look at this. It's about the helicopter."

He pulled over to the side of the road. Other vehicles were doing the same. A stretched black limo with tinted glass pulled in behind them. They were now only a few minutes from South Miami Beach where they had planned to spend the day enjoying the festive culture which had grown up around the mysterious helicopter. The chopper had materialized on the beach a week before. Coastal waters had been closed several days due to a sudden surge in shark activity which had seemed to accompany the chopper's arrival.

Now, people were all abuzz. Some had pulled over to watch their PhaseScreens while others had attempted to speed up and race ahead to the beach. The broadcast even prompted some to flee . . .

"Ladies and gentlemen, Jess Neely, BNN, reporting live from South Miami Beach. Well, just as suddenly as it appeared here one week ago, the helicopter has disappeared yet again. Fifteen minutes ago, the Twin Ranger vanished.

"Officials are clearing the beach. Regrettably, Zorro's appearance has been canceled. At least a hundred thousand were expected to fill the arena in back of the Eastmore to hear the young entertainer's tribute to the famous Glorietta Zomata, whose life apparently ended in that helicopter many years ago. Zorro also promised to introduce a famous star from the past who was to announce her comeback and perform with him.

"Uh, wait. This just in. I'm being told there has been another development. My director is now informing me — Wait. Let me show you this image.

"What we are looking at is a live shot taken by the Prater moon-based telescope. We've been watching Asteroid Bella-2 closely this year as it makes the final leg of its journey toward a collision two months from now with Jupiter. Thousands of pictures have been taken during the past few years, but look carefully at this live shot. See this blip? It was not there earlier today. Now, enlarge it and what do you see?

"This image is not fake. We can clearly see the helicopter sitting near this crevice on the surface of Bella 2. I'm hearing in my headphones a suggestion

that this may prove we aren't alone in the universe. Science knows of no earthly technology capable of moving an object from this beach to that asteroid in a matter of minutes.

"So, what's going on here? Years ago, scientists spotted another mysterious image on this asteroid. It was nicknamed 'Squadcar' because it somewhat resembled a black SUV. It was never conclusive, however, and it disappeared when a large space rock collided with Bella-2. Scientists never —"

Ryan turned off the sound but left the video playing.

"Dad, did you make the helicopter move?"

"Yeah, Dad, did you move the helicopter?"

Knoxi cut off the video. "You boys don't need to see this!"

"Mom, what do you mean we don't need to see this?"

"Yeah, Mom, what do you mean we don't need to see this?"

"Ryan! Quick. Hit the *Phazaar!* We need to talk!"

"Again?" Ryan punched the yellow Phazaar button, placing an eighteen-second time warp in the "quantum zone" between the front and back seats, making the front occupants invisible and inaudible to those in the back.

In their instant privacy, Knoxi whispered, but *loudly.* "You said you had no idea where the helicopter went, then after all the years, it shows up on this beach? Now, a week later it disappears and shows up on the same asteroid where the SUV went? Can't you get a grip?"

"Me? Get a grip? You call outta nowhere wanting me to move a helo, and then call again and ask me to make an SUV disappear. Do you know how crazy that sounds?"

"Certifiable!" She giggled, then laughed so hard she cried.

"I mean, its—it's not as simple as rocket science!" he explained. "And, no need to whisper. The boys can't hear us."

"I know that!" she whispered again, trying to catch her breath.

The time warp disintegrated, returning them to visibility.

"Mom, Dad, what were you doing? Were you making out?"

"Yeah, Mom, Dad, were you making out? Why's Mom crying?"

"Your mother and I were just talking."

"Dad, did you invent Phazaar? Can I get one for my Hover-Buggie?"

"Yeah, Dad, can we get Phazaars for our Hover-Buggies? I mean, Phazaar is just a series of elementary fusiform gyros with a deuron superflexor, right?"

"You guys aren't legally old enough yet."

"Are we old enough to know why Mom knew Rolfe Sagan?"

"One day, your mother will tell you her story. You need to hear it, but not 'til you're older."

The black limo parked behind them pulled back onto the road. As it whizzed past, Knoxi sat straight up. "Did you see that?"

"See what?"

"The slogan! The slogan on the back window of that limo!"

Ryan looked through his binoculars.

— No Hostages Beyond This Point —

The End

Epilogue

The world never learned of Knoxi's excursion from playing college basketball to doing God's work in pirate country. Her connection to Rolfe Sagan was never divulged.

Pirates in the Caribbean scattered immediately, making it difficult for authorities to find them. But piracy on the high seas and in coastal shipping lanes became a thing of the past, especially in waters where ships came equipped with Saint Maria flags waving atop the mast. Some claimed that Saint Maria had died a martyr's death at Maria de Dios that night, while others said she had escaped in a yellow airplane which still patrols the skies in maritime regions.

Rolfe Sagan became a folk hero/martyr of sorts after his bold revelations had exposed globalists plotting to gain control of the world's wealth by preying on the weak and vulnerable. Although reports of Sagan's death were confirmed by eyewitnesses, his burial place was never found.

Knoxi and Ryan were never able to determine why former DEA Agent Virginia Cutter had shown up to play the role of Saint Maria. Sagan had told Knoxi that Saint Maria would protect her on the mission, but no connection between Cutter and Sagan was ever disclosed.

Ryan attempted unsuccessfully to discover how Rolfe had obtained the technology to send the encoded messages to Knoxi's phone. It would remain a mystery, like nearly everything else about Sagan. He covered his tracks well and left no trail to follow.

Jeremy McNair played fourteen seasons with the Dodgers, building a solid reputation for a hard-nosed style of play, and a soft touch when somebody needed a jump-start. His personal involvement in community projects such as athletic training for at-risk teens and his support of feeding centers like Carlos Santana's were widely-noted.

Robbie and Peaches Ahusaka finally moved to Montana, where Robbie was able to fulfill his dream of becoming a cowboy. After working for eight years as a ranch hand, he bought his own fifty-acre spread. Peaches attended the University of Montana where she eventually received a Ph.D. in forensic science and became a state-wide problem-solver for the cattle industry.

Their daughter, Strawberry, was their only child. At the age of eleven, she accompanied her parents to hear Knoxi Musket Maxwell speak at a governor's banquet in the state capital of Helena. That night, she heard Knoxi say, "The future belongs to the bold, the adventurous, and the committed."

The next day, Strawberry announced she had changed the direction of her life. She was now committed to someday traveling farther than any human had ever gone, determined to plant the Ahusaka family shield on the surface of Mars, along with a four-foot cross engraved with a verse from Psalm 19:1 — "The heavens declare the glory of God."

Deputy Ulysses Fox, the man who warned Cody of Sheriff Colton's treachery, had been working undercover for the Texas Rangers. He was killed in the line of duty two years later. Cody and Shawn both shared thoughts at his eulogy in Austin, and both men accompanied his body to the burial site at Arlington National Cemetary for a full military 21-gun salute.

Carlos Santana's wife left Carlos again six years after returning. She declared that Carlos would never amount to anything unless he stopped "depending on God and Jeremy McNair for everything." She wanted the wealth other American women reveled in, and she would never achieve that married to a man who gave everything away. Even

Annie could not convince her that her self-centered desires would someday leave her bitter and disappointed in the end, the way of so many "wealthy" women who have everything, and who have nothing.

Carlos' two daughters, Maria and Lucia, stayed with their father. They loved seeing smiles on the faces of the poor who had come off the street, and they particularly liked hanging around Jeremy when he was in town. Carlos let each of his daughters preach in English once per month, and their Jeremy McNair impersonations were a huge draw.

Cody and Brandi Musket spent five years helping the planet recover from the residual carnage done by the Abdullas and Carascos of the world. Their Planned Childhood facilities overflowed with liberated victims and suicidal patients. During Brandi's later years she gained a reputation which earned her the nickname "Mama Brandi." Her constant presence among so many victims was a life-changer for thousands, so much so that she was eventually awarded a Nobel Prize for peace.

Zorro became a Tejano legend. When he finally introduced his mother on stage and revealed her identity, it sent the music world into a frenzy. Her fans, advanced in age, had never forgotten. They poured into giant venues to hear her old songs, and most of all, to hear about her journey as told from her own lips.

Zorro did not remember the aircraft ride or the crash which had occurred the night he was rescued. Annie and Jeremy never discovered Knoxi's part in their son's return. Ryan and Knoxi wanted to keep it that way.

Knoxi resumed her basketball career at Texas University and eventually regained her enthusiasm for the sport. She struggled with her feelings for several months until she and Ryan were introduced to Carlos Santana, the pastor/plummer/fixer-upper who worked two jobs to support his family and provide food for the homeless at his mission near the Dodgers' spring camp.

Carlos never addressed big audiences, and he possessed no dazzling public profile, yet his daily prayer, asking God to direct him to someone who needed a hand, had led him to an encounter with Jeremy and Annie. His kindness to them had bound the McNairs together with one tiny thread of hope in a time of crisis, and now the Dodgers' center fielder and his family were blessing thousands across the land. What if Carlos had not taken the time to stand in the rain and be a friend?

And, what if she and her friends had not reached out to the tearful Alex, masquerading as a police officer while running for her life? Alex would have died, would never have become Annie, Jeremy's wife, and the worldwide consortium of evil would never have been exposed.

In her later years Knoxi tended to shy away from addressing large crowds and venues. She found her passion again in meeting with smaller groups where she could interact with struggling individuals. During those years she was fond of saying these words:

> *"Never strive so much to be adored by the great masses, and don't crave the limelight. Rather, look for the stranger, and always be willing to stop for just one. You never know when you might change the history of the world."*

Made in the USA
Lexington, KY
05 March 2018